Mermaid's Demise

RIVIAND LOST
BOOK 2

KRISTY DIXON

For Mary Coleen

Riviand
Colter's Lake
Goblin Mountain
Tyran
Troll's Retreat
Troll City
Serpent's Hill
Desert
Kinton
Dragon's Cove
Pyramid

1

— · —

CHAPTER 1

Mateo sat at a table and blew wood shavings from the sign he was carving. "Doesn't this feel like we're giving up?"

Kaylee tilted her head as she studied the sign. "How so?"

"If we actually open a store here, it's like we're saying we aren't ever getting out of Riviand."

Kaylee's mouth turned down. "We aren't giving up. I'm sure we'll figure a way out, but who knows how long it will take? We can't just waste away, hoping to get home."

"I guess," he said, making another nick in the wood. He didn't want to brag, but the sign looked good. He had gone with all capital letters because carving lowercase Es was hard, and *Kaylee's Snakes and Bakes* had a lot of Es. Kaylee had wanted their store to be called Kaylee's and Mateo's Snakes and Bakes, but Mateo thought that was too long. He didn't mind having his name eliminated.

"It was nice of Claret to let us use the old bakery," Kaylee said. "Have you asked Odie if he wants to join us?"

Mateo frowned. "Not yet." Kaylee and Mateo had been in Riviand for four weeks, but Mateo still wasn't sure he

1

trusted Odie. The guy had spent most of his life working with the goblins. True, he had helped them save Riviand, but a few weeks couldn't make up for a lifetime of siding with the goblins.

"The sign looks good," Kaylee said. "I feel like we'll probably mess it up when we paint it. Maybe we should leave it."

Mateo stood and walked across the almost empty bakery. He held up the sign so she could look at it from a distance. "I don't think people will be able to see it if we don't paint it."

Kaylee squinted from across the room. "Yeah, I guess you're right. We should make a checklist of things we need to do in here."

Mateo looked around. "Definitely paint. It looks like it hasn't been painted since before we were born."

She nodded. "Everything in the kitchen needs major scrubbing."

Mateo looked at the wooden floor planks. They were chipped, and some appeared to have water damage. Fixing the floor was probably beyond their abilities. A good scrub might be all they could manage.

"We should probably be done for the day," he said. "We need to get cleaned up in time for dinner with Claret's aunt."

Queen Claret ruled over Riviand. She was sixteen just like Kaylee and Mateo, and they had worked together along with Odie when the goblins stole the Blade of the Phoenix. Without the blade, the entire continent had been in danger of drowning. Riviand was under the ocean, and the Blade of the Phoenix was what kept it down.

Now that problem was over, but Kaylee and Mateo didn't know how to get out of Riviand. Only the goblins knew the way. There was also the fear of the goblins trying something else, and rumors said that the goblins were forming an army.

Claret's aunt and advisor hadn't been at the castle when Kaylee and Mateo had arrived, and then she had been sick, so they hadn't met her. She'd started improving, but then taken a turn for the worse. Mateo wasn't really looking forward to meeting her, but he was tired of it getting postponed. They were supposed to meet her three times before and each time she had canceled.

"I'm ready," Kaylee said, brushing wood shavings from her pants. She stood and straightened her green tunic, then climbed under the table to get her knee-high boots. She sat on the floor and tugged them on. "What?"

Mateo shook his head. "Nothing." He'd been staring again. Whenever he got lost in thought lately, he seemed to zone out when he was staring at Kaylee. There were a lot worse things to look at. Kaylee had the prettiest brown eyes he had ever seen, and her face—well, it was a nice face to have.

"Hello? Mateo? You're scowling at me again."

"Sorry." He didn't know why he always looked angry when he was thinking.

She stood. "Do you think Claret's aunt will actually show up this time?"

"I don't know," he said, opening the front door. "It's strange she keeps canceling. Maybe she doesn't want to meet us."

Kaylee pulled the door closed and locked it. "Claret said her aunt always needs a lot of rest after she comes home from touring the kingdom. This seems excessive, though. She's been putting us off for over two weeks."

They started down a paved street, passing small shops that were empty for the day. The sun was setting and a cool breeze blew Kaylee's shoulder-length black hair away from her face. Mateo sighed. He wondered if Kaylee might like him more if they had started out better. He knew she didn't hold their first few interactions against him, but she definitely wasn't feeling what he was feeling.

He told himself he was being ridiculous. They had only known each other for a month. It felt like a lot more. They'd already been through a lot together, beginning on Earth and ending up in Riviand.

"You wanna race?" he asked.

She turned and arched her brow. "Not at all. I hate the way you hold back and let me think I'm going to win, and then you shoot ahead at the last second."

"I won't do it this time. Ready? Set? Go!"

Kaylee shook her head as she watched Mateo race ahead of her. She wasn't in the mood to run, but if she didn't, he was going to get to the castle way before her. She wasn't terrible when it came to running, but Mateo did it regularly, so she couldn't come close to beating him. Her legs picked up speed, and she frowned when Mateo turned around and grinned. There was no way she was catching up.

The glass structure that held the replica of the Blade of the Phoenix was in the middle of town, and she ran past it without giving it a second glance. She was one of the few people who knew the sword was a fake. The actual sword was hidden in her room in the castle, where no one would find it and threaten Riviand again.

By the time she reached the castle steps, she was panting. Mateo stood at the bottom, waiting for her, a big smile on his face. That smile made her want to wake up early every morning to run so she could get better than him and wipe that smile from his face.

"Nice effort," he said.

She punched him softly in the shoulder. "You're so annoying."

He laughed. "I know." They went up the steps and waited for the guards to open the door. The guards knew them now, so they didn't have to wait long.

They entered the castle, and Kaylee pushed her black curls behind her ear. "See you at dinner."

Mateo waved, and she took off down the long entryway and up an enormous staircase. Her room was one of the first doors to the right.

She hurried in and grabbed a brush. They should have come back earlier. Dinner was in fifteen minutes and she was sweaty. She pulled the brush through her hair and wished for at least the third time today that she knew how to do box braids. When she had come here, her little braids had been neat and kept her hair from her face, but she'd had to take them out because they were always getting dirty.

There wasn't a lot she could do in fifteen minutes. She tossed the brush on her bed and opened the large oak wardrobe across from her bed. A blue dress stood out, so she grabbed it. She didn't like dresses, but it was fun to wear them here. It felt like Halloween because they were fancy and looked like they were from the Renaissance. She pulled it over her head and gave herself a quick glance in the mirror. It would do. Claret's aunt probably wouldn't show up, anyway.

Odie sat in the dining room of the castle, his knee bouncing up and down. He'd gotten here early, and he was nervous. He ran his hand through his brown hair and glanced up at the large crystal chandelier that hung over the table. It made small rainbow shapes on the walls when the sun hit it just right. He felt out of place, and he was nervous to see Claret's aunt again. She only knew him as the goblins' ridiculous messenger. If anyone could get Claret to kick him out of the castle, it was her.

Silver plates and goblets adorned the long table. The tablecloth was light blue and so were the napkins. Claret must like light blue. He'd noticed the color in most of the rooms. Claret's castle was so much brighter than the goblin castle Odie had grown up in. Most things there were made of obsidian, which was beautiful, but not very cheerful. It had been a strange few weeks, living in a place so different from what he was used to.

Some days, Odie wondered if he should leave. It felt strange living off Claret's charity after all he had put her through. She didn't seem to hold a grudge, but she might be good at pretending. He'd been the one to come and demand money in return for Riviand's safety. Even if Claret had forgiven him, he wasn't sure Mateo and Kaylee would ever accept him.

He thought about leaving at least once a day. He wouldn't, though. As much as he thought he should, he was a coward. The only life he knew was with the goblins. If he left the castle, he had nowhere to go, and he didn't know how he would live. There was also Dovin. Dovin was a middle-aged man who came to Riviand with Kaylee and Mateo. He was quickly becoming like a father to Odie, and he didn't want to lose that.

"You're here early," Dovin said, entering the room. His leather jerkin fit him perfectly, and he walked confidently to the table and pulled out a chair.

"Yes, I didn't want to make a worse impression on Claret's aunt than I already have."

"I wonder if she'll show up this time," he said, relaxing in his chair. "I'm starting to wonder if she's avoiding us."

Odie nodded. He wondered what reason she could have to keep putting them off. Odie didn't mind. She probably didn't want to see him. He thought of all the times he had stood in Claret's throne room, relaying messages from the goblins. Durdessa had always been by Claret's side, her eyes burning holes in him.

"Are you nervous?" Dovin asked.

"A little. Claret's aunt hates me."

"Well, people can change their opinions. Claret did, after all."

"I suppose."

"Don't worry. It will all be over soon."

Claret's teeth ground together as she faced her aunt. Durdessa stood before her in a beautiful green dress that flowed past her feet. Her long blond hair fell in soft waves over her shoulders. She didn't look sick.

"You cannot put this off forever. My friends are going to think you are avoiding them. Why can't you come to dinner?"

Durdessa sighed and glanced at her hands. "Can't you give me one more week? By then, I'm sure I'll be up for it."

Claret's brows came together. This wasn't like her aunt. Durdessa liked people, and she was social. Why was she avoiding Claret's friends? This was the first time in her life she'd had any, and she thought her aunt would be thrilled.

"They're going to think you are unreliable." Usually, Durdessa was the one lecturing Claret about things like this.

Durdessa walked over to Claret and straightened her small tiara. "There are things about me you don't know, Claret. Things I've never told you."

"Like what?"

"Things that I need to keep secret for my safety. Your parents knew, but no one else."

Claret's mouth turned down. "I don't see why that stops you from meeting people. Kaylee and Mateo are really nice. Even Odie is growing on me."

"I still can't believe you allow that boy to stay in the castle after all he put you through."

"Don't change the subject."

Durdessa put a hand to her forehead. "The truth is, I've already met your friends."

"What? Where?"

She shook her head. "It doesn't matter. What matters is that they know my secret. If they see me, there is nothing to stop them from telling the world, and then terrible things could happen."

"I haven't known them long, but I trust them. If you tell them not to say anything, they won't."

"Can you tell them not to speak of how or where we met first?"

"All right," Claret agreed, pushing down her confusion. "I bet they're already down waiting for us."

They rushed from the room and Claret went into the dining room. Durdessa waited outside the door. She wondered what Durdessa's secret could be and how Kaylee and Mateo knew it.

Kaylee, Mateo, Odie, Dovin, and Padmire sat at the table. They all looked up when she came in. Padmire sat on a high stool that had been fashioned just for him. Being a bungle, he was only a foot tall and had a hard time reaching.

Dovin's brow arched. "Is everything all right?"

"Yes. It appears my aunt has already met Mateo and Kaylee, and she would like them to promise not to tell where they met or give any information from their meeting. I guess they know a secret she doesn't want anyone to know." It was irritating that Claret wasn't allowed to know the secret. She would pry later.

Kaylee and Mateo looked at each other with confused expressions.

"I promise," Kaylee said, "but I can't think of anyone we've met that told us any secrets."

"Neither can I," Mateo said. "But I promise."

Durdessa stepped into the dining room and Kaylee gasped. "Oh, I see." She clasped her hand over her mouth and Mateo's eyes went wide. Claret would not rest until she knew Durdessa's secret.

Dovin stood quickly, knocking his chair to the floor. Durdessa's gaze shifted to him and all the color left her face. "Dovin?"

Dovin stared as if he'd seen a ghost. "Here? But how?" His eyes teared up, and he walked slowly around the table until he was facing her.

Durdessa reached out for Dovin and he caught her in his arms. Tears ran down her cheeks and she sobbed. She pressed her face into his neck and he ran a hand over her hair. Claret watched in confusion.

Claret glanced at her friends. Odie was staring at his plate, and Kaylee and Mateo were watching Dovin and Durdessa and looking awkward. Padmire was ignoring it all and eating some fruit.

"I should have listened to you," Durdessa cried. "I was stupid and careless, and I got too close to the whirlpool."

Dovin kissed her forehead. "I thought you were dead or that you couldn't resist the ocean anymore."

"I tried to come back so many times. I could never find a way."

They stood hugging for an uncomfortable amount of time. Claret wanted to grab her friends and leave, but she didn't know the best way to go about it.

"I've missed you so much," Durdessa said, pulling back and looking at him.

"Not as much as I've missed you." Dovin leaned down and kissed her.

Claret motioned to her friends, and they all filed out the door. All except Padmire. Claret carefully closed it behind them.

"Well, that was awkward," Mateo said.

Kaylee punched him in the shoulder.

"Ouch."

"Let's go eat in the kitchen," Claret said, leading the way. Her mind was a flurry of confusion. Claret knew Durdessa wasn't really her aunt. Durdessa had fallen into Riviand through the waterfall when Claret was young and had become friends with the king and queen. Durdessa had become a part of the family and had always been there for Claret. She'd never mentioned leaving someone special behind.

They entered the kitchen and sat around the servants' table.

Mateo turned to Kaylee. "It all makes sense! When we were sailing on Oscar's ship and Dovin was telling us about mermaids, he sounded sad. That must be why."

Kaylee covered Mateo's mouth with her hand. "Shhhhh! You promised not to tell."

Mateo pushed her hand away. "Oops."

Claret leaned forward. "Mermaids? What about mermaids? Durdessa can't be..." She slumped back into her seat. Her aunt was a mermaid. Everything made sense now. All the times Durdessa left the castle and came back so weak and tired, it must be because she was out at one of the lakes. Legend had it that changing from a mermaid back into a person was painful and exhausting.

"I'm sorry," Mateo said. "I didn't mean to let it slip."

"You'll have to tell Durdessa that," Kaylee told him.

Claret drummed her fingers on the table. "Durdessa didn't want me to know her secret because it could be dangerous for her. I would never tell, though." They all looked at Odie.

He narrowed his eyes. "Why are you all looking at me? I'm not going to tell. Who would care anyway?"

Claret frowned. There were lots of people who might care. Being a mermaid was something ordinary people might want to be. Mermaids were not natural. They only changed because of a magical stone that was placed in a locket. Anyone might try to steal it.

Mateo shrugged. "It's hard to trust someone who spent years listening to the goblins."

Odie frowned and pushed his black feathered cape over his shoulder. "You're the one who told her secret to begin with. And who do you think I'm going to tell? The goblins will never trust me again and you all are the only people I know."

Claret reached out and took Odie's hand and stared into his eyes. "I trust you. I'm sure you won't ever let us down."

He pulled his hand away and leaned back against his chair. "Thanks," he mumbled.

"How is the shop coming?" Claret asked, taking the attention off Odie. She tried not to think about the fact that her aunt was a mermaid or that she had just grabbed Odie's hand.

Kaylee grinned. "Mateo finished carving the sign. It looks good. We dusted everything and swept the floors, but they need to be scrubbed."

"I still don't think we should mix animals and food," Mateo said. "It's unsanitary."

"There's a big room off the back of the bakery. We can put a few snakes in there and people can go look at them. Or... people can bring us any sick or injured animals they find and I'll nurse them back to health! There isn't anything like a vet in Riviand. Not that I'm qualified or anything."

"I think we need to separate the rooms with a wall," Mateo argued. "If people come for animal-related things, they can go in the back door. I don't want to sell people cookies and then have them get sick because of the animals. Besides, who wants to eat a cookie when they can smell animal poop?"

Kaylee nodded. "We could separate them. Odie, do you want to help us with the shop?"

Mateo's jaw went taut, but he didn't say anything. Claret tried not to be upset that they didn't ask her to join them. She was the queen, after all, and she didn't really have the time. Still, it would be nice to be asked.

Odie glanced from Kaylee to Mateo. "What would I do?"

"You're good at making things," Claret said. "You might be great at baking. I bet alchemy and baking go hand in hand."

"They do," Odie said, pushing his brown hair from his eyes. "I can bake a little."

"Wonderful," Kaylee said. "You can come help us to-morrow. Then, if you end up enjoying it, you can take it all over when Mateo and I figure out how to get out of Riviand."

Claret tried to smile. She felt like a bad person. Something inside her hoped they never figured a way out. She knew that was terrible of her. She had never had friends before and she was enjoying their company.

2

—·—

CHAPTER 2

Kaylee sat at the foot of Dovin's bed and watched him put his belongings in a bag. She had never seen him smile so much. "So you and Durdessa are married. That's huge."

Dovin grinned as he folded a tunic. "Yes. I cannot believe she's been here all this time. When Claret mentioned her aunt's name was Durdessa, I had a small spark of hope that it was her, but I thought it was silly of me, since Durdessa couldn't have been her aunt. I've always thought the pull of the ocean was too much for her when she never came back. I'll never forgive myself for not looking harder."

"So now what? This changes things."

"What do you mean?"

Kaylee rubbed her arm. Dovin meant a lot to her. If he stayed here, who would be there for her? "It means you won't want to leave Riviand now."

Dovin shook his head. "I still want to leave. So does Dessa. She's wanted to come home since she first came here."

"But what about Claret? I think she's a little lonely, and she doesn't have anyone but Durdessa."

Dovin paused and ran a hand over his sandy blond hair. "We might have to think about that. Claret is young, and she needs someone to look out for her. She has a lot of responsibility and that can be hard even on an experienced person."

Kaylee grinned. "Experienced? You mean old?"

He just smiled and kept packing.

She sighed. "I guess we don't have to worry about it now. We still don't know how to leave, and Claret might still be in danger."

"True," he said, tying his bag shut. "We will stay until things feel more settled." Dovin glanced around the room, making sure he didn't miss anything. He was moving across the castle to Durdessa's rooms and Odie was taking this one. It was bigger than the one he was currently in.

"Do you think the goblins will really start a war?"

"It's possible. Especially with Garin encouraging them. Goblins are lazy and are prone to giving up easily, but I don't think Garin will stop. From what Williams said, Garin was quite the criminal before he came here."

"Where is Williams?" Kaylee asked. "I haven't seen him in days." Coach Williams wanted them to call him William, but habits were hard to break. They had finally compromised and were calling him Williams. He had been the gym teacher at her high school and she had found out recently that he was from this world. He hadn't wanted to come back, but he had so he could warn them about Garin, and now he was stuck.

"He's getting a classroom ready for you and Mateo. He's collecting books and things that might be useful."

Kaylee groaned. "I don't see why we have to do school things while we're here."

"You don't want to fall behind."

"We're missing school, anyway. Doing the stuff here isn't going to count when we go back."

"But it will be easier to make up if you know the material."

"When do we start?"

"Tomorrow."

"Maybe Odie and Claret could join us."

"They're welcome to. I'm sure they would enjoy it as much as you."

Kaylee shook her head. If that was true, it was going to be hard to get them to agree to it. Kaylee went to find them to see what they thought. She knocked on Mateo's door and entered when he said, "Come in."

Mateo was next to his bed doing pushups. His face was red, and he was sweating.

"That looks fun," she said.

He sat back and wiped his forehead with his hand. "Just because I'm in a different world doesn't mean I should let myself go. I have to work harder because I don't have any weights."

"Well, lucky for you, Dovin is going to make us start schoolwork tomorrow, and that includes gym."

Mateo groaned. "That sounds awful."

"He said Claret and Odie can join us."

"That should be interesting. Do you want to have a planking contest?"

Kaylee grinned. "I do, actually." She got down and put her forearms on the floor. Kaylee was great at planking, and she was lighter than Mateo, so she didn't have to hold up as much weight. He had also just finished doing pushups, so he might be worn out.

He copied her and grinned. "Ready? Go!"

Kaylee lifted her body at a slant and kept herself straight. She felt her ab muscles tighten, and she turned to look at Mateo. He was doing the same thing and focusing his eyes on the rug. One minute went by, and then two.

"Give up?" Mateo asked, a slight tremble in his voice.

"Nope. It's only been a couple of minutes."

"It's okay to give up."

She grinned. "Planking is my favorite ab workout. I can do this forever." In reality, she was already beginning to shake. She hadn't kept up her usual workout routine, and she could feel it. The longest she had ever gone was ten minutes, but there was no way she was going to be able to do that.

Mateo's arms were shaking a lot more than hers. He looked at her and she smiled. She was sure the vein in her forehead was poking out. He frowned and then tipped, knocking her over in the process.

She shoved him over. "I win."

He sat up. "No way. You hit the floor first."

She poked him in the chest with her pointer finger. "That's only because you fell on me."

"Excuses, excuses. Well, it wasn't fair, anyway. You weigh less than me, so you didn't have to hold up as much."

"Yeah, but what are your massive arm muscles for if they can't even hold you up?"

He flexed his arm. "They are pretty impressive, aren't they?"

She shook her head. "They aren't as big as your head. I'm going to go talk to Odie and Claret and see if they want to join us tomorrow."

He grinned. "Can you imagine either of them doing gym class? I bet Odie wears his feathered cape and Claret wears a dress."

Kaylee giggled. "I could see that."

"You know you still owe me a foot rub?"

"What are you talking about?" She remembered, but she'd hoped he had forgotten.

"From that time I beat you in a race on the ship."

"I don't think you can hold me to that. I think the time has expired."

"Nope. I let you put it off last time." He took off his socks and Kaylee frowned.

"You've been exercising. I don't want to touch your nasty foot."

He jumped up and went to the wardrobe. "I'll put on clean socks. You won't have to touch my bare feet."

"Fine," she grumbled. "But shouldn't you owe me? I just beat you at planking."

"I'll rub yours after." He sat on his bed and held his foot out to her.

She cringed. "I don't want you touching my feet."

"Foot rubs are the best. They give you a new bounce to your step."

"Sure they do." She took his foot and began rubbing it. "I can still smell your sweaty foot through the sock."

He grinned. "Well, maybe next time you'll try harder to win."

The door opened and Odie came in. He raised his eyebrows. "Is this another Earth thing?"

"Have you never had a foot rub?" Mateo asked.

Odie shook his head. "No, and I'm beyond surprised you could get Kaylee to do it."

Kaylee scowled. "He's a poor winner. He can't just win and move on."

Odie looked more confused. "I'm going to leave. This is too weird even for me."

"On your mark, get set, go!" Williams blew his whistle and Odie, Claret, Mateo, and Kaylee all took off running. Odie had always wanted to attend school, but he'd never thought it would be like this. He darted ahead of Claret and Kaylee and ran across the dirt road next to Mateo. He'd heard Mateo say he was good at running, but Mateo hadn't seen what Odie could do.

Odie had never had friends, unless you counted his goblin brother, Tipp. Since most goblins didn't accept him, he had spent a lot of time running around the goblin mountain by himself. He could run up the mountain without breaking a sweat. He also chased Tipp around a lot because Tipp was always messing with his experiments.

"This isn't a competition!" Kaylee yelled from behind.

"Yes, it is!" Mateo called back.

Odie smiled. If it was a competition, he wasn't holding back. He focused ahead and tore past Mateo and easily left him behind. It felt odd to run without his cape on. He was rarely without his black feathered cape. Every time his pet puffin, Gregor, lost a feather, Odie scooped it up to use for his capes. Most of the feathers he found were from crows that liked to stay around the woods where he grew up. He had left the other capes in the goblin castle, so he only had one with him.

"Good job, Odie!" Williams yelled.

Odie grinned and went to his full speed. He touched the tree they had been instructed to run to and ran back. Mateo was frowning and ignored him when he passed. Kaylee wasn't too far behind Mateo, and Claret was bringing up the tail. She wasn't even running. She was walking fast and holding her side.

When he got back to the place they started, he stopped and bent over to catch his breath.

"That was impressive," Williams said. "If we were back on Earth, I would have you try out for my basketball team."

Odie wasn't sure what basketball was, but he was pretty sure the coach had complimented him. Odie had been a little scared of the man at first. He was tall, with broad shoulders, and he wasn't quick to smile. He had a picture of a sword on his arm. Odie was curious about it, but he didn't dare bring it up.

Mateo ran up next to him and skidded to a stop. "You could have warned me you run," he said. "I would have tried harder."

Odie didn't say anything, and Williams chuckled. Kaylee came in next, and they all waited for Claret. She had only just turned away from the tree.

"I guess they don't teach queens to run," Mateo said.

Williams nodded. "Why would they? School is different here, and she's always had a tutor, from what I hear."

"I hope she doesn't give up," Kaylee said. "I don't want to be the only girl."

Mateo smirked. "Why? Because then you'll be the slowest?"

Kaylee crossed her arms. "No, and I'm not going to come in behind you for long. You're only faster because you've been doing it for so long. Once I put my mind to something, I make it happen, and I'm going to be faster than you before three months are over."

Mateo laughed and Odie smiled. He didn't doubt she would get faster than she was, but her legs were a lot shorter than Mateo's and he had the advantage, since he was already good at it.

Odie cupped his hands around his mouth and yelled, "You can do it, Claret!" Her head came up and a determined look settled onto her face. She picked up her speed and ran the rest of the way.

"I... am... not... ready... for that!" she said, dropping to her knees. Her long blond ponytail hung almost to her waist, and she was wearing a tunic and pants. It was easy to think of her as a normal sixteen-year-old girl and not a queen right now. Sweat rolled down her forehead, and she dabbed at it with a handkerchief.

"You did fine," Williams assured her. "It's hard when you first start a new routine, but if you don't give up, you'll get better faster than you think."

Claret nodded. "I won't give up. I'm glad you invited me to participate. This is something I should get good at so that I can be the best leader I can be. My father told me princesses shouldn't run, but now that I had that last unfortunate experience with Vigh, I think being able to run is a good thing."

Odie's mouth turned down. Vigh had been a guard in Claret's kingdom. He'd tricked Claret and tried to steal the Blade of the Phoenix. It hadn't ended well for him, and his death had bothered Claret.

"Why don't you all go get changed so you can start on your other lessons?" Williams said.

Odie held his hand out to Claret, and she took it. He helped her to her feet and quickly let go.

"Race you all to the castle!" Mateo said, taking off.

"No way!" Kaylee called after him. She linked her arm with Claret's and the two of them walked leisurely toward the castle.

Odie watched Claret and smiled. She was determined. It would be hard to be the slowest person and still not give up. The more he got to know Claret, the more he admired her. His smile faded. There was no point in thinking about her. She was a queen, and according to the goblins, he was a joke.

"Anything wrong?" Williams asked.

Odie shrugged. "No, I'll see you back in the classroom." He followed slowly after the others and wondered if he would ever really be part of their group.

Mateo leaned his chair back on two legs and watched Williams write 'The history of Akkron' on a large standing chalkboard. They sat in a room in the castle where Claret had been tutored and it was just big enough for the four of them to all sit at small desks. Mateo had scooted away from his because his knees were too high to sit under it. Odie could get his knees under his but only just.

"Why are we learning the history of Akkron?" Mateo asked. "It has nothing to do with things in Riviand."

Williams leaned against the front wall and crossed his arms. "There are several reasons. It's good to know about other places. Claret, Odie, and Kaylee know nothing about the continents up above. It might be interesting for them."

"That's only one reason," Mateo said, rocking back on his chair.

Williams grinned. "The biggest reason is that I don't know anything about Riviand. I can teach about the upper continents or Earth."

Claret leaned forward. "I'm eager to learn anything I can about the upper world. All we know is what we read in the old history books and they are only about things that happened two thousand years ago."

Kaylee glanced at Mateo. "Don't do that with your chair. You might fall on your head."

He grinned. "I'm not going to fall."

Kaylee rolled her eyes and turned back to the board. "What's the point in me learning this? I'm not even from this world."

"But what if you get stuck here?" Odie asked. "There's a big possibility you won't ever be able to leave."

Kaylee glared at him. "We're going to get out of here."

Mateo wasn't sure how he felt. He missed his family, but he enjoyed being here. On Earth, he wasn't allowed to do magic, and here he could learn more.

"But what if you don't?" Odie said. "I'm not trying to scare you. I just think you should prepare yourself in case you never leave."

"The goblins know how to get out of Riviand," Kaylee said. "That means there is a way, and I'm not spending the rest of my life using an outhouse."

Mateo wasn't a fan of outhouses, but if it meant learning magic, he could deal with it. He opened his mouth to speak, but his chair leg slipped and he slammed back into the floor. He blinked as he stared up at the ceiling. "Ouch."

Kaylee looked down at him and shook her head. "Nice."

"Are you all right?" Williams asked, holding out a hand, and pulled him to his feet.

"Fine," Mateo mumbled. He picked up his chair and set it upright.

"Great. Then let's talk about the history of Akkron, shall we?"

3

— · —

CHAPTER 3

Kaylee looked at her canvas and wrinkled her nose. Her painting didn't look a thing like the trees to the west of the castle. Her canvas was backed against Claret's, so she couldn't see how hers looked in comparison. She'd been sitting on the roof of the castle with Claret, trying to paint a picture for the last hour. Her back ached from trying to match Claret's perfect posture.

"I give up," she said. "Mine looks like a five-year-old painted it."

Claret leaned to the side and looked at her. "I'm sure it's not that bad."

"It's bad."

Claret stood and came around to see. She smiled. "It is certainly—unique."

Kaylee grimaced. "That's a nice way to say terrible." She got up and went around to see Claret's. She frowned when she saw perfect trees and a pink and purple sky. It was something a person might frame and hang up. "Yours is fantastic."

"I messed up several times," she said. "I have been painting all my life, though. This is your first time, so you can't expect perfection."

"My mom makes me take a lot of classes. I'm surprised she never made me do art. Your sky is so pretty."

"I take liberties with the skies. They're my favorite things to paint."

Kaylee heard people laughing and walked to the small wall that surrounded the roof and looked down. Mateo and Odie were standing in the flower garden, talking to Williams. Odie's puffin was walking around their feet.

Claret came up next to her. "I wonder what they are up to."

"Who knows? It's good to see Mateo with Odie. They could be friends if Mateo gave him a chance. I understand why he's suspicious of him, but I also understand why Odie obeyed the goblins. I think he should get points for realizing the goblins were wrong and switching sides."

Claret nodded. "I used to fear him. I'm not sure why. He was never threatening or anything. I'm surprised how quickly my opinion of him changed. He made me nervous for years, and now I trust him almost completely."

"How are you doing?" Kaylee asked. "Are you feeling better about Vigh?"

She shivered. "It still keeps me up some nights, but I know it was all necessary. I'm beginning to feel better about it. I should have listened to Captain Nerman when he said Vigh was a problem."

Kaylee put her hand on Claret's shoulder. "He fooled all of us."

Her lips turned up slightly. "I've never had a friend I could talk to about things before. Thank you."

"You can talk to me about anything." It would be nice to have someone here she could talk to. Claret was a lot different from her, but she was sure they could be friends.

"I've never had friends before," Claret admitted. "I was always envious of the girls in the village. They would sit around in groups laughing and, I assume, talking about clothing styles and boys. I had Durdessa, but that isn't the same. She was more of a parent."

Kaylee laughed. "I am always available to talk about boys."

Claret looked down at Mateo and Odie. "He is really handsome."

Kaylee nodded. "He's pretty immature, though."

"I think most boys our age are."

"Probably." Kaylee wasn't sure why she wanted to make Mateo seem less impressive in Claret's eyes. She wasn't interested in him, so why should she care?

"I've always loved romance," Claret said. "I used to have one of my maids sneak out to the library and bring me books about love. My father didn't approve of that kind of thing. Do you like to read?"

"Yes, but I prefer adventure books more than romance. I like it to have a bit of romance, but nothing over the top."

"I am so happy for Durdessa. That has to be the best love story I've ever heard. Being apart for so long and then finding Dovin after all these years."

"It is crazy. I didn't even know Dovin had been married and I've known him for years. I'm glad they get a happy ending."

"It's nowhere near an ending. I imagine they will have many happy years ahead of them. She's not very happy right now. I saw her earlier and her eyes were red and puffy."

Kaylee frowned. "Why?"

"Something about her daughter. I guess she made some bad choices and ruined her relationship with Dovin. Durdessa didn't give me all the details, but she was pretty upset. She said she'll be fine by tomorrow. I guess she just needs to cry it out."

"I didn't know Dovin had a daughter," Kaylee said, wondering what else her mentor had kept from her.

"It sounds like she did some really bad things," Claret said. "Like, she's a criminal or something."

"I can't imagine daring to defy Dovin. My friend on Earth used to tease me because I always did what he said."

"It's probably different when it's your own parent."

Kaylee nodded. She had obeyed Dovin better than she had her mom. "Maybe he was more strict with me because of his daughter. I mean, he wasn't super strict, but he made sure I wasn't getting into any trouble." A small lump formed in her throat when she thought of what Dovin and Durdessa must be going through. Dovin had become as good as a father to her, and she wasn't going to let him down.

Claret looked down at Odie again. She wasn't sure why he kept catching her eye. How had he gone from feeling like her enemy to being someone she daydreamed about? And she'd admitted she fancied him to Kaylee. There was nothing good that could come from thinking about Odie that way.

She turned back to Kaylee's painting. It did look like a child had painted it, but that didn't make it a poor effort. Everyone had to start somewhere. Not being able to paint wouldn't affect Kaylee's life. Kaylee had life skills that Claret could only dream of having. She was going to improve herself, even if that meant running pathetically behind her friends until she was better at it.

"It's neat you can come up here," Kaylee said. "I never would have thought of going to the top of a castle. The view is magnificent."

Claret nodded. "It's one of my favorite places."

The door to the roof flew open, and Captain Nerman rushed toward them. He went to one knee and bowed.

Claret motioned for him to rise. "What is it, Captain?"

He stood. "It's the goblins, Your Highness. I sent spies up into the goblin mountain and there is no doubt they are forming an army. They are forging weapons and making armor."

"We cannot have that," she said, her stomach dropping.

"No, Queen Claret. What do you want me to do?"

Claret tried to look confident, but she could feel her hands trembling. "What would you suggest?"

"We need to act. It will take them time to build up an army sufficient to come against us. We should stop them before they become a threat."

Claret nodded. She hated being in command of everything. If she made the wrong choices, people's lives would be at stake. "I will think about it," she said. "Thank you for your hard work, Captain."

"I feel this isn't something we can ignore for long."

"Meet me tomorrow at noon. We can discuss it then."

He bowed again. "Yes, Your Highness." He turned and disappeared the way he'd come.

"Why do the goblins have to rebel now? My father was much better at these things."

Kaylee's mouth turned down. "I'm sure you'll make a good decision. Do you have a council that helps you with these things?"

"No, only my aunt and Captain Nerman. A council would be helpful. My father didn't like anyone except Durdessa and my mother helping him."

"Let's gather up the others and maybe we can help you. I'll find them all and tell them to go to your council room."

Claret gave a half-hearted smile. "Thank you. Tell them to come in twenty minutes. I need to do something first."

"Sounds good."

Claret rushed to her room and looked in her mirror. She didn't want to appear anxious when she met with everyone. Her face was a little red, but that could be from being outside. She quickly changed into a fresh dress and ran a brush through her hair. By the time she met the others in the meeting room, she was feeling better.

The meeting room had a large round table that could hold twelve to thirteen people. When she walked in, she saw she was the last to arrive. Kaylee, Mateo, Odie, Dovin, Williams, and Durdessa all stood when she entered.

"Please sit." They all sat, and she went and stood at an empty space at the table. "I have been informed that the goblins are building an army." No one's expression changed. "I believe they need to be stopped before they are a threat, but I am not sure the best way to go about that."

Odie frowned. "We already knew they were planning on it. Why is it more pressing now?"

Claret took a deep breath. "Captain Nerman sent spies to watch the goblins, and they saw the goblins building weapons. I didn't worry as much before because they seemed to be in the first stages and I hoped their planning wouldn't come to anything."

"Goblins will only fight with motivation," Odie said. "Gold will usually get them to go to war. Power might, but only for some. Most of them are lazy and don't like to do anything they don't have to do. There is a good chance they won't follow through."

Mateo narrowed his eyes. "What is their motivation this time? We know there's the human they're listening to, but is that all?"

Odie shook his head. "I don't know."

Williams leaned forward and rested his arms on the table. "Garin is from Basura. From what I learned, he jumped from a ship and purposely swam to Mermaid's Demise and must have been sucked down into Riviand. He probably has nothing to offer the goblins."

Dovin rubbed his chin. "But he is a criminal and a good one. He is probably persuasive."

"Yes, and there is something unsettling about him," Odie said. "His eyes are like fire. They are literally orange."

Claret tried to keep her face from showing fear, but her stomach was tied into knots at the thought of Garin. He had wanted to kill Dovin just to make a point. "I'm not sure how to deal with this. If I send in soldiers to stop their preparations, it might just speed up a war. Is there a way to do this without fighting?"

Durdessa's mouth turned down. "Goblins are difficult to deal with. I don't like to advocate bribing, but it might be the best way. Goblins rarely resist gold."

Odie was nodding. "It's true. Having gold is most of the goblins' goal in life."

"I don't like bribery," Dovin said. "Once you bribe someone, you spend the rest of your life giving them more. You don't want to be stuck giving everything to them."

"I could go to the castle and talk to the king," Odie said. "He might have me locked up, but there is more chance of him listening to me than anyone else."

"But he might not, then we would have to go rescue you," Mateo said.

Kaylee rubbed her lips together. "It would be hard to rescue you because you're the only one who knows the goblin lands."

Dovin's eyes landed on Mateo. "What if I teach Mateo to teleport? He could go with Odie, and if things go poorly, he could bring them back here. Since people down here don't know how to teleport, no one would think to stop you because you would be gone before they knew what happened."

Mateo's eyes lit up. "That would be awesome."

"I don't know," Kaylee said. "It sounds dangerous. So many things could go wrong."

"Like what?" Mateo asked. "At any sign of danger, we would be out of there."

"Do you really think the goblins are going to welcome you in with open arms?"

"Who knows? They don't know anything about me. For all they know, Odie made a friend and went back home."

Claret took a stabilizing breath. The last thing she wanted to do was send her new friends into danger. "I'm not willing to risk someone getting hurt."

Mateo crossed his arms. "You can't prevent that. If we go, we could be in danger, but if we don't, others are sure to get hurt. War is much bigger than we are."

"Should we vote?" Dovin asked.

Claret frowned. She wanted to remind them she was the queen and whatever she decided should be the end of it. Still, she had asked for their guidance, and she was inexperienced in things like this.

"All right," she said. "I vote no. Kaylee?"

Kaylee glanced at Mateo. "I vote no."

Dovin looked at Durdessa. "Dessa?"

Durdessa shot a sympathetic look toward Claret. "I vote yes."

"As do I," Dovin said. "Williams?"

"I'm going to say yes."

Odie nodded. "Yes from me."

"And me," said Mateo.

Claret looked hopelessly around. "Where is Padmire?"

"He's playing with Gregor," Odie said.

She didn't know why she asked. Padmire would probably vote yes as well.

"Fine," she said. "But I think it's a bad idea."

"Does that mean you like us?" Mateo asked with a grin.

Claret scowled. "Yes, I do. For the first time in my life, I feel like I have a group of..." She wanted to say friends, but she wasn't sure if they all felt the same. "A group of people I can talk to. I don't want to lose any of you."

"Don't worry," Odie said. "I don't think my father would actually lock me up. He'll probably figure I got angry and ran off, and he'll forgive me for that."

She tilted her head. "But you helped me escape."

He shrugged. "I still think he'll get over it. King Ummi has always had a soft spot for me, even though I am an embarrassment."

Claret knew she wouldn't win. If she commanded them not to do it, she was certain they would, anyway. She might as well make sure they were well prepared. "All right. You may do that, but I want you to promise you will teleport the moment you sense danger."

Mateo and Odie shared a look and then nodded. Claret sighed. It would have to do.

4

— • —

CHAPTER 4

"Mateo, you're not concentrating," Dovin said, keeping a firm grip on Mateo's arm. "Close your eyes and try again."

"I'm trying my best," Mateo muttered, wiping the sweat from his brow. He had thought teleporting would be easier. He'd been trying all morning and all he had to show for it was a headache.

"Shut your eyes and imagine yourself as a closed door. Your entire body needs to feel like it's closed into a tight ball. Picture the inside of Claret's castle. Once you feel yourself get warm and fall, you open yourself up, and you should be at the place you are imagining."

Mateo was letting the humid air and the chirping birds in the nearby trees distract him. "Can't we go somewhere quiet? And preferably not so hot?"

"You never know where you are going to be when you need to teleport. If you learn in uncomfortable situations, you will be able to teleport from anywhere."

"It would be better to start easy and work my way into harder spots."

Dovin cocked his head. "Is that what you've been doing with your levitating?"

Mateo nodded. He'd shown Dovin the way he could levitate a fist-sized rock but nothing bigger.

"That might be the reason you can't lift bigger things." Dovin raised his hand and a four-foot boulder rose several feet into the air. "You see this? It is no more difficult than raising a small rock. The only reason you can't do it is because you think you can't do it. You are holding yourself back because you know it's heavy. When you levitate, nothing is heavy."

"I know, but I can't change the way my brain works."

"Sure you can. It takes practice, but it's possible."

"How long did it take Sen to learn to teleport?"

Dovin shook his head. "That is irrelevant. Your brother differs from you."

"He got it on the first try, didn't he?"

Dovin flashed his teeth. "He did."

"Can we take a break? Maybe eat lunch?"

Dovin's smile slid. "We don't have a lot of time. Kaylee is going to come get us when everyone else eats."

"Fine," Mateo mumbled. He shook his hands and head. "I'm ready." He closed his eyes and tried to close himself off to everything. He pictured himself as a door closing, and then he pictured his room in the castle. There was no falling sensation. He squeezed his eyes tighter and focused more on closing himself off.

"Don't make it a chore," Dovin's voice said, cutting into his concentration. "This shouldn't draw sweat. It's a graceful, quick movement."

Mateo gritted his teeth together. He'd wanted to learn to teleport for a long time, and now that he had the chance, he was failing. When Dovin had first begun teaching some of the kids in Boztoll, Mateo had been irritated that he wasn't old enough to learn to teleport. Now he was glad he hadn't failed in front of the others. Bringing up a ball of light was simple. Maybe the reason he was having trouble now was because of all the years he'd spent not doing magic. Learning as a child might have an advantage.

"What if I run?" he asked.

Dovin's brows came together. "What do you mean, run?"

"Standing here and trying to teleport feels impossible. What if I run and then try?"

"I don't see how that would help."

"Can I try?"

Dovin let out a slow breath. "I can't have you teleporting without me. What if you end up somewhere you shouldn't?"

Mateo grinned. "Can you run?"

"I am not running while you try to teleport. It doesn't sound safe."

Mateo opened his mouth to speak but stopped when he saw Kaylee come through the trees. Her hair was in two braids that went to her shoulders and she was wearing a red tunic. Red was an excellent color on her.

"Hey, guys. It's time for lunch."

"Lovely," Dovin said. "We'll pick this up after we eat." He rushed toward the castle.

"How's it going?" Kaylee asked. "I thought Dovin said it wouldn't take long."

He frowned. "Yeah, well, I guess teleporting isn't my talent."

"Have you been able to do it at all?"

"Nope. I think I could if Dovin let me do it my way."

"What's your way?"

"Running."

Her eyebrow arched. "Running?"

"Yeah, I think it would be easier to run and then try it, but Dovin won't let me. I think it's because he knows he can't run like I can."

"You could try it now," she said. "I'll even go with you."

He smirked. "You trust me?"

Kaylee grinned. "Not at all, but it sounds like an adventure."

"It's probably not a good idea."

"Chicken?"

"No."

"Then let's do it." She held out her hand and Mateo took it.

"All right, we run to that half-dead tree over there. As soon as we take a step past it, I'll try."

"Sounds good."

"Okay, ready? Run!"

Kaylee kept her grip on Mateo's hand as they ran across the dead weeds. Now that they were running, she was regretting her decision. Anything could happen. What if Mateo teleported them to the wrong place by accident?

Either she was getting faster, or Mateo was going slower for her. As soon as they ran past the dead tree, she closed her eyes. Her foot slipped, and she felt herself falling. Instead of falling on her face, her entire body felt like it did a slow-motion flip. She opened her eyes and saw nothing but blackness and Mateo. She squeezed his hand and, in a flash, she smashed into the castle dining room floor.

"Ouch," Mateo said, lying at her side.

Kaylee stared up at the ceiling and took several deep breaths, then rolled over to her hands and knees. She pushed herself into a kneeling position and glared down at Mateo. "Nice landing."

He looked up at her and didn't give any indication of getting up. "Hey, I got us here. The landing was as much your fault as mine."

"I can't believe we flipped like that."

"Where did you just come from?" Claret asked from her seat at the head of the table. "It was like you fell from the sky."

Kaylee jumped to her feet. Durdessa and Odie were sitting at the table, staring at them. "Mateo was having trouble teleporting, and he thought it would be easier if we ran instead of holding still."

Durdessa raised her perfect brow. "And was it?"

Mateo grinned up at them. "Yeah, but the landing was rough."

Dovin entered and frowned when he saw Mateo. "How did you get here before me and why are you lying on the floor?"

Kaylee grabbed Mateo's hand and helped him get to his feet.

He rubbed the back of his neck. "I teleported us."

Dovin crossed his arms. "Without supervision?"

"Kaylee supervised me."

He rolled his eyes. "That doesn't count."

"We ran."

"And that's why you were on the floor."

"Yeah, the landing didn't go as planned."

"I would imagine not."

"But I did it."

Dovin didn't say anything else. He just sat down next to Durdessa.

Odie placed his napkin on his lap. "If we have to run to teleport, that might cause a problem. Running would alert the goblins and they would try to stop us."

"But now that I've done it, I might be able to do it without running."

Padmire entered the dining room with Gregor at his heels. He climbed up on his stool and grabbed a small piece of fish from a platter and threw it down to Gregor. The puffin devoured it and moved from foot to foot, begging for more.

Williams was the last to arrive. As soon as he came, the servants began bringing in plates of food. Kaylee sat between Odie and Mateo and dug eagerly into her mashed potatoes. Whatever gravy they made here was turning potatoes into her favorite thing to eat.

"I might need to take Gregor when we go," Odie said. "My father and brother know I would never leave him anywhere."

Padmire frowned. "If you must leave quickly, he might get left behind. It's best to leave him here with me and tell them he ran away."

Odie tore a piece from his roll and frowned but said nothing. Padmire had all but taken Gregor from Odie. He fed him and spent a lot of time with him. Kaylee wasn't sure, but she thought from the side glances Odie gave the bungle that Odie wasn't happy about it. Gregor liked Padmire, though, and followed him all over the castle.

"I won't allow you to go until you can teleport from a standing position," Dovin said to Mateo.

Mateo took a gulp of water. "You won't allow it? Who put you in command?"

Kaylee glanced at Mateo. "Of course Dovin is in charge. He's the only one who knows what's going on most of the time."

Mateo scowled but began eating his food. The room was quiet for the next few minutes, with only the sounds of silverware on the plates. Kaylee still wasn't convinced sending Odie and Mateo to deal with the goblins was a good idea. She would feel better if Dovin went with them, but the goblins knew who he was. They knew nothing about Mateo, so they would easily assume he was just a boy Odie met somewhere.

"The queen has great potential as far as magic goes," Padmire said through a mouthful of food. Everyone turned their gaze from him to Claret.

Claret froze with her fork halfway to her mouth. She placed it on her plate. "What do you mean?"

Padmire grinned, showing his sharp yellow teeth. "I can see people's magic potential. That is how I help them when they come into my cave. I see what they have and what they need. Queen Claret should be able to learn even the most difficult magic. It only takes time and patience."

"What about me?" Mateo asked.

Padmire narrowed his eyes. "You have potential, but you allow insecurities to get in the way. If you can lose those feelings that block you, then you can do great things."

Mateo frowned and took another bite. Kaylee wouldn't feel bad for him. She couldn't do magic at all. She still had the Blade of the Phoenix, and she had shot magic from it once before, but she didn't know how to do it. It had happened when she was scared and she wasn't sure what she had done.

"They don't educate children in magic the way they used to," Padmire said. "Nowadays they leave all the teaching to the parents and the parents get lazy with it."

"My parents aren't lazy," Mateo protested. "They live in a place without magic, so teaching it to me could have caused problems."

Padmire shook his head. "If I knew how to get out of here, I would take you all to my cave, although that is like cheating. Once you go through the cave, you get a special type of magic that you can do without even trying."

"Just one kind?" Kaylee asked.

"Well, if you have no magic and you go through, you get one special type, as well as becoming magic like other people. Each time a person goes through, they get something new. I try to give them something they need."

"Are you magic?" Durdessa asked. "I remember the legends of the cave at Meegore, but there is a lot I never understood."

"I can see magic potential, and I can do what you might call magic inside the cave. I am very aware of what happens inside, but I can't do magic when I leave."

Kaylee put her fork down. "Couldn't people keep going in and out until they were really powerful?"

Padmire sighed. "That is the reason the cave is usually sealed off. Too many people tried to take advantage of the cave. It was a sad thing to see, so I sealed it. I am the only one who can allow anyone in now."

Kaylee wondered what it would be like to have magic, but she wasn't convinced it was a good thing for everyone. She could see herself getting incredibly lazy if she didn't have to get up to do everything. Why clean up if you could sit in a chair and levitate stuff around? No, it was best she didn't have it.

5

— · —

CHAPTER 5

Odie sat on a large rock and watched Mateo fail to teleport again and again. Dovin must have nerves of steel because he stood holding on to Mateo's arm, hoping something would happen. Odie only stayed because Gregor wanted to be outside. The bird hopped around, looking through the tall grass.

Mateo had teleported by running again another time, but he had smashed into a wall in the castle and Dovin had forbidden him from doing it again. Dovin said he'd never had a person struggle this much. That hadn't helped Mateo's mood. Kaylee was wandering around behind Odie, trying to find snakes near the trees. So far, she'd had no luck.

"All right, that's all for today," Dovin finally said. "We'll start again first thing in the morning."

Mateo nodded and wiped his brow. Dovin went toward the castle and Kaylee came over.

"I'm not getting any better," Mateo mumbled. "I don't know why I can't practice running. It would be easier to learn to control that."

"You want to run into walls?" Kaylee asked.

"No, but I think it would be easier to control that than to keep trying this way. I'm not getting anywhere."

"Why don't we go to the goblin mountain now?" Odie asked. "Kaylee could tell the others we went."

Mateo moved his mouth from side to side. "Dovin would be really mad."

"Maybe, but it's that or spend who knows how long trying to do it his way."

Kaylee put her hands on her hips. "You can't go against Dovin. He might be a little strict, but he knows what he's talking about."

"Anyone can be wrong," Odie said. He wasn't thrilled to waste time while Mateo tried to learn something for days.

Kaylee narrowed her eyes. "Dovin won't be happy when he has to go save you."

"He won't have to," Odie said confidently. "I can get my father to listen. He might see me as an embarrassment, but that doesn't mean he doesn't respect my opinions." Odie knew he was being overly confident. King Ummi did care about Odie regardless of how others saw him, but that didn't mean he was going to listen to him. Especially not when it was a matter of war. Still, he might be happy to have Odie and his experiments.

"Well, I don't see me catching on to Dovin's way," Mateo said. "And I don't see him ever letting us go until I do. Let's go."

Kaylee's lips came together, and she poked her finger into Mateo's shoulder. "You can't go. That could be disastrous. You don't have a plan or anything."

Mateo shrugged. "We can't make a plan until we see what we're up against."

"Don't go."

Mateo grinned. "Why? Are you gonna miss me?"

Odie and Kaylee rolled their eyes.

"No, but you are both being stupid. So many things can go wrong."

Odie stepped forward. "Lots can go wrong if we don't go."

"Tell the others not to worry," Mateo said. "We've got it under control."

Odie picked Gregor off the ground and thrust him at Kaylee. "And ask Padmire to watch Gregor."

Kaylee took Gregor, but she was still frowning. "This is a bad idea."

"It'll be fine," Mateo said. "Ready?"

Odie nodded and checked to make sure his feathered cape was secure.

Mateo turned to him. "Hold on to my cape and run."

Odie grabbed his cape, and they took off running. Kaylee yelled something that he couldn't understand. Odie's feet felt like they were ripped out from under him and he was flying through black space. This wasn't what it felt like when Dovin teleported them. Before he had time to analyze it, they slammed into the earth. His face hit first, followed by the rest of him.

Odie groaned. He could hear Mateo moaning to the side of him. Odie got onto his hands and knees and sat back on his heels. He brushed dirt from his face and looked at his hand to make sure he wasn't bleeding. Mateo was spitting dirt from his mouth to the side of him.

"Nice landing," Odie said.

Mateo wiped his mouth on his hand. The corner of his mouth was bleeding but not enough to cause concern. "But we're here, aren't we?" he said before spitting again.

Odie looked up at the goblin mountain. Mateo couldn't take them to the castle because he'd never seen it before. He had only been to the mountain once, and that was when they were trying to keep the continent from rising. The black mountain rose until it disappeared into the clouds. It was always cloudy around the mountain. Odie had only been up to the top twice in his entire life.

"Now what?" Mateo asked, pressing a piece of his cape to his bleeding mouth.

"We have to go around the mountain because we're on the wrong side. Then we have to walk up. Without a portal, it will take us about an hour to reach the castle. Unless we run."

"Lovely. Let's go then."

They began walking in silence. This was going to take forever. Odie could run pretty fast, and that was how he usually got around the mountain. He couldn't make Mateo run. Not that he wasn't good at running, but running up a mountain took a different type of leg muscles. If Mateo wasn't used to it, he would have sore legs, and that could be a bad thing if things didn't go the way they hoped.

"You let them go?" Dovin asked, putting a hand to his forehead.

Kaylee crossed her arms. "Let them go? I told them they were stupid and not to do it, but they didn't listen. What do you think I should have done? Tackle them?"

Durdessa sank into a chair in the queen's council room. "Why are teenagers so impulsive?"

"How long has it been since they left?"

Kaylee sat next to Durdessa. "Not long. I came and found you as soon as they went."

Dovin nodded. "Then we don't have time to debate. I'll teleport over and try to stop them before they get to the goblins."

Durdessa frowned. "I just found you, Dovin. My heart can't take losing you again."

He smiled and put a hand on her shoulder. "You won't. Goblins can't take me down."

"We keep telling him the mentor always dies, but he still isn't careful," Kaylee said.

Durdessa gave her a slight smile. "It isn't easy to kill Dovin. Many have tried."

Kaylee grinned. "You forced too many people to do chemistry for too many hours a day?"

He winked. "Something like that. Now I need to go. There isn't time."

Durdessa stood and gave him a hug. "Be careful and try not to get hurt."

"Of course," he said, kissing her on the forehead. He took a step back and disappeared.

"I'm sure he'll be fine," Kaylee said. "He knows everything."

"He thinks he does," Durdessa said. "Thinking you are indestructible can be your undoing."

A knock on the door startled Kaylee.

"Come in," Durdessa said.

The door opened, and Captain Nerman entered, dragging a woman behind him. Her long brown hair was snarled and her gray dress was torn and dirty. Red circles rimmed her eyes, and she tried to yank her arm away from the captain.

Captain Nerman bowed, his gaze on Durdessa. "This woman was outside the window, trying to listen to your conversation. What would you have me do with her?"

Durdessa tilted her head and studied the woman. "What is your name?"

The woman gave one last tug of her arm, then her shoulders slumped. "I wasn't doing anything wrong," she said, her gaze fixed on the floor. "My name is Isadora. I was trying to find the kitchens to ask for a crust of bread."

"Where do you live, Isadora?" Durdessa asked.

"Wherever I can."

"We were just about to have lunch. Will you join us?"

Isadora's eyes flew up to meet Durdessa's. "Eat with you?"

"Yes, of course."

"I... that wouldn't be proper. I'm filthy. If I could just have some bread and maybe a little cheese, that would suffice."

"Nonsense. You will eat with us. Release her, Captain."

Captain Nerman frowned and let go. Isadora rubbed her wrist with her hand and she glared at him.

"That's all, Captain. Thank you."

Kaylee watched Captain Neman's face turn red. He looked like he wanted to argue but changed his mind. He bowed and stood by the door. "I'll escort you all to the dining room."

"Thank you," Durdessa said. "Come, Isadora, Kaylee." The three of them walked through the castle to the dining room, with Captain Nerman walking beside them.

Claret was already seated, waiting for them. When they entered, she stood. "Who is this?"

"Claret, this is Isadora," Durdessa said. "She will be dining with us. Isadora, this is Queen Claret."

Isadora's eyes widened, and she dropped to her knees.

"It's good to meet you, Isadora. Have a seat," Claret said.

Isadora popped up and sat in the closest chair. Kaylee wasn't sure what she thought about the woman. She was probably around thirty and pretty, even with her dirty face. She wasn't bone-thin like Kaylee imagined a beggar would be, but who knew her circumstances?

Kaylee didn't fail to notice Captain Nerman was still in the room. He was standing in the corner where he would be out of the way, but he could still observe things. Heaping plates of food were brought and set before everyone and Isadora dug in. She shoveled food in faster than even Mateo could. The woman was starving.

They all ate silently until Isadora began slowing down.

"Where are you from, Isadora?" Claret asked.

Isadora dabbed her mouth with a napkin. "Here and there. I never stay in one spot for too long. I've fallen into a few problems in the last year and I'm trying to get over near Colter's Lake. Do you know it?"

Kaylee glanced at Durdessa, and Durdessa looked at Claret. Colter's Lake was the place Kaylee met Durdessa. When she found out she was a mermaid. Durdessa didn't know Mateo had accidentally let Claret know her secret.

"I know it," Durdessa said, placing her fork on her plate. "Why do you want to go there?"

"It's not Colter's Lake specifically, but I have family in the surrounding area. I'm hoping to get there and make a better life for myself. My uncle owns a shop in a nearby village, and I'm almost sure he would give me a job. I've been traveling for so long, but I think it will be worth it."

"It's too bad Dovin isn't here," Claret said. "He could get you there in no time."

"Oh?" Isadora asked. "How?"

Durdessa shook her head slightly at Claret.

"Oh... um... he is quite experienced at travel. Perhaps if you wait, he could take you when he returns. You're welcome to stay at the castle if you wish."

"Really?" Isadora asked, her mouth turning up at the corners. "Thank you. I promise I won't get in the way."

"Are you finished eating?"

"Yes, thank you. It was wonderful."

Claret turned to the place Captain Nerman stood, trying to blend into the wall. "Captain? Will you take Isadora to an empty room? Have the servants draw her a bath and get her something clean to wear."

Captain Nerman's mouth turned down. "Oh course, Your Highness." Kaylee watched the captain's face. He didn't trust Isadora. Kaylee hadn't decided if she did yet. It was the captain's job to be suspicious and keep Claret safe, and he had a lot of experience.

Isadora and the captain disappeared around the corner.

Durdessa looked at both of them. "I can take Isadora to her uncle."

"That's really far away," Kaylee said. "It will take forever."

Durdessa's jaw moved from side to side. She looked like she was contemplating something. She sighed. "I can teleport."

Claret's eyes went wide. "You can?"

"Dovin taught me when we first met."

"Why didn't you tell me?"

"When I came to Riviand, I decided it was best to keep it quiet. Being the only person here who could teleport could cause unwanted attention. I could take her and be back in a few minutes."

"That would ruin your secret," Kaylee said. "Isadora might tell people."

"I could ask her not to."

Kaylee looked at Claret. "I don't trust her."

Claret blinked. "Why is that?"

"I'm not sure. There's just something about her that makes me nervous. I'm not trusting by nature, so it might be nothing. I don't think Captain Nerman does either."

Durdessa smiled. "He doesn't trust anyone."

"Why was she at the castle? If you are going to beg for food, is that really the best place to do it?"

Claret nodded. "We have people come to get food often. They usually go to the kitchen doors and wait."

"Huh," Kaylee said, pulling on one of her braids. "I didn't know people did that."

"We have plenty at the castle, so if anyone is in need, I welcome them. People who return are referred to a member of the staff and helped. We get them trained and find jobs they are suited for."

"That's really... great." Kaylee was impressed. Royalty wasn't always aware or concerned about the poor. It was nice to know Claret was.

"Taking her to her family won't hurt anything," Durdessa said. "If she has fallen on hard times, family is probably what she needs."

"I think that would be fine," said Claret. "A new start will be good for her."

Durdessa nodded. "Then it's settled. I'll take her tomorrow after breakfast."

Kaylee still didn't think it was a good idea, but she didn't have a good argument. She hoped they wouldn't regret it.

6

CHAPTER 6

Mateo had never seen anything like the goblin castle. When they got to the castle, he'd worried about being captured, so he hadn't paid much attention to the outside. All he had noticed was that it was all black, and it shined. When they got to the doors, the two goblins who were standing guard opened the door and let them in when they saw Odie, without asking questions.

Odie rushed him down a black hallway and into a throne room. Mateo had never seen so much obsidian in one place. The entire castle seemed to be made of the stuff. An obsidian throne sat on top of five steps, but the king wasn't there.

Mateo squatted and ran his hand over the floor. "This is so cool."

"Careful," Odie said. "Obsidian was a strange thing to use when building. The first goblin king in Riviand was obsessed with it, but it isn't as strong as it could be. Pieces flake off all the time and leave sharp edges. I've cut myself more times than I can count."

Mateo nodded. "It still looks neat. So how do we find your father?"

"I'm sure he'll find us. He spends most of his time here. I'm always surprised he doesn't bore himself to death."

The tall black door behind them creaked open. Mateo spun around to see a goblin peek in at them. He was wearing a vest and tan pants. Most of the goblins Mateo had seen had been wearing loin cloths and nothing else.

"Odious! It is you," the goblin said, entering the room. "One of the guards said you were here."

"Hello, Tipp," Odie said. "Where's Father?"

"A guard is looking for him. Where did you go? Where's Greg?"

Odie frowned. "Gregor. Not Greg. He got lost."

The goblin's mouth turned down, and he looked like he might cry. "That's terrible."

"I'm sure he'll turn up."

"Who is this?" he asked, pointing at Mateo. "You know Father doesn't like humans wandering around here."

"He isn't wandering. This is Mateo. He's my new friend. Mateo, this is Tipp. He's my brother."

Mateo wanted to laugh at the thought of the short goblin being Odie's brother, but he held it in. "Hi."

Tipp just gave him a blank stare with his large eyes, then looked back at Odie. "Father isn't happy you left with the prisoners. He tried telling everyone they captured you and forced you to go with them, but one of your sleeping potions knocked out the guards at the prison door. That had to be you."

"They could have stolen it," Odie said.

Tipp shook his head. "But I bet they didn't. You wanted to save the queen. She got cuddly with you for a minute and you lost your mind and swapped loyalties."

Mateo grinned. "You and Claret got cuddly?"

Odie's mouth turned down. "It wasn't like that. Tipp's just being annoying."

"Odious!" a voice boomed, echoing through the room. Mateo turned, expecting to see a giant, but saw a three-foot goblin wearing a crown almost half as tall as he was. He had rings on every finger and enough gold necklaces to appear excessive.

Odie bowed his head. "Hello, Father."

"You leave without a word and with my prisoners, and that is all you have to say for yourself?" The king scowled at him as he walked up the steps to his throne. He sat down and drummed his fingers against the armrest.

"There were… circumstances," Odie said.

"Who is this human? You know better than to surround yourself with humans."

Mateo raised his brow. Did the king forget Odie was a human as well? "My name is Mateo. Odie told me I could join the goblin army if I came here with him."

The king narrowed his beady eyes. "Why would you want to join us?"

"My family was wronged by Queen Claret's parents," he lied. "I want nothing more than to see that family out of power."

"Your accent is odd."

"He's from the other side of Riviand," Odie said.

The king rubbed his gray chin. "I knew you would be back, Odious. A punishment would usually be in order, but there isn't time for that. Garin is preparing the goblins and we could use you and your experiments in our ranks. Just think of what we could accomplish with your sleeping drought. We could probably take over with that alone."

"I thought my experiments were embarrassing to you."

The king waved a hand in dismissal. "That was before."

Odie's fists clenched and unclenched. "So now I'm suddenly useful?"

"Careful," Mateo said under his breath. They didn't need a fight right now. Not when the king was willing to let a punishment slide. Mateo had thought it would be a lot harder to convince the king to let them join him.

The door opened again, and Mateo turned to see a man dressed all in black. His blond hair poked out at strange angles and his eyes glowed an unsettling orange. This had to be Garin. His clothing was a lot like Odie's, but he had a regular black cape, not feathers.

"Garin, you see?" the king said. "Odious returned, just like I said."

"I see," the man said. "But how can we trust him? He caused a lot of trouble, letting the queen out."

"I didn't let her out," Odie said. "It was that man who was locked up with her. He took us all out against my will."

Garin's brow rose. Mateo couldn't tell whether he believed him.

"He should be put to work immediately," Garin said.

"Doing what?" Odie asked.

"Making sleeping potions, of course," the king said. "As many as you can. We've been filling your room with supplies, hoping you would come back. Now that you have, you can get started right away."

"Who is this with him?" Garin asked.

"This is my friend, Mateo. He's going to help me."

Mateo nodded. He didn't want to speak and give himself away. Since Garin was from Basura, it was possible he would recognize Mateo's accent.

"Can he be trusted?"

Odie nodded. "Completely."

The king nodded. "Very well. You will start immediately."

"It might take a while," Odie said. "When my supplies were moved last, some of my papers were lost. I don't know the exact ingredients that I used, so I'll have to experiment again."

"And how long will that take?" Garin asked.

Odie shrugged. "Anywhere between a month to three months."

His eyes narrowed. "To figure something out you've done before?"

"It was rather complicated."

"Let Tipp know if you need any ingredients you don't already have," the king said.

Tipp crossed his arms and glared. "I'm going to be a captain in the army and you are making me be Odie's delivery boy?"

Garin patted Tipp on the head, causing his glare to deepen. "Don't worry, Tipp. Your time will come."

Odie led Mateo to his room. How was his father so dense? If King Ummi thought Garin was going to allow him to be king of Riviand, he was daft. Garin wanted power for himself, and the goblins were going to hand it to him. He couldn't take over Riviand himself, but if he got the goblins to do it, he had a better chance.

Odie came to a stop when he entered his room. His shelves that had been sent to the dungeons earlier had all been returned and filled with vials of all sorts of things. It was hard for Odie to get the things he needed, and now it looked like he had everything he could have dreamed of.

His bed and wardrobe hadn't been returned, but his table was in the middle of the room, just waiting for him to start his experiments. Of course he couldn't really make sleeping potions. That would be the advantage the goblins needed to fight against Claret. Without the potion, they weren't likely to win.

"This is your room?" Mateo asked. "Where do you sleep?"

Odie shrugged. "I used to have a bed. I guess they don't think that's important."

"How long are you going to be able to pretend you are trying to make something?"

"I don't know. With luck, we can take down Garin quickly and we won't have to worry about it."

Mateo picked up a vial full of blue liquid and shook it in front of his eyes.

Odie rolled his eyes and took it away. "If that breaks, it will eat a hole into whatever it spills on. I wouldn't touch any of this stuff without asking."

Mateo got a sly grin on his face. "So what is the story with you and Claret?"

Odie felt his neck get hot. "There is no story."

"Oh? What was your brother talking about, then?"

He sighed. "The dungeon was full of bugs and it was making Claret uneasy. I made a potion that killed the bugs, but it made them fall like rain onto everything in the dungeon. Claret was startled, and she clung to me for a few minutes while she was crying. Tipp came down and took it for something it wasn't."

Mateo tilted his head and grinned. "And that's all there is to it?"

"That's all."

"That's disappointing."

Odie secretly agreed, but he wouldn't admit it. "The chances of anything happening between me and Claret are the same as the chances of Kaylee ever falling for you."

Mateo smirked. "That good, huh?"

Odie shook his head and scanned the shelves, trying to catalog what he had in his head. "You're delusional if you think Kaylee is ever going to be interested in you."

Mateo sighed. "Yeah, I know. Still, you should have seen us when we first met. We've come miles since them. I'm sure she hated me for the first week. Give us a year and you might be surprised. You shouldn't give up on Claret so fast."

Odie forced a laugh. "Give up? Who says I'm interested?"

"I'm guessing."

"There's no reason to set my sights on someone like Claret. I'm a bit of a clinker if you haven't noticed."

"You're not a clinker," Mateo said. "A nerd, maybe, but not a clinker. I don't actually know what a clinker is."

"What's a nerd?"

"It doesn't matter. I'm just saying, if you don't let a girl know you like her, then you won't ever get anywhere."

Odie grabbed a vial from the shelf. "I'm not delusional. Does Kaylee know you like her?"

Mateo sat on the corner of the table and crossed his arms. "Maybe. I've hinted a few times and joked about it. Joking is the only way I deal with these situations."

"That doesn't sound useful."

"Yeah, it's probably not. Still, live with hope."

"Perhaps. I'm not going to sit around hoping Claret sees me any differently than she sees anyone else. It sounds like a colossal waste of time. You don't seem to be taking your own advice anyway.

"It's different with me and Kaylee. I already know she's not interested, so telling her outright would just make her feel weird because she would have to tell me she doesn't like me. Claret watches you. That might mean something."

Odie laughed. "She doesn't watch me. And if she does, it's because she thinks I'm odd."

Mateo grinned. "You are odd, but some girls like that."

Odie just shook his head. He would never tell Claret that he admired her. He didn't need that kind of heartache.

Mateo got on his knees and looked into a small glass jar. "Are those dead bugs?"

Odie looked into the jar. "Yes."

"Why do you have dead bugs?"

"There are lots of bugs you can use to make things. You can mash those up and put them in a warm liquid. It makes the person who drinks it tired."

"A sleeping potion?"

"No. I do use them in my sleeping potion, but if it's by itself in liquid, it just makes a person tired. It's for people who have trouble sleeping."

"You could probably open a shop and sell things like that."

Odie nodded. It wasn't a bad idea. He'd thought about it a time or two, but there was a lot of planning that would have to go into that.

"Have you ever had a girlfriend?" Mateo asked him, still looking in jars.

"A girlfriend? A friend that is a girl?"

"No, like a special girl that you like and she likes you."

Odie frowned and moved some things around so they would be better organized. "No. I've never even had a friend. I've always been around goblins and most of them only tolerate me. What about you?"

"There were some girls who tried to hang around me a few times, but I wasn't pleasant, so they stayed away for the most part."

"Not pleasant?"

Mateo shrugged. "My parents moved me to a world with no magic. I was a bit of a punk and I didn't cooperate well.

Most people avoided me because that's how I wanted it. Then my parents sent me to a different country to try to straighten me out. That's when I first saw Kaylee."

"And then you turned your life around and decided to be a better person?"

Mateo laughed softly. "No. Kaylee has a confidence that just drew me in. It didn't hurt that she's also beautiful. I was still a brat, and she called me on it. I don't know if I'm becoming a better person, or if I changed because I finally got what I wanted, which was to come here."

Odie couldn't feel too bad for Mateo. He'd grown up in a family that cared about him. He hadn't had friends because he'd chosen not to have friends. Odie had always wanted to fit somewhere and never had. He was starting to think he might be able to be friends with Mateo. He was confiding in him after all.

"So what are you going to do about Claret?" Mateo asked.

"Nothing."

7

CHAPTER 7

Claret and Kaylee sat on the edge of the balcony off of Claret's room. The view wasn't as good as from the roof, but it was still nice. Claret could see the pink of the sunset over the trees. She wondered what Odie was doing and wished he had at least told her goodbye. It shouldn't bother her, but it did.

Kaylee stared up at the colors. "It amazes me every time I look at the sky that Riviand is even possible. The sky looks the same as it would up above. People must have been really powerful back in the day."

"I think they were. It doesn't seem strange to me since I grew up here."

"Isadora cleaned up nicely," Kaylee said.

"You still don't trust her?"

"Not really. I can't even say why. I think I feel a little hesitant to trust after Vigh. He seemed like a great guy."

"That's true. I don't see a reason not to trust Isadora. All she wants to do is get to her family."

"I know. And she'll be gone tomorrow, so we don't have to worry about her for long."

"What do you think Odie and Mateo are doing?" Claret asked.

"Who knows? I hope they stay out of trouble."

Claret stared at the sky. "I hope Dovin finds them before the goblins do."

Kaylee nodded. "I can't believe they took off like that. I should have tackled them and tried harder to keep them from leaving."

"That would have only temporarily stopped them. You couldn't watch them all the time."

"You're right. Did you hear that?"

Claret strained her ears. "No, what?"

"I think someone knocked on your bedroom door."

Claret stood and walked toward the balcony door. "I can never hear anything when I'm out here." Kaylee followed her, and they went inside. Claret opened the bedroom door to see Captain Nerman.

"Durdessa is gone," he said. "I have men out already."

Claret's eyes narrowed. "Gone where?"

"Someone stole her locket. She was tearing her room apart trying to find it. That woman you all invited in is gone as well. I think she stole the locket and Durdessa is trying to find her."

Kaylee didn't look surprised. "It figures."

Claret was more than a little shocked. She had trusted Isadora and look where that had gotten her. "I'm sure Durdessa will be fine. If anyone should be worried, it's Isadora. Durdessa loves that locket."

"Should I send more men out looking for her?"

"Yes. She couldn't be far."

Captain Nerman nodded. "We'll find her." He turned and disappeared down the hall.

Kaylee looked nervous.

"I'm not worried. Durdessa is strong, and she is good at getting what she wants."

"You know what that locket is, right?" Kaylee asked.

"I know she really likes it. She showed it to me once, but I've never seen her wear it. She said it's a family heirloom and she can't risk losing it."

"It's the necklace that turns her into a mermaid."

Claret's eyes went wide. "Are you sure?"

"Pretty sure."

"Do you think Isadora knows what it is?"

Kaylee shrugged. "Probably not. Those lockets came from the upper continents. People down here probably don't know about them."

Claret covered her mouth with one hand. "What if Isadora puts it on? Will she automatically turn into a mermaid?"

"I only know a little from what Dovin told us, but I think so."

"We can't have that. We have to find it."

Kaylee paced a few steps and back. "Do you think Isadora was really going near Colter's Lake?"

"Wouldn't that be careless of her to tell us?"

"Yes, but what if she hadn't planned to steal anything but then she saw it and couldn't resist it?"

Claret nodded. "I suppose that's possible."

"I wish we could teleport."

"I have alicorns. That will save time."

Kaylee grinned. "I rode on an alicorn. She was so pretty. We don't have alicorns where I'm from."

"That's too bad. Should we go now?"

"It's going to be dark soon. Can you fly in the dark?"

"I never have, but can it be any harder than in the day?"

Kaylee shook her head. "Don't ask me. I only controlled one once, and I think controlled is the wrong word. I think she was the one doing everything."

"Can you ride a unicorn?" Claret asked.

"I've never seen a unicorn. I can ride a horse."

"Riding an alicorn is the same, except you pull up when you want to fly and lean forward when you want to go down. If you aren't comfortable flying one, you can ride with me."

Kaylee took a deep breath. "I should ride on my own. Then if we find Durdessa, we can take her back."

"But she can teleport."

"Riiight. It still might be nice to have extra space, just in case."

"All right, let's go to the stables."

Kaylee grabbed her arm and pulled her to a stop. "Should we tell someone what we're doing?"

Claret bit her lip. "I don't think so. Well, perhaps I'll leave a note in my room in case something happens." She rushed to her night table and opened it, then pulled out a pen and paper. She wrote a hasty note and put it on her pillow. "There."

Kaylee leaned against a stall in the stables and grinned. "Is this Willow?" she asked, looking at a black alicorn.

"Willow?" Claret asked. "This is the alicorn Vigh flew in on. I don't know her name."

"It is Willow," she said, holding out her hand. Willow leaned in, allowing her to rub her mane. "Do you remember me?"

"Is that the one you wish to take?" Claret asked.

"Yes."

Claret unlatched the stall and Willow walked out. She opened another and led out a brown alicorn with a white spot over her eye. "This is Melody. My father gave her to me when I turned twelve."

Kaylee let Melody smell her hand. "I never knew alicorns could be different colors. I thought they were all white. Well, I didn't know they were real, but on TV they're always white."

"What is TV?"

"That's hard to explain."

"Alicorns come in a lot of colors." She rubbed Melody's neck and the alicorn bent down so she could mount. Kaylee did the same thing. Mounting an alicorn was as easy as mounting a horse.

They rode out of the stables and into the chilly evening. The moon was full, and the stars were beginning to appear.

"It's easier to get them to fly if you get a running start," Claret said. "Are you ready?"

Kaylee nodded and tried to ignore the butterflies in her stomach. Claret and Melody trotted off down the dirt path leading away from the stables. Kaylee urged Willow to follow. When they were at a run, Claret and Melody lifted off the ground. Kaylee swallowed and pulled gently up on the reins. The reins made it a lot easier. Willow left the ground with ease and Kaylee sucked in a breath. The feel of the wind in her face made her smile. This was the best way to travel.

The sun shone in Claret's eyes. She blinked several times and urged Melody to fly down. If they didn't stop, she was going to fall asleep. She couldn't remember the last time she'd been this tired. Melody landed, and she heard Willow land behind them. The alicorns ran a few paces before they came to a stop.

Kaylee slid off Willow's back. "Are we there?"

Claret hopped down. "No, sorry. We're close, but I'm so tired. We need to sleep."

Kaylee half smiled. "Thank goodness. I've been hoping you would stop for hours. We should have made a signal or something. I could use an outhouse right about now."

Claret's eyes scanned the forest. "I don't think you're going to find an outhouse. Maybe a bush."

Kaylee wrinkled her nose. "Watch Willow. I'll be back in a minute." She hurried off into the trees.

Willow and Melody both began munching weeds. They weren't going anywhere. Claret looked at the ground. It wouldn't be a nice place to sleep, but she didn't care at the moment. She could sleep on a rock and hardly notice.

When Kaylee came back, Claret took her time in the bushes and then they both found the clearest places they could and tried to sleep.

"We should have brought blankets and food," Claret said, putting the hood of her cloak up so bugs wouldn't get on her.

"Yeah, we should have." Kaylee copied her with her hood and lay down.

Claret frowned as soon as her head touched the earth. Perhaps sleeping on the ground would be harder than she thought. She'd never slept outside before. She squeezed her eyes shut and tried to relax.

"I'm suddenly wide awake," she said, turning to face Kaylee.

Kaylee yawned. "Count sheep."

Claret's mouth turned down, and she looked around. "There aren't any sheep."

"In your mind," she said, yawning again. "Picture sheep going by and count them. It's supposed to help you fall asleep."

Claret closed her eyes and pictured a sheep walking past. "One," she said out loud.

"Do it in your head or you'll never fall asleep."

"Right." She pictured another sheep. It didn't move past. It stopped and started barking at her. She shook her head. Now the sheep was wearing a crown. She wasn't good at this. "Kaylee?"

Kaylee didn't answer. Her eyes were closed, and she was breathing deeply. Claret let out a slow breath. They were in the shade, but the sun was still bright. She closed her

eyes again and tried not to think about sheep. The sheep
in her imagination were not very cooperative.

74

8

— · —

CHAPTER 8

O die added a pinch of hods bark powder to his mixture. Hods bark wasn't hard to come by, but it only worked if you crushed it into a fine powder first. Odie used it often enough, and he had the crushing down to an art. Mateo wanted to help, so Odie had given him a piece to crush. He was determined, but he didn't have Odie's skill.

"Do you really think you can make something that will make us invisible?" Mateo asked.

Odie dropped in two moakberries and began stirring. "I hope so. I've tried before and never succeeded. It's possible, though. My father got an elixir that turns a person invisible, but I think he got it from someone shady. He said he could make it, but it was easier to buy than find ingredients. I know it's expensive, and he was only able to get it once."

"And you used it to steal the Blade of the Phoenix?"

"Yes."

"So how will you figure it out?"

"I'm not sure I will. When my father gave it to me, I tried to study it before I used it. It was a finely ground powder and there wasn't much to go by. I had to mix it in water and drink it. It was the color of a moakberry and it smelled like a hods tree. Everything else is a guess."

"I never liked moakberries," Mateo said. "My mom used to make them into pie when I was little. They make my tongue feel fuzzy."

"I like them if they are washed well. One thing you'll find around here is dirty food. Goblins don't mind a little grit in what they eat."

"Gross," Mateo said, trying to smash the bark with the back of a knife. There were easier ways to do it, but at the moment, Odie just wanted to keep Mateo busy and out of his way.

"It probably has something like squished acalin or something like that. Most good things do."

Mateo stopped smashing. "Acalin? The bugs that explode?"

"Yeah. I use them in a lot of things."

"Does that cause explosions?"

Odie's eyes sparkled. "Not always, but a lot of the time."

Mateo grinned. "Let's try it."

"Grab me the jar on the second to top shelf. It's got a blue lid." Odie kept mixing.

Mateo grabbed the jar and brought it to him. "It's weird you keep a jar of squished up bugs."

"You would be amazed at how many things they can be used for." Odie opened the jar and measured out a teaspoon of acalin and put it in the bowl. "You might want to stand back. If it's going to explode, it's going to be when I'm mixing."

Mateo backed up against the wall and Odie gently stirred the mixture.

"You should get some protective goggles or something to go over your face. Especially if you blow stuff up often."

"I can usually tell something is going to blow up before it happens."

"Oh yeah? How?"

"It starts to bubble up." Odie frowned. The mixture was bubbling. "Get out!" he yelled, rushing for the door. Mateo was right behind him. Before he could open the door, he felt the mixture hit him in the back of the head.

"That was awesome," Mateo said, sticking his head in the stream again. "I've never seen anything bubble like that before. When you said explosion, I thought of like, you know, fire and stuff. Not a bubbly purple goop." He put some funny-smelling soap Odie had brought in his hair and tried to scrub it. "That stuff is sticky."

"You never know what's going to happen when you use that stuff," Odie said, picking goo from his hair. "I've had a lot of weird stuff happen when I experiment with it. Occasionally, it's something awesome, but usually it's a mess."

"How are we going to clean your room? The entire place was covered."

Odie shrugged. "One great thing about being a prince is you never have to clean up. There are servants for that."

Mateo laughed. "Prince Odie. It has an odd ring to it."

Odie ran his hand through the water. "And unfortunately, it's Prince Odious."

"I wondered about that. You weren't very fortunate in the naming game."

"Goblins are like that. There aren't many good names around here."

Mateo ran his fingers through his hair. He couldn't feel any more goop. "Now what?"

"We start over."

"Won't your father get suspicious if you fail too many times?"

Odious laughed. "He would be more suspicious if I succeeded quickly. I make a lot of messes before I figure something out. It's all part of the process."

"But they think we're trying to make sleeping powder. If you've done it before, they might expect fast results."

"I think we'll be fine for a while."

Mateo nodded. "I've been thinking. We know there's a way out of Riviand, and it's probably somewhere on this mountain. Could we look for it when we aren't making messes?"

"I don't know how it works. When I went up, I couldn't see anything, and they did something to me, so I felt confused. My guess is that we would have to go higher up the mountain, but I'm not sure."

"Would anyone be suspicious if we went looking?"

"No. I run all over the mountain. Goblins expect it. I don't usually go higher than the castle. No one does. The air gets funny up higher and there isn't much to see."

"So we can go up?"

"It would take time. We would have to do it sometime when we wouldn't be missed."

Mateo wiped a drip of water from his face. "Like when the servants are cleaning your room?"

"Perhaps. I could tell one of the servants to tell my father we're out looking for more rednax venom. Rednax are difficult to find. The last time I went looking for one, I was gone for a week."

"Let's do that."

"Do we really want to be gone for a week? Shouldn't we be here trying to figure out how to stop the goblins from going to war?"

Mateo shrugged. "They're preparing, and they haven't gotten very far. I don't think it will hurt."

"But we don't need to leave Riviand," Odie protested.

"No, but I don't want to be stuck down here forever. This might be my only chance to find the way out."

"You don't like it here?"

"I like it fine, but my family isn't here, and Kaylee doesn't want to stay here. Her family isn't even from this world."

"All right, but I have another idea about the invisibility potion. Let me try it, and tomorrow we can go up the mountain."

"Fine." Mateo hadn't had regrets about coming here with Odie, but being stuck in his room trying to grind up bark was boring. He half suspected that Odie had given him that task so he wouldn't bother him. "Do you think your servants could get me some ingredients if I asked?"

Odie raised an eyebrow. "What type of ingredients?"

"Flour, sugar, eggs. That kind of thing." If Kaylee and Mateo were going to start a bakery, he needed to figure out how to cook in Riviand. It might be different than in Mexico.

"Sure. Those are easy things. The cook probably has it all in the kitchen."

"Great. You can make your little potions and I'll make cookies. It might revolutionize this place."

Odie just stared at him like he was speaking another language. Mateo didn't care. Once Odie tasted his first cookie, he would understand. They started their walk back to the castle. The stream was close by, so that was convenient. Mateo couldn't imagine bathing in the stream. The water wasn't freezing, but it wasn't warm either.

"So rednax are hard to find in Riviand?" he asked.

"Not everywhere, but there aren't many in the mountains."

"Where I grew up in Boztoll, they were everywhere. My mom used to get super mad when me and my brothers got sprayed."

Odie jumped over a rock. "You got sprayed?"

"Lots of times."

Odie chuckled. "I've worked with rednax lots of times and I've never been sprayed. Tipp has, though."

Mateo grinned. "My brothers and I like to compete. That occasionally gets us into trouble. Once we went to Earth, we didn't have a problem. They have skunks but not rednax."

When they got back to the castle, they went to the kitchen. Mateo loved this place. The kitchen was like everything else. Made from obsidian. There was a large fireplace in one corner and black countertops going around three of the walls. They were so low a person could step up on one with no trouble at all.

Sconces lined the wall, their candles giving some light, but probably not enough in the dark room. The main source of light came from a large window on one wall. There were several cupboards above the counters, and Mateo had the urge to open every one to see what was inside. He didn't know much about goblins, and he was curious. He felt like a giant in here.

A goblin with a white apron and a blue bandana tied to her head turned and growled at them. She was the first female goblin Mateo had seen here. Stringy brown hair hung to her shoulders, and she wasn't wearing a hairnet.

"Prince Odious," she said with a scowl. "I hope you haven't come to blow up my kitchen again. And it appears you've brought a friend to help you."

"Good to see you too, Vivi. I'm not blowing anything up today."

She put her hands on her hips. "No? I heard you've already caused a mess in your room. All my workers had to leave me to go help clean it."

Odie smiled. "Well, I'm not blowing up anything else today. This is my friend Mateo. He wants to cook something. Is that all right?"

She muttered something under her breath.

"He won't blow anything up."

"Have you cooked before?" she asked, sizing up Mateo with her eyes.

"Yes. Don't worry, I won't make a mess."

"Hmph. You tell me what ingredients you want, and I'll get them for you. I can't have you searching all around and messing up my system."

"All right," Mateo said, racking his mind for his cookie recipe. He made it enough that he should have it memorized. "I need butter, sugar, brown sugar, eggs, vanilla, flour, baking soda, salt, and what was that stuff called? Cocoam?"

Vivi and Odious were both staring at him with looks of puzzlement.

Vivi grabbed a small black step stool and put it up to the cupboards. "I can get you some of that stuff, but I've never heard of brown sugar or baking soda." She climbed to the top of the ladder and opened a cupboard.

Mateo frowned. They had to have baking soda. "It's a white powder that helps things rise."

"Oh, probably this." She handed him a canister.

He unscrewed the lid and smelled it. "I think so. Do you have molasses? I can use that instead of brown sugar."

Mateo was glad he'd been the brother who always helped his mom with the baking. His brothers all thought it was boring. Vivi took down more ingredients and lined them up on the counter. He looked down and wondered if it would be easier to sit on the floor while he mixed everything. Sitting would probably make the counter a little high, but better than trying to squat or bend over.

"Here's some cocoam powder," she said, handing it to him.

Odie turned to him. "It's no good unless you add something to it. Sugar and stuff like that."

"Do you know a way to make it more solid? Like something you can bite, but isn't a powder."

"Not really, but I can figure something out," Odie said.

"We would need to break it into small chunks about this size," he said, holding his thumb and middle finger as if he were holding an invisible chocolate chip.

Odie nodded. "I'll get started on it." He took the cocoam powder and grabbed a small bowl from the cupboard.

Vivi sighed. "I'm not staying in here to watch you mess up my kitchen. I'll be back in a few hours and I expect everything to be clean. Do you understand?"

Odie grinned. "Of course, Vivi."

She rolled her eyes and mumbled as she left.

"I like her," Mateo said.

Odie laughed. "Me too. She's not someone you want to cross, though. Let's try to be clean so we don't have to deal with her wrath."

9

— · —

CHAPTER 9

Kaylee's eyes popped open, and she sat up. From the look of the sun, it must be afternoon. A noise had woken her, but she couldn't place where it had come from. She scanned the trees but didn't see anything strange. Claret was rolled up in a ball, her hair covering her face. She was snoring softly.

Kaylee got to her feet and listened. She wished she'd brought the Blade of the Phoenix. There were good reasons to leave it hidden, but it would be nice to have some sort of protection. What had they been thinking?

"What's going on?" Claret asked, sitting up. She pulled her hood down and pushed her messy hair from her face.

"I thought I heard something. We should get moving. We've slept away the first part of the day."

Claret yawned and got to her feet. She ran her fingers through her messy hair. "Where are the alicorns?"

Kaylee looked around in a panic. "I don't see them."

"I'm sure they're close," Claret said. "Alicorns don't wander far unless they're lost. If so, Melody will fly home. I don't know about Willow. She might not consider the

85

castle her home yet. Blast these knots." Her fingers weren't getting through her hair without a lot of work.

Kaylee touched her own hair and found her ponytail intact. She rarely left her hair down, and she was used to having it tight. It came as an advantage when you needed to get up and go quickly.

"Someone's coming," Claret said, pointing into the trees. A woman was running toward them, her hair blowing behind her. "Is that Isadora?"

Kaylee squinted. "I think it is. Should we try to take her down?"

Claret bit her lip. "How? We didn't bring any weapons."

"I can run at her and try to knock her over, then you can help hold her down."

"Um…"

Kaylee shook her head. "Never mind. We'll see what she says when she gets here." Isadora must have seen them. She was running right to them.

When she reached them, she stopped and bent over, holding her side. She breathed deeply and glanced at them. "You have to help me!" The new green dress she had gotten from the castle was already dirty and ripped. She looked behind her as if she were being followed.

Kaylee stepped forward. "Help you? Why would we help you? You stole Durdessa's locket."

"I had to!" Isadora exclaimed. "Can we discuss it later? We need to get out of here now! Run!"

Isadora ran, and Kaylee glanced at Claret. The queen had a troubled expression.

"I guess we better run?" Kaylee said. Claret nodded, and they took off after Isadora. Even if there wasn't anything coming, they needed to get Durdessa's locket back. Isadora changed directions, and they followed. If the alicorns hadn't been lost before, they would be for sure now.

Isadora let out a yelp and fell, disappearing from view. Kaylee and Claret ran to the spot and saw her at the bottom of a ten-foot drop. She was sitting and staring up at them.

"Are you all right?" Kaylee asked.

"Yes," she said. "Just a little clumsy."

Kaylee sat on the ground and slowly lowered herself. It was slightly sloped, so not too difficult. When she got down, she looked up at Claret. Her brow was furrowed, but she sat down and began slowly inching forward. She slid down and landed on her feet, letting out a relieved breath.

Isadora stood and brushed off her dress.

"What are you running from?" Kaylee demanded. "And why did you take the locket?"

Isadora pushed a lock of hair behind her ear. "Do you know what the locket is?"

Kaylee and Claret nodded.

"Then you know how powerful it is. I wasn't at the castle to beg for food. My mother forced me to go and take the locket. She threatened me with horrible things if I failed. After I took it, the guilt was overwhelming. I knew my mother couldn't have that kind of magic. She's already too powerful."

"Why does she want it?" Claret asked. "I don't see how it could help someone be powerful."

"Do you not?" Isadora asked. "A mermaid can go in any water. People aren't expecting it. There are great advantages to it."

"Durdessa is after you, as well as the castle guards," Claret said. "Is that who you are running from?"

She shook her head. "I don't fear them. All they would do is lock me up. And Durdessa is no longer after me."

Kaylee's eyes narrowed. "What do you mean?"

"My mother captured her. Mother is the one I'm running from."

Claret frowned. "Why would she take Durdessa?"

"To use her, I'm sure. Durdessa has been a mermaid for years. She knows the tricks."

Kaylee crossed her arms. "How did your mother even know Durdessa is a mermaid? She keeps that a close secret."

"My mother knows many things. Have you ever been to Colter's Lake?"

Claret shook her head, and Kaylee nodded.

"Durdessa spends a lot of time there. My mother sees her. It's hard to get anything past her. My mother is a powerful witch."

"A witch?" Kaylee asked. "How many witches are there? Vigh's mother was a witch as well."

Isadora looked at her shoes, her mouth trembling. "Vigh was my brother. That is the reason my mother is striking now. She's angry about his death."

Claret put a hand to her stomach and went pale. Kaylee touched her arm. Claret was still feeling guilty about Vigh's death.

"So your mother uses her children to get what she wants?" Kaylee asked. "Why is she after you?"

"I threw the locket into Colter's Lake instead of taking it to her. I thought it would be better to lose it than to give it to her."

"Does she know you did it?"

"Yes. She saw me."

"And she didn't go in for it?"

"Mother is terrified of the water. It's the only thing I know that scares her."

Kaylee tapped her fingers against her arms and tried to think. Saving Durdessa should be their priority. The locket would come second. They could go back to the castle and hope Dovin was back, but it would take far too long on foot.

"How did you find us?" Claret asked. "It seems odd we would end up in the same place, hundreds of miles from where we last parted."

Kaylee hadn't thought of that. What were the chances?

"I didn't find you on purpose. I saw you when I was running. I was as surprised as you."

Claret smoothed back her hair. "How did you get here so fast? You were on foot and we had alicorns. There is no way you covered that much distance on foot."

"I told you, my mother is a powerful witch. She can open portals."

"Where is Durdessa?" Kaylee asked. "We have to save her."

"At my mother's manor. That's where she keeps everything she collects."

"Collects?"

"Yes. It's a large house, almost like a castle. She keeps different... creatures there. I had thought she meant to use the locket for herself, but I wonder if she really wanted to have Durdessa wear it so she can show her off to people. She has other mermaids."

"That's terrible." Claret gasped.

"Most people think my mother is just a noble woman, but she also caters to a darker crowd. She likes to show them the things she has stolen."

"That must be one reason she wanted the Blade of the Phoenix," Kaylee said.

Isadora nodded. "One of the reasons."

"Can you take us to your home?" Claret asked.

Isadora bit her lip. "Perhaps. If we go there quickly, we can probably enter without my mother knowing. She's still looking for me and wouldn't expect me to go back home."

"Then let's go now," Claret said. "We have to save her."

Kaylee had a bad feeling about this, but Claret looked determined.

Isadora nodded, but her forehead was creased with worry. "We need to hurry. If my mother finds us, it will go worse for me than you. I can never return once we find your friend."

"Don't worry about that now," Claret said. "I can help you begin a new life once we finish."

"Thank you. Follow me and let's be quick."

<hr>

Odie stared at Mateo's creation and frowned. "I'm not trying it until you do."

Mateo grinned. "You distrust me? Fine." He took a bite of one of the round desserts and chewed. "It's not bad. A little burned, but the next batch will be better. I've never cooked in something as confusing as that oven, but I'll figure it out."

Odie picked up a cookie and turned it in his hand. He'd helped Mateo figure out a way to turn the cocoam powder into small solid chunks, but he wasn't sure he trusted it. He took a bite and his eyes lit up. It would require another bite just to be sure it was as good as the first.

"Good, huh?"

"It is. So these are the things you want to sell if you open the bakery?"

"One of the things, yes."

"You are going to make a fortune."

Mateo laughed. "I'm glad you approve."

Odie grabbed a platter and put the remaining cookies on top. "Once it's full, I'm going to take it around and pass them out. Most of the goblins have never liked me, but this might give us points."

The door creaked open and Vivi peeked in. "Any explosions?"

Odie grinned. "No. Come in, Vivi. You have to taste this."

Vivi scowled but entered the kitchen. Odie held out the platter, and she hesitantly took a cookie. She turned it over cautiously and smelled it.

"Just try it," Odie urged.

She licked it, and Mateo chuckled. She glared at him and then took a small bite. Her expression remained the same. She studied it again and took another bite, then shoved the rest into her mouth.

"Well?" Mateo asked.

She wiped crumbs from the corner of her mouth. "If you ever need a job, come see me." She grabbed two more cookies and stormed from the kitchen.

Odie looked at Mateo and they burst out laughing.

"From Vivi, that is a great compliment," Odie said.

"I probably shouldn't be doing this," Mateo said. "We came here to stop a war, not make cookies."

"I don't know," Odie said. "Goblins are easily distracted. This will definitely get their attention."

"But not enough to stop a war."

"It takes time to prepare for a war," Odie assured him. "Years even. We just need to take it a step at a time. Goblins usually join wars. We don't start them. *They* don't start them," he said, correcting himself. "I think we should try to get them to stop preparations, but I think there is a huge chance they would never get to the actual war part. There is very little chance of the goblins defeating the capital city of Tyran, let alone all of Riviand."

The door flew open and Tipp ran in. King Ummi and Garin were behind him.

Tipp looked around until his eyes rested on the platter of cookies. "Vivi said your friend made one of the best things she's ever tasted."

Mateo raised the platter and held it out to him.

Tipp grabbed a cookie and stuffed the entire thing in his mouth. "This is sooo good," he said, with crumbs falling from his mouth.

"Just wait until the next batch," Mateo said. "They should be better, and they taste better hot. They're probably done." He went over to the oven and peeked in.

"It's just a cookie," Garin said. "Nothing to get too excited about." Odie couldn't help smiling when Garin picked two from the platter.

"A what?" King Ummi asked, picking one up.

"A cookie," Mateo said, carrying over a hot pan. He placed it on the low countertop. "Give these two minutes and then try one."

King Ummi took a bite, and his eyes widened. "I like it. I command you to teach Vivi how to bake these."

Mateo grinned. "Sure, but I don't think she likes me."

Kind Ummi nodded. "Vivi doesn't like anyone."

Garin ate his cookie slowly and watched Mateo. He had an expression Odie couldn't read.

"Have we ever met?" Garin finally asked.

Mateo pointed at himself. "Are you talking to me?"

"Yes. I've been trying to figure out why you look familiar since I first saw you."

Mateo shrugged. "I don't think so."

"Where are you from?"

Mateo paused and glanced at Odie. Odie's heart started racing. They hadn't come up with an explanation for who Mateo was and where he was supposed to be from.

"Here and there. Most recently Tyran."

"Hm. Your accent doesn't sound like anything I've heard here."

Accent? Odie frowned. Mateo and Garin had the same accent. That should be a dead giveaway.

Mateo scooped the cookies onto the cooling rack. Garin took another and left. King Ummi and Tipp did the same. Well, Tipp took a few.

Odie turned to Mateo. "Have you ever seen him before?"

Mateo shook his head. "No. I would remember those eyes."

10

—·—

CHAPTER 10

"There it is," Isadora said, pointing at a mansion in front of them. It was three stories tall, with lots of windows and a red brick facade. Claret frowned. Someone with an estate this large should be known to her. She supposed a witch might stay hidden for obvious reasons, but it still seemed like she should have at least heard of the witch before. Of course she didn't know the witch's name.

"We need to go in the back. Preferably a window."

"Why?" Kaylee asked. "Your mother isn't here."

"But it would be preferable if the maids didn't see us."

"Do the maids know you and your mother had a falling-out?" Claret asked.

"No, I suppose not. Still, I don't trust my mother. She might have popped back in to tell someone to hold me here or something."

"How did Durdessa even get here?" Kaylee asked. "It seems like too many coincidences."

"When my mother made a portal, I ran in. As soon as I was through, Durdessa was standing there with me. She

95

must have run through with me. We might as well start in the basement either way. That is where my mother keeps… things."

Isadora led them in a large circle around the house. Claret's mind kept telling her to go back to Tyran and seek help, but it would take so long she didn't dare.

"Come on," Isadora said, running toward the house. Claret and Kaylee were on her heels. When they got to a ground level window, Isadora pulled on it and it opened. Isadora sat on the ground and stuck her legs through. She dropped out of sight.

Kaylee frowned. "The witch leaves her window unlocked?"

Isadora's face appeared at the bottom of the window. "She doesn't. I do. This is how I come and go when I don't want my mother to know."

"This is a bad idea," Kaylee muttered so only Claret could hear.

"It will be fine. We have to find Durdessa."

"I don't trust Isadora."

Claret shrugged and went through the window, and Kaylee followed. The drop was more than she'd expected, but she landed on her feet. She blinked while her eyes adjusted to the light.

"Now we need to go to the basement," Isadora said.

Claret's eyes widened. "I thought this was the basement."

"The basement doesn't have any windows." The room they were in was painted white and didn't have anything in it. Isadora pulled open a door to reveal a staircase. "Come."

"I've got a bad feeling about this," Kaylee said. "A creepy witch's basement with no windows?"

"You can leave and I'll go," Claret said. "I can't leave Durdessa."

Kaylee shook her head. "I'm coming."

The stairway wasn't what Claret was expecting. It was painted white, and it was well lit with candles every few feet. Claret feared it would be more like the goblins' dungeon, dark and full of spiderwebs.

When they reached the bottom, a long hallway greeted them. It was wide and to the sides, there were creatures in cages. It was set up the same as the goblin dungeon, except well kept.

Claret frowned at the first cell. Inside was a troll. He was sitting at a table, writing on a piece of parchment. His long, quill-like hair fell past his shoulders. He didn't even look up. He wore a tunic and cape, even though it was warm. The cell was decorated neatly with a tan rug and a bed and other small furnishings.

"Zute?" Kaylee asked, grabbing the bars.

The troll turned. "Ah. Kaylee. Pity you're here. Pity any of us are here." He went back to his writing.

Kaylee turned and looked at Isadora. "We have to free him."

Isadora nodded. "It won't be easy. Let's find the queen's aunt first," she whispered.

Claret looked at the cell across from Zute's cell and saw three monkeys. There was a tree growing out of the floor and the monkeys looked content. Her eyes fell on a small sign that explained the species of monkey and their names. She turned and saw the same with the troll.

Kaylee's eyes narrowed. "It's like a zoo."

"We don't have much time," Isadora said. "We cannot be found."

Each cell they passed had a different creature. There were unicorns, alicorns, a goblin, a small dragon, and a few animals that weren't unique. The spaces were all well kept and appeared comfortable and some looked almost fancy with their rugs and fancy candle holders.

"Hundo!" Kaylee said, looking in the cell of a giant. He was at least ten feet tall and wore small round spectacles and an apron. He was holding a book in his hand and sitting in a comfortable chair.

The giant turned and gave a sad smile. "Kaylee and Queen Claret. I wondered what became of you."

"Don't worry," Kaylee said. "We're going to get you out of here. We just need to find someone first."

He shook his head sadly and gazed at Isadora. "Not unless you get rid of that one."

Isadora frowned and put her hands on her hips. "I am not my mother."

Hundo scratched his head and opened his book. "I don't understand you."

"We're almost there," Isadora said. "The water section is next."

Claret's eyes felt like they might bug out of her head. From the floor to the ceiling was a glass wall, and behind it, water. It looked like pictures Claret had seen depicting the ocean. No one had ever seen the ocean because it was above Riviand. There were beautiful plants, some floating in the water and some coming out of the ground.

"How is this possible?" Claret asked.

Kaylee didn't seem overly impressed like Claret.

Isadora put her hand on the glass. "My mother's magic is strong. She can do things others can't even dream of."

A school of little creatures swam up to the glass. They had the head of dragons and the body of a seahorse. They were gold, blue, and tan. Claret had never seen anything like them before. She'd also never seen a seahorse, but she'd seen a picture once.

"These guys, I remember," Kaylee said, tapping the glass where the creatures bobbed up and down. "They have a nasty sting."

"Yes, the wellers," Isadora said. "They are only found in Colter's Lake."

"How do they sting?" Claret asked.

Kaylee tapped the glass harder, and the wellers began moving up and down, their color changing to bright red and blue. Long barbs shot from their mouths and harmlessly hit the glass and fell slowly to the sandy floor. "Like that."

"The mermaids are on the other side," Isadora said, pointing. They turned to see an identical enclosure to the one the wellers were in, but there were four mermaids swimming around.

Claret walked up to the glass, her mouth hanging open. She'd never seen a mermaid before. One was black, with long hair waving behind her. She wore a golden crown. One had shoulder-length black hair. She was glaring at them as she swam in place. A red-haired mermaid swam quickly behind a plant so they couldn't stare at her. The last one had brown hair that had been secured in a braid that hung down to the center of her back. She ignored them.

This prison went back farther than the others. An arched hallway gave the mermaids space to swim. They all wore red silk shirts, which seemed out of place, but who knew what mermaids really liked?

"Why is one of them wearing a crown?" Kaylee asked.

"It's a game my mother plays. The mermaid that she is the most pleased with gets to wear the crown for the day. They all try to outdo each other. Well, most of them. Jayah doesn't care if she wins or not."

"That's an odd thing for your mother to do."

"The mermaids are my mother's favorites. Mother doesn't really want Durdessa's locket. She wanted Durdessa. She likes a variety, and she has longed to have a blond mermaid."

Claret hugged herself. "Your mother has a serious problem. I don't see Durdessa."

Kaylee's eyes narrowed. "Your story has holes."

"Durdessa isn't there yet," Isadora said, ignoring Kaylee. "She's in the last cell, next to the mermaids. If I know my mother, she's unconscious. She'll give her time to rest before she puts her with the others. My mother may be a witch, but she cares for her captives quite well."

Claret hurried past the mermaids to the last cell. This cell only had a small carpet and a table with two chairs. It had fewer candles than the other spaces. Durdessa lay on the rug, one arm thrown above her head. Her chest rose and fell. Claret grabbed the bars and pulled on them. "How do we get her out?"

Isadora pulled a key from her pocket. "I stole a key years ago. I used to sneak down here to play with the dragons. It's a pity there is only one now." She turned the key, and the lock popped open. She pushed open the cell door and frowned. "How will we get her out? Mother probably gave her something to keep her sleeping for a while."

Kaylee frowned. "I doubt we can carry her. Maybe we can wake her?"

Claret rushed to her aunt and fell to her knees. She shook Durdessa's shoulders, but she didn't show any sign of waking.

"If you threw Durdessa's locket into Colter's Lake, Durdessa won't be able to become a mermaid," Kaylee said, not entering the cell.

Isadora nodded. "Mother is terrified of the water, but she will get someone to find it. She's very persuasive."

"We are so stupid," Kaylee said. "We shouldn't have come down here."

Claret frowned, and Isadora's brows came together.

Kaylee took a step away from Isadora. "We walked right into your trap. Your mother will be so proud."

"What are you talking about?" Isadora asked.

"I think you know."

Isadora smiled, and Claret felt a chill run down her spine. "I don't even have a mother," Isadora said.

Kaylee swung her fist at Isadora. The woman disappeared and reappeared five feet away. "You are the witch."

"It's true. And now you get to stay here, forever."

Claret ran toward the cell door, but Isadora waved her hand and it slammed shut. Kaylee dove at her and knocked her over. Before they could hit the floor, Isadora vanished, and Kaylee slammed into the wooden floor. Isadora appeared and pulled backward with her hand. The cell door opened, and she pushed her hand forward. Kaylee slid across the floor and into the cell, the door slamming behind her.

Isadora waved her arms through the air, and her dress changed into a long, glittering, yellow gown. Her hair twisted around itself and she smiled. "I've never had anyone walk so willingly down here before. I could have just brought you here by magic, but where is the fun in that?"

Claret stood tall and walked to the bars. She took them in both hands and glared at the woman. Her heart was pounding in fear, but she wouldn't let it show. "People will come for us."

Isadora laughed. "You mean people will come to see you. You are now part of my exhibit. A queen and a girl with no magic. And not just any girl, the girl who used the Blade of the Phoenix to secure the continent. My friends will be thrilled. I need to get Claret a crown. A queen should always wear a crown, don't you agree?"

"You have to let us go," Kaylee said. "We won't be part of this."

Isadora smiled. "But you have so many friends here. Zute and Hundo. I know you only met them once, but you got along."

"You captured people I know?"

"People is a strange word."

Kaylee seethed. "Have you been watching us?"

"When I can, and it's been interesting. Don't waste your time on things you can't control. With the queen gone, Riviand will fall to the goblins, and the goblins will fall to me. Of course I know goblins. It won't be hard to get them on my side."

"Please don't do this," Claret said.

Isadora's smile fell and her eyes flashed with anger. "You know you deserve to be here. You killed Vigh, my only son."

"It wasn't her," Kaylee said.

Claret wanted to throw up. She hated thinking about Vigh. It had been her fault.

"I saw it happen. I have more magic than anyone in this pathetic place has had in over a thousand years. When I rule, you will be entertainment for my friends." Isadora pulled Durdessa's locket from her pocket and held it up. She tossed it through the bars and onto the floor. She waved her arms and disappeared.

Claret sank to the floor and covered her face in her hands.

"Don't let her get to you. Vigh was trying to kill you at her command. If anyone is to blame, it's her."

Claret looked up. "I know." She knew, but that still didn't stop her nightmares. "I didn't listen to your concerns and now we're stuck here."

"Don't let yourself feel down. It's because of me that Hundo and Zute are here. I'm almost sure she took them because I talked with them. I don't know why, but it can't be random. We aren't going to blame ourselves. All these problems are because of Isadora. Instead of worrying about what we can't control, we are going to figure out a way to get out of here."

Kaylee went to the bars and tried to look past them. "Hundo?" she called. "Can you hear me?"

"Yes," Hundo said loudly.

"Have you been mistreated?"

"No. Isadora may be a witch, but she has been accommodating. The food is quite delicious, and the room is comfortable."

"We're going to get out of here, somehow."

"I am patient," the giant said.

Claret took a deep breath. She wished she could say the same.

11

CHAPTER 11

"What do you want to talk to me about?" King Ummi asked.

Odie looked up at where his father sat on the throne. "About Garin. I don't think you can trust him."

His father sighed and straightened his crown. "I don't trust Garin."

"Then why are you siding with him?"

"I've met no one like him before. There is something dangerous about him. I fear offending him."

"You'll spend years planning a war so you don't make him angry? He's one person. The goblins can surely defeat him."

"Perhaps, though I wouldn't count on it. He wants to overthrow Riviand and I cannot understand why. He's from the upper lands, and he came here on purpose. I think he was like others who came here believing Riviand would be a land full of treasures. When he came and realized it wasn't, he must have decided to take over. He says when we win, I will rule Riviand, but I am no fool. He wants it."

"So why are you following him? It's dangerous."

"Yes, but I don't know a better solution."

Odie frowned. "The world doesn't need a war."

"I have no problem taking gold from the queen. Garin's plans are much more sinister. I've been thinking and I might have a solution that would benefit everyone. I wish to keep it to myself for now."

Odie leaned forward. "Tell me. I might be able to help you."

"If my plan works, you will be the one to help."

"What do you mean?"

"We make an alliance with Queen Claret."

"That won't be hard if we promise peace. She isn't a violent person."

"I mean to give her an option. War or marriage. To you."

Odie blinked twice. "Marriage? Father, that's the craziest thing you ever said. I'm not old enough to get married and even if I were, Claret won't agree to something like that."

"You wouldn't have to marry her immediately. A year or two would suffice. If you marry her, Garin could feel he was controlling you. It might be enough to stop any talk of war."

Odie threw his arms in the air. "Father, do you hear what you're saying? Garin would be controlling me. A man like that shouldn't be in control. Do you really think he'll be happy with that kind of role for long? Eventually, he'll want to be the one people look to. Then he would end up getting rid of me and probably Claret."

King Ummi stoked his chin. "Hmm. You could be right. It makes sense to arrange that marriage, though. You are the only prince in all of Riviand and she is the only princess. Well, I suppose there is Tipp, but he can't marry a human."

"It's ridiculous to think about. We need to get rid of Garin. He's dangerous, and he needs to be dealt with."

"Let's not get ahead of ourselves. It might be wise to get rid of Garin, but to wait until we've secured Riviand."

"I thought you didn't want to do that? Leave Riviand alone."

"Gold is my motivation, but if we were in command, all the gold would be ours."

Odie let out a breath. His father didn't even know his own mind.

King Ummi tapped his fingers against his throne. "I'm having a thought. Leave me now so I can think about it."

Odie bowed curtly and stormed from the room. It was good to know the king didn't trust Garin. That was one step in the right direction. Still, the king didn't seem eager to part with the man, either.

Odie opened the door to his bedroom and went in.

Mateo sat at the table in Odie's room, sorting the ingredients Odie had asked him to. Odie kept finding jobs for Mateo so he wouldn't get bored. The door opened and Odie entered. He slammed the door and sat at the table.

"My father is impossible. He doesn't trust Garin, but he doesn't dare to go against him. He's trying to find ways to get out of war, but his ideas are ridiculous."

"Oh? Like what?"

Odie looked sheepish. "He thinks we should tell Claret she has to go to war or marry me."

Mateo burst out laughing. He could only imagine how that conversation had gone. "It sounds like a good idea to me."

"Claret would never agree to something like that."

"She might. If it was to avoid war."

"No. She wouldn't marry the enemy to keep peace. She's smart enough to know that wouldn't go well. It would be obvious the goblins were still trying to manipulate her."

Mateo nodded. "But you forget. You aren't her enemy."

"I know."

"At least your father is trying to come up with things that might lead to a happier ending. I bet I could take Garin. He doesn't look that strong. We could ambush him and force the king to tell us how to send him back up to the other continents."

Odie shook his head. "He could come back. He came here on purpose. Remember? He also has magic that is making my father nervous."

"I still wonder about his eyes. I've never seen anything like them."

"Neither have I." Odie grabbed a canister and twisted the lid. "It would be helpful if I could figure out this invisibility thing. We could probably scare Garin so badly he would leave and never come back."

"Can't you ask your father? He's the one who gave it to you before."

"No. He wouldn't approve. I'm probably not going to get anywhere. If the ingredients are so hard to get even my father can't manage it, what are the chances I have the right things here? Pretty much zero."

Mateo leaned his arms against the table. "Is there a library here?"

"In the castle? No. Goblins can read, but they don't like to."

"Do you know where we could find one? Maybe we could find a book about spells or something."

"I know Tyran has a library and the giants."

"I've been to the giants' library. I wonder if giants know more magic than we do. The giants up above are really smart and they have strong magic. They don't use it a lot and they don't talk about it. I wonder if they could help us. I met a giant that I might be able to persuade."

"The giants are far away. It would take us forever to walk."

Mateo grinned. "But now we can teleport."

Odie groaned. "I don't mean to offend, but teleporting with you is not a pleasant experience."

He laughed. "No, it's not. But I won't get better if I never practice. What do you say?"

"What about going to the upper continents?"

"That can wait."

"Why not go to Tyran?"

Mateo shook his head. "If Tyran had books about things like being invisible, I think everyone would know. Giants might keep things to themselves."

"Invisibility isn't our only option," Odie said. "It would be helpful because we could spy on Garin, but if it takes too much time and effort, we might lose sight of our goal."

Mateo nodded. "I suppose. Still, being invisible would be neat."

"Believe me, I would like nothing more than being invisible. Not having magic in Riviand is limiting."

"In Basura there used to be a lot of people without magic. Out of all my brothers, only two of us have magic."

"But now everyone has it?"

"That's what I understand. It didn't help my brothers because they were in an entirely different world when it happened."

Odie rubbed his chin. "But it means a person who has no magic can get it."

Mateo didn't want to get Odie's hopes up. He hadn't liked Odie at all when they first met, but he'd quickly grown on him. "It was a huge event that caused it. Something that probably won't happen again."

"I try not to care about not having magic. I try to do things that make it look like I have it. Experiments and stuff."

"That's more impressive than having magic. Anyone can have magic, but not everyone can do what you do." He wanted to grin when Odie's eyes lit up. Kaylee would approve of the conversation. He wished she'd been there to witness it.

Odie sat down. "Perhaps we should go talk to the giant. There are legends that say giants have magic that people can't comprehend. It's hard to know if it's true since they don't like to talk to humans. We could also see what the giants think about the goblins going to war. I bet they would side with Claret."

"The giant we met was the only one in his village. He said the others all left to find another giant village so they could all be together if something bad happened when the continent was rising. I'm not sure if they've returned now that the threat of that is over."

"Giants are very loyal to each other. If one accepts you, they all will."

"So we teleport there, I can ask Hundo about invisibility, and we can be back by dinner."

Odie's brows came together. "Nothing ever seems that smooth. I'll tell my father we are going to go looking for ingredients for something. They won't question it if we don't return for a few days."

"All right. Why don't you go tell him now, then we can go?"

Odie stood and nodded. "While I'm gone, you should think of a way to land softer when you teleport." Odie left, and Mateo sighed. It felt like they were always doing something. Once they fixed things with the goblins, he was going to take two days to just have fun.

Ten minutes later, Odie returned. He had a small brown pack over his shoulder. "All right, let's go."

"What's in the pack?"

"Some food and a few stink bombs. You never know when they might be useful."

Mateo laughed. "I can get behind that. I've been thinking. If we run and teleport, maybe we shouldn't stop running when we land. That might be the reason we fell."

Odie's eyebrow arched. "But if we land somewhere and keep running, we might run into something."

"There isn't a lot of stuff around the giant village. I can take us outside the village. There won't be anything for us to run into."

"No trees?"

"Well, there might be trees. Just run, keep your eyes open, and try not to fall."

"This plan seems flawed."

Mateo frowned. "I can go alone."

Odie sighed. "No, I'll come."

"I wonder if I can teleport us from this room. There isn't a lot of space to run, but any motion makes more sense to me than standing still."

"That's probably why you can't teleport unless you're moving. You've decided that it makes more sense to do it that way, so you've created a block for yourself."

"Probably. I'll work on it later. Grab my cape."

Odie grabbed his cape, and they walked to the back wall. "I'm ready."

"Three quick steps and I'll do it. Ready? Go." They rushed forward and teleported. As soon as the wind hit Mateo in the face, he took three more steps and crashed into a tree.

12

CHAPTER 12

Kaylee sank to the floor and took a deep breath. She couldn't see any way out of here. Durdessa was moaning in her sleep, so with luck, she would wake soon. Claret had been sitting on the floor, sniffling and blaming herself. Kaylee wouldn't give up, but she didn't know what to try first.

Durdessa's eyes fluttered open, and she frowned when she saw Kaylee. Sitting up, she put a hand to her head. "Where are we?"

"In a witch's dungeon," Claret said. "We tried to save you, but Isadora tricked us."

Durdessa put a hand to Claret's cheek. "You shouldn't have come. Is that my locket?"

Kaylee crawled over to the necklace and grabbed it. She handed it to Durdessa.

"Thank you. I should have known better than to follow Isadora. She was much too easy to follow. Once I caught up to her, she grabbed me and pulled me through a portal. That's the last thing I remember. Why would she give my locket back?"

Kaylee stood and pulled Durdessa to her feet. "I'm not sure if you can see from here, but Isadora collects different creatures." Kaylee looked through the bars, but it was hard to see from this angle. "She has a huge glass wall with water behind it. And mermaids."

Durdessa's eyes widened. "Mermaids? I just got a chill. I knew other mermaids had fallen in before, but I've never met them."

"There are four. She's going to make you go in with them."

"Interesting. I never would have thought a witch would want a collection of mermaids. Why not use the locket herself?"

"She pretended to be Vigh's sister, but she's actually his mother. She told us the witch was scared of water. Maybe that part of her story was true."

"Hmm." Durdessa's eyes fell on Claret. "Why are you crying?"

Claret wiped at her eyes. "It's all my fault that Kaylee and I ended up here. I never seem to do the right thing."

"It's not your fault," Kaylee said, even though it kind of was. "I didn't have to come."

"But you didn't trust Isadora. I should have listened."

"Crying about it won't help."

Claret's eyes went wide and her lips trembled.

Kaylee resisted rolling her eyes. "I'm not trying to hurt your feelings. We're in a dangerous situation, and we need to get out of here. We can cry about it later. Right now, we need to act."

Durdessa held out her hand and a ball of light appeared in her palm. "Look, I can do magic."

Kaylee grinned. "Does that mean you can teleport?"

"Possibly. Sometimes people put spells over things like prisons so that people can't teleport or summon things. It's possible she wouldn't do it because I've never heard of anyone in Riviand who could teleport. Still, the occasional person can make a portal, so there might be a charm that would keep people in."

"Can't you try?" Kaylee asked.

"Not yet. If I go, I won't know how to come back because I don't know where we are."

"And we have to free everyone."

"How many creatures are in here?"

"I don't know," Kaylee admitted. "Isadora has been watching us. I don't know how, but she knows a lot. There's a giant and a troll here who helped us. She brought them here because of it. Maybe she has a crystal ball or something."

"What's a crystal ball?" Claret asked.

"A round ball about this big," Kaylee said, showing her with her hands. "You look into it and it shows you things."

Claret's eyes went as wide as saucers. "That sounds terrifying."

Durdessa shook her head. "I've never heard of anything like that. I doubt she has one."

"Well, she was seeing things somehow. Maybe she can see us now."

A voice clearing caused Kaylee to jump. She turned to see a short man in a fancy brown suit and top hat standing in front of their cell.

"Hello and welcome to Isadora's. My name is Korum. If you wish to enjoy your stay, mind your manners and try to be interesting when Isadora brings people in to see you. If there is anything you need to make your stay more comfortable, please let me know."

Kaylee walked over to the man and grabbed the bars. "Are you serious? Why are you talking like we are guests and not prisoners?"

"It all depends on your point of view. The way you act determines the way you will be treated. Your room will be decorated according to your preferences. Please decide together the way you would like to live. The mermaid will, of course, be placed with the others."

"Our room?" Kaylee asked. "You mean our cell."

"Once it is decorated, you will see it differently. If you give it a chance, you will come to like it."

"Vigh said his mother wanted to start a war. None of this makes sense."

"Isadora is a complex woman. She has many desires and interests. Keeping you here will help her start a war, and she also gets a queen and a non-magic person in her collection. For her, that is two wonderful things."

"Why did she take the giant and troll who helped us?" Kaylee demanded.

"She likes all the creatures to live harmoniously. If you know some of your neighbors, she feels the morale will be better. I must go now. If you have more questions, you may ask me when I return with your dinner." He walked away.

Kaylee turned to Claret and Durdessa. "This is so weird. I don't know what to think."

Durdessa joined Kaylee at the bars and watched the man walk away. "I'm going to try something." She disappeared and reappeared on the other side of the bars. "I can teleport. Lovely." She vanished and popped back by Kaylee. "Let's wait until Korum returns with dinner. We can eat and then get everyone else out of their cells. That was careless of Isadora."

"Why not do it now?"

"I have a feeling he'll be back soon, and we don't want to be in the middle of anything when he returns. I don't know what Isadora can do, but it would be best if we treat her as someone more powerful than the three of us put together. Besides, I haven't eaten in a while and I feel a bit dizzy."

"Claret, you're going to have to pull yourself together," Kaylee said. "Do you think you can do that?"

Claret nodded and got to her feet. "I'm sorry. I should never be weak and scared."

"Anyone can feel weak and scared. Let's just try to get out of here before we give into it. All right?"

Claret nodded and wiped her nose on a handkerchief. "I know. It's just hard to know you aren't suited for what you are supposed to be."

Durdessa put a hand on Claret's shoulder. "We all grow into who we need to be. It's a process."

Kaylee nodded. "You should have seen me a few years ago. I shiver every time I think back to what a spoiled little brat I used to be. I know I still have my issues, but I can see the progress I've made."

Kaylee really hated thinking back to the ten-year-old she had been. She had been rude and horrible to her cousin Graham, even though he had been one of the best people in her life. It had cut her to the center when he had left and never came back to visit. She'd blamed herself for years. Now that she knew he had gone to a different world, she felt a little better. It still would have been nice if he'd come and explained things to her.

"What do we do when we get out of the cell?" Claret asked. "How do we get the others out?"

"I can teleport everyone out into the hallway. If everyone holds on to one another, I might be able to take everyone out at once. I've never taken over three people at a time, though, so I'm not sure what will happen."

Kaylee sat cross-legged on the floor. "Isadora seems very attached to this place. What is she going to do when all her *collection* disappears? She's going to be angry."

Claret felt sick to her stomach. Kaylee was right. Isadora would be fighting mad if they succeeded. The witch already had reason to hate her, and she wouldn't endear herself anymore by freeing her prisoners. It needed to be done, but that didn't make it less of a problem. Claret wished she were more like Kaylee. She didn't seem to be scared of anything.

"Do you think Isadora has alliances with anyone?" she asked. "I worry about retaliation. We already have the goblins preparing for war. I don't know if we can handle trouble from two sides."

Durdessa sat next to Kaylee. "It's hard to know for sure. I've never heard of her before, which makes me think she keeps a low profile. Even if the goblins and Isadora come at Tyran at once, I think we would win."

Kaylee's mouth turned down. "It seems weird that Riviand is so big and only has one ruler."

"Two if you count King Ummi," Claret said.

"Yes, but it's still a lot of land and people to keep track of."

"I tried to talk Claret's father into separating it," Durdessa said. "It is too big for one person to rule."

"What did Father say?" Claret asked. She'd never heard anyone suggest breaking up Riviand.

"He said it was a bad idea. He worried there would be wars between people who thought they should rule. It's true, but I still think it would have been a good idea."

Claret's brows came together. "What is it like on the upper continents?"

Durdessa scooted back so she could lean against the gray wall. "The two continents are different. One is divided into two kingdoms. The other continent is run by governors who are voted into office. Akkron is the main city and the governor of Akkron lightly rules over the rest of the governors. They have their own say in things, but he can make decisions that affect the entire continent."

"Mateo said something about the governor of Akkron being a woman," Kaylee said.

Durdessa smiled, but it didn't touch her eyes. "It's been a long time since I was there."

Claret began pacing across the cell. Dividing Riviand would put a lot less stress on her, but what if it caused discontent among the people? It would be nice to spread out some of the responsibility, but she didn't want to be the cause of chaos, either.

"What if you remain in control of Riviand but have elected governors in all the cities?" Kaylee asked. "That way, they could deal with the city's problems and only come to you if completely necessary."

Claret tried to run her fingers through her tangles. "That might work."

Durdessa frowned. "It might. Now isn't the time to do it, though. We need to deal with Isadora and the goblins first."

"Right. I can't lose focus. After we escape, I'll worry about the goblins. One thing at a time."

Kaylee nodded. "I wonder how Mateo and Odie are doing. It's too bad there aren't cell phones or something here."

Claret didn't know what a cell phone was, but she didn't need to spend time worried about something they didn't have. "How will we get the mermaids out?"

"The same as the others," Durdessa said, biting her lip. "I worry, though. As soon as they remove their necklace, they will begin to change back. It's a painful process and slow, so we should free them last."

"How long does it take?" Claret asked.

"It depends. The longer a person stays a mermaid, the longer it takes to change back. I've had it take as long as five hours."

"Five hours?" Kaylee asked. "I'm starting to feel nervous. Can they walk while they're changing?"

Durdessa's face fell. "No. There is usually a lot of writhing on the ground, waiting for legs to return."

Claret raised her brow. "And you keep doing it?"

"It's hard to explain the pull of the water," Durdessa said with a far-off look in her eye. "Once you put on the necklace and swim around, it does something to a person. I can't explain it. You almost forget about the pain you know will be waiting for you."

Kaylee sighed. "So if we have a giant, a troll, a bunch of animals, and four mermaids in excruciating pain, how are we all going to hold on to each other and teleport?"

"It's going to be difficult," Durdessa admitted. "We'll have to do the best we can."

Claret tried to see through the bars to the other cells, but she couldn't see much. "I think Isadora cares for all the creatures. If we have to leave the animals, I think they'll be all right. They looked happy."

"We can't leave them," Kaylee protested.

"But if we have to leave someone behind, I think it would be best." She turned to see Kaylee glaring at her. "People have pets. She has given them a lot of space and their cages are clean."

"There's a dragon in here," Kaylee said. "There's no way dragons are supposed to be locked up."

"Perhaps not, but some animals might actually do better here than in the wild."

Durdessa sighed and rubbed her eyes. "We will do the best we can. It's difficult to say what will happen, so we need to be ready for anything."

Footsteps echoed from a distance, and they all fell silent. After a moment, Korum appeared in front of them with a large serving tray. The cell door popped open, and he slid the food across the floor. Before they could think, the door slammed shut.

"Sorry to do it this way," he said. "I don't want to get close until I determine whether you are a threat."

"We understand, thank you," Durdessa said.

Korum nodded, and they listened to his footsteps retreating.

Claret picked up a piece of chicken and smelled it. "Do you think it's safe?"

Kaylee grabbed a piece and took a bite. She grinned. "There's only one way to know."

13

— · —

CHAPTER 13

Odie touched a long scrape on his arm and cringed. He couldn't believe Mateo had run them into a tree. Actually, he could, and he wasn't looking forward to teleporting with him again. Mateo looked worse. He had hit the tree head-on and had a big bump on his forehead. Now they were walking around the giant village, looking for any sign of life. So far, they had seen no one.

The village was small, but the structures were large. The doorways were as tall as the doorways in Claret's castle. Mateo took him to a bakery and a library because that was where he had talked to a giant before. Both places were deserted. Since they had come to see the library, they stayed in the building and looked at the books on display.

The giants' books were larger than any books Odie had ever seen but not too big to hold. The books were all laid out on big stone tables. There were ten books on each table, their covers facing up. They were all leather-bound and plain, with only a title and the occasional author's name.

"I don't see anything about magic," Mateo said from a few tables away.

Odie shut the book he'd been looking at. "Me neither. It makes sense. Giants hold their magic close. No one knows what they are capable of. They aren't going to lay it out for anyone to see."

Mateo let out a long breath. "Now what? Hundo was the only giant here. He must have gone looking for the other giant village. That could be anywhere."

"There are a lot of buildings we didn't look at. He might still be here."

"I suppose. Let's go look." Mateo hurried out the door and Odie followed. "I guess I could yell for him. It's not like there is anyone around to get disturbed by it."

Odie shrugged. "It's worth a try."

Mateo cupped his hands around his mouth. "Hundo! Hundo!" They began walking down the dirt path that went through the town. Every few feet, Mateo would call out.

"You won't find him here," said a voice from behind them. They spun around to see a fairy fluttering near them. It was the same one they had met back when they were trying to hide the Blade of the Phoenix.

"You scared me to death!" Mateo said, holding a hand to his heart.

She tilted her head. "I think you are mistaken. You are very much alive."

Mateo grinned sheepishly. "It's just an expression."

"Hmm," she said, and then she flew away. Mateo took off after her, so Odie followed. She went behind a large hut and flew inside a barn. They ran in after her and the barn door slammed shut.

Odie wrinkled his nose. There weren't any animals inside, but it smelled like there had been recently. When the giants left, they must not have cleaned up first.

"I cannot talk to you out there," she said. "The other fairies will hear."

Odie glanced around. "And they can't hear us here?"

"Not without trying." She landed on the ground and grew to human size. She pushed her long, flowing black hair over her shoulders. "Fairies can't hear through structures. That is probably something I shouldn't share. My name is Arelia if you have forgotten. I know humans have short memories."

"Do you know where Hundo is?" Mateo asked. "We need his help."

"You need more help than even you know," Arelia said. "You have gone back to the goblins with plans of betrayal. The goblins will not take that lightly."

"We aren't trying to betray anyone," Odie said. "We are trying to get them to stop preparing for war."

"There is trouble from more than the goblins. Your friend Hundo was taken by the witch."

"What witch?" Mateo asked. "Why?"

She narrowed her eyes and stepped closer. "Her name is Isadora. She collects different... species. I see a pattern in those she has taken lately. The last two helped you."

Mateo rubbed a hand over his face. "Who else?"

"A troll named Zute."

"Why would she go after creatures we know?" Mateo asked.

Odie glanced at him. "I don't know them."

"She has something against you and what you stand for. And your little group killed her son."

"Vigh," Mateo muttered. "His mother was a witch."

"Yes, and she wants revenge."

"How would she know who has helped us?" Odie asked.

She frowned. "All fairies have their loyalties. Some fairies have sided with Isadora. Fairies hear and see everything because there are so many of us. Keep anything you wish to be a secret quiet if you are ever out in the woods."

Odie already knew this. He'd had a run-in with fairies that he hoped his friends never found out about. With luck, the fairy would keep the story to herself.

"How many fairies are loyal to the witch?" Mateo asked.

"I cannot say, but it is enough to cause you great trouble. No one thinks to fear fairies. If they decide to fight with her, Riviand will fall."

"Can you tell us where we can find Hundo?" Mateo asked.

Odie shook his head. "I don't think we have the resources to go save a giant from a witch."

"I have to try," Mateo said. "If she took him because he helped us, I owe it to him."

"You would run there if you knew what else she possesses," Arelia said.

"Do we want to know?" Mateo asked.

"I am on your side, but I cannot help you. The other fairies cannot know my loyalties are with you. The witch lives in a vast manor near Colter's Lake. She has your friends."

Odie's heart sped up. "Which friends?"

"I think you know which friends." The fairy shrank back down and disappeared through a window.

"She has to have Claret and Kaylee," Odie said. "What do we do?"

Mateo was clenching and unclenching his fists. "I'm not sure. She could be lying."

Odie nodded. "Fairies are known to lie, but she seems different. I think she's on our side, like she said."

"What are the chances of finding the witch? I've been to Colter's Lake, but the area around there seems to be empty fields."

"I don't know. I think we should go back to the castle and get Dovin."

Mateo started for the door. "You're right. Dovin knows everything. He'll figure something out."

"I'm not excited to teleport," Odie admitted.

Mateo rubbed his head. "Neither am I. I need to get over my block."

"I don't have magic, so I can't understand, but it seems like you could do it standing if you can do it running."

"I think it's because it makes sense to run and disappear. The movement makes sense. Standing and getting somewhere is hard to wrap my head around."

Odie nodded as they walked out into the sun. He would prefer walking but not when Claret might be in danger. For Claret, he would risk running into another tree. He would do it for Kaylee as well, but somehow it seemed different. Maybe because Kaylee was still close to a stranger.

He'd known her as long as Mateo, but he'd spent more time with him. Odie liked to think of him as a friend, even though Mateo had hated him not too long ago. He'd thought he would never get over it, but he had pretty fast. Odie knew he was lucky to have fallen in with the people he had. Others might not be so forgiving.

"Ready?" Mateo asked. "I can take us to the front of the castle, where there aren't any trees."

Odie grabbed Mateo's cloak and nodded. They ran a few steps and Odie's eyes widened as the scenery changed. They were still running, but they were by Claret's castle. Odie dropped the cloak and stopped. Mateo ran a few more steps, then turned and grinned. "We didn't crash! That was completely smooth."

Odie was glad but not ready to celebrate. They had to find Claret. And Kaylee. "Let's go find Dovin."

Mateo took the castle steps two at a time. Before he could get to the top, the doors opened and Dovin came out. He stared at Mateo and Odie with a blank expression. Mateo stopped and swallowed. He wasn't sure what to make of Dovin's reaction. Dovin turned and went back into the castle. Mateo looked at Odie and shrugged. They followed him in and down the hall to Claret's meeting room. Dovin took a seat at the table and kept his eyes on them. They both sat down and waited.

"I assume telling you what you did was careless would be falling on deaf ears. I spent two days climbing around the goblin mountain trying to find you."

"We're sorry, but we thought it was important," Mateo said, stopping when Dovin's gaze landed on him.

"We are a team. A team cannot go sneaking off to pursue their own goals."

"Are the girls here?" Odie asked.

Dovin rubbed the stubble on his chin. "No."

Mateo leaned forward. "A fairy told us a witch took them."

Dovin's eyes widened. "This is getting out of control. I had to leave to look for the two of you. When I came back, it was to learn that a beggar woman had come to the castle. She stole Durdessa's locket. Durdessa went after her and Claret and Kaylee went after Durdessa. If I hadn't been looking for you, it wouldn't have happened."

"Let's go find them," Mateo said. "We know they're in a manor by Colter's Lake."

Dovin's eye twitched. Mateo felt his stomach drop. He'd never seen Dovin appear nervous. "If I lose Durdessa again, I will not take it well."

The door opened, and Padmire and Gregor entered. Gregor squawked and hopped over to Odie. Odie scooped him up and ran a hand over his feathers.

"I need a map," Dovin said. "I'm not trusting your teleporting."

Mateo nodded. He would normally get defensive, but he knew Dovin was worried.

Padmire grinned, his pointed yellow teeth making Mateo cringe. "Are we getting into trouble again?"

Everyone ignored him.

"If a fairy told you something, there is a huge chance she lied," the bungle said. "Fairies lie more than they tell the truth."

Mateo scratched his head. "I think this one was telling the truth. She said that most of the fairies are on the witch's side."

Padmire snorted. "I have never met a fairy who was up to any good."

"They can't all be bad."

Dovin sighed. "I'm with Padmire. Of course we have only known fairies in the upper world. Things could be different here."

"They aren't," Odie said. "This one seemed nice, though."

"They want you to think that," Padmire said.

"What is our other option?" Mateo asked, throwing his arms in the air. "Whether or not the witch took them, they are missing."

"We could be walking into a trap," Dovin said.

"So what do you suggest?"

Dovin shook his head. "I don't know."

Mateo's heart thudded. Dovin always had an idea, or at least felt confident they would figure things out. "You always know what to do."

Dovin chuckled bitterly. "I usually do. Things are different here. In Basura, I know the world. I know the people and the different creatures. Their habits are familiar to me. I am still figuring out Riviand, and it hasn't been easy."

"If you feel lost, then I don't have any hope."

Dovin stood and patted Mateo on the back. "Don't lose hope. Just because I'm having a weak moment doesn't mean we won't have this straightened out. Let's go look at the map and then give me a few minutes to think. I'm never down for long. We will save them whether the fairy was lying or not."

14

— • —

CHAPTER 14

Kaylee, Claret, and Durdessa all stood in front of the glass that separated them from the mermaids. Durdessa had teleported them out of the cell and they were undecided about what to do next.

"Can you hear me?" Durdessa asked them. The four mermaids stared at them, their hair floating behind them. Durdessa pointed at her ear. "Can you hear me?" she repeated.

The one with a braid shook her head. The red-haired mermaid swam back so they couldn't see her and the other two just watched.

Durdessa pulled out her locket and the three mermaids that were still watching gaped at it. "I can't use this," she muttered. "If I do, I won't be able to get everyone out. I just want them to know I have it."

"How will you explain things to them if you are still human?" Kaylee asked.

Durdessa rubbed her lips together. "I'm not sure. Let's free everyone else and figure the mermaids out later."

"We aren't going to be able to take the other water creatures," Claret said, pointing at the tank behind them.

Kaylee nodded. "I suppose that's all right. They have a lot of space and it's clean."

"I would like to leave," Hundo called from his cell. "If it wouldn't be too much trouble, that is."

Durdessa walked down the hallway, her shoes clicking against the wooden floor. When she came to Hundo's cell, she disappeared and then reappeared with Hundo at her side. Next she got Zute.

"Are there any others here who are not animals or mermaids?" Durdessa asked.

"I do not believe so," Hundo said. "Except the goblin."

"Leave me be!" the goblin yelled. "I'm happy here and I'll bite anyone who tries to take me!"

Durdessa was in and out with the goblin in a flash. "Bite me and see what happens."

The goblin swallowed and rubbed his arm nervously.

Durdessa glanced at Kaylee. "I'm not going to be able to take all the animals. I'm sorry, there are too many."

Kaylee sighed but nodded. Once they escaped, they could figure out a way to get the other animals.

"Do you have any pets in your world?" Claret asked.

Kaylee let out a slow breath. "No. I had a dog when I was younger. Walter. He was a good dog, but I didn't take the time to care for him. My cousin Graham did everything for him and eventually took him when he left. I've always felt guilty about it. I guess that's why I want to free them all."

Durdessa looked at all the animals. "The dragon shouldn't stay," she said. "Neither should the alicorn and

Pegasus. They can't fly in here and they need that freedom. We should take the unicorn as well so she doesn't feel lonely. Unicorns don't do well on their own."

One by one, she brought the animals into the hallway. It was feeling crowded. Claret was eyeing the dragon suspiciously and keeping her distance.

"Now the mermaids," she said. The mermaids were watching them all with puzzled expressions.

The mermaid with a brown braid came against the glass. "Leave us alone," she said. "We like it here. We have plenty of room and we don't have to fear for our safety."

Durdessa frowned.

"Why can we hear her and they can't hear us?" Claret asked.

"As a mermaid, she can project her voice."

"So we leave them?"

"I'm conflicted. If they're happy, then I don't want to ruin that, but they are being held here by a witch."

"Can you take me with you?" the mermaid with short brown hair said. "I want to be free."

"Don't leave, Jayah," said the mermaid wearing a crown. "We are free. As free as we have ever been."

Jayah crossed her arms and frowned. "We are not free. I dislike sitting in here while people gawk at me like I'm some type of freak."

"It's dangerous for any of you to stay," Kaylee said.

"Dangerous how?" asked the mermaid with the braid.

Claret put her hands on her hips. "I thought you couldn't hear us?"

"We don't talk to just anyone."

"Isadora might take care of you, but she's holding you here illegally," Kaylee said. "And she is a witch. Eventually, things are going to get messy."

"Messy how?"

"We don't know, but it won't be safe."

The mermaids all shared glances.

Durdessa was concentrating on the mermaids. A vein in her forehead stood out. "I can't teleport in."

"Teleport?" all the mermaids said at once.

"We thought that was a joke," Jayah said.

"Haven't you seen her teleporting in and out of all the cells?" Claret asked.

"We can't see down that way. Isadora put some type of protection on this glass. That is probably why you can't get in."

"If you can't teleport, we are going to have to break the glass," Kaylee said to Durdessa.

Claret wrung her hands together.

"That sounds dangerous. That's a lot of glass and a lot of water. I'm going to have to teleport everyone else out first," Durdessa said. "I'll only take you a quarter of a mile away. With luck, I'll be able to bring myself back. Since I don't know where we are, it might be difficult."

"Just use the door," Korum said from behind them. They spun around to see the short man standing there. "It isn't locked, and Isadora left to go brag to her friends about her recent additions."

"Why would you help?" Kaylee demanded.

"I don't want to be here any more than you do. I will lead the animals out if you let me leave as well. Leaving on my own has always scared me. If I disappear with you, Isadora will assume you took me, and I can be free."

"All right," Durdessa said. "We will trust you, as we have no choice."

"Do not speak in front of the fairies," he said. "They hear almost everything you say outside and they obey Isadora. She could be back anytime, so let's go. Don't worry about us. We will move fast and be gone before Isadora gets back."

Hundo put a hand on the Pegasus and alicorn and guided them toward the stairs. Zute hurried behind them, and Korum encouraged the unicorn to follow. The dragon watched stubbornly from his spot on the floor. If it all came down to it, Kaylee would pick him up and carry him. He wasn't very big.

Kaylee grabbed a chair that was leaning against the wall near the stairs. She made her way back to the mermaids and slammed the chair into the glass. Nothing happened.

The crowned mermaid snickered. "You really think you can break magic glass with a chair?"

Kaylee frowned and slammed the chair into the glass again. The chair broke, and splinters flew across the way. There wasn't so much as a nick in the glass. "What are we going to do?"

"Leave us alone," said the one with brown hair.

"I can get out the top," Jayah said, looking up. "The only problem is, I wouldn't survive the fall."

"Do you have magic?" Claret asked.

"Yes, but I can't use it as a mermaid."

Claret looked at Durdessa.

"That happens to some mermaids," Durdessa said. "You go over the top, and I'll levitate you down."

Jayah nodded and swam to the top.

"Stop!" one mermaid called.

"I can't stand it here, Havva!" Jayah burst out of the water and it splashed over the side. She held on to the top of the large aquarium. Kaylee hadn't noticed the top was open earlier.

Durdessa raised her hands and lifted Jayah from the top of the tank. She lowered her slowly. As soon as she got to the ground, she curled up in a ball and took off her locket. She clasped it in her hand and gritted her teeth.

"You're going to regret it," Havva said, adjusting her crown.

Kaylee took the small green dragon and grabbed a piece of Durdessa's dress. Claret clasped another piece. Durdessa touched Jayah's shoulder, and they teleported to Claret's bedroom at the castle.

Jayah lay on the floor shaking, her arms wrapped around her knees... or her tail. It was still there, but it was splitting apart. Durdessa grabbed the quilt from Claret's bed and put it over her. She continued shivering.

"The beginning is the worst," Durdessa said. "You two go tell someone we're here. I'm sure the guards are out searching for us. I'll take care of Jayah."

Kaylee and Claret left the room. Kaylee still had the small dragon under her arm. Thankfully, it hadn't tried anything.

"You should put that down," Claret said. "It might blow fire or bite you."

"He seems all right," Kaylee protested.

"I've never heard of a friendly dragon. Unless you count what Dovin told us a while back."

"Dovin knows a lot about dragons. If he thinks they are safe, I trust him."

Rounding a corner, they saw Dovin, Odie, and Mateo standing in the hallway. They appeared to be arguing. They all stopped and turned when the dragon jumped out of Kaylee's arms.

A grin spread across Mateo's face, and he ran over to them. "We were just going to find you!" He put one arm over Kaylee's shoulders and one over Claret's. "A fairy told us you were captured by a witch. Where did you get the dragon?"

"We were captured by a witch," Kaylee said. "So was the dragon."

Dovin and Odie approached them. They were both frowning.

"Did you find out what happened to Durdessa?" Dovin asked.

"She's in my room," Claret said, moving out from under Mateo's arm. "She's with a mermaid. The mermaid is changing back into a person—or whatever they do."

Dovin's face relaxed. "Thank goodness."

Odie bent down and held his hand out to the dragon like a person might do to a dog. The dragon sniffed him and wandered to a different part of the hall.

"The witch had a bunch of creatures. We freed all the ones we could," Kaylee said.

"So some are still there?" Dovin asked.

"Yes, but Durdessa got out all the ones who cared. There were three more mermaids who wouldn't come."

"Four mermaids all together?" Dovin asked. "That's astounding. I didn't know there were that many still in existence."

"We have a couple that live in Tyran," Claret said. "They fell in years ago and made lives here. Most people don't know about the mermaid part. We promised to keep it a secret, so no one knows who they are. I don't even know who they are. My parents helped them start new lives."

"From what I was told, there were only about fifty to begin with. I assumed they had all died by now and the lockets were lost at the bottom of the ocean. I wonder how so many ended up here."

Durdessa rounded the corner. "Are you talking about mermaids?"

"Yes," Dovin said, wrapping her in a hug. He kissed the side of her forehead. "I was worried about you."

She smiled. "Jayah wants to be alone while she changes back. It's a horrible thing to watch. As to why mermaids end up down here, I can tell you that." She snuggled in closer to Dovin. "When mermaids are in the ocean, there are different feelings in different areas. I swam near Mermaid's Demise and the water was warm and almost soft. It's hard to describe. The closer I went, the more pleasant it was. I knew I was getting too close to the whirlpool, but I kept going anyway. By the time I decided I'd come too far, it was too late. The whirlpool had me. The next thing I knew, I woke up in Riviand."

"Do you think the same thing happened to the others?" Kaylee asked.

"Probably. It was almost as if it was calling to me."

"There had to be a reason it was called Mermaid's Demise, I suppose," Dovin said.

"How did you get your locket?" Kaylee asked Durdessa.

"My mother had it, and she got it from her mother. My mother never used it. She hated the way my grandmother seemed so dependent on it. She didn't want to give it to me, but I convinced her. I should have gotten rid of it. My older brother begged me to destroy it, but the thought of being a mermaid was exciting to me."

"Arving will be happy to know you're all right," Dovin said. "He was crushed when you didn't come back."

Durdessa frowned. "He had already lost so much. I'm sorry I added to his pain. How is he?"

Dovin shrugged. "It's hard to say. He keeps to himself and rarely lets anyone visit him."

"He was that way after Neva and Pax's boat went down."

"True, but he's worse now. He won't even see me."

"Who are Neva and Pax?" Mateo asked.

Durdessa frowned. "My brother Arving's wife and son. Neva loved the ocean. Arving didn't want them to go out because it was raining, but Neva wouldn't listen, just like me. They never came back. I need to get up there to see him."

Dovin narrowed his eyes. "Odie, don't bother the dragon. Most dragons are easy to tame, but he will bite you if provoked."

Odie glanced over from where he was following the dragon. "I've always wanted a dragon," he said. "I've never heard anyone but you say a dragon was easy to tame."

"Keep him away from Gregor," Claret said. "I don't know what dragons eat, but I wouldn't risk it."

Odie's eyes widened. "I didn't think of that."

Kaylee decided she'd let Mateo drape his arm over her for long enough. She moved away and went near Odie and the dragon. "He's a cute little thing. He must be a baby."

"Perhaps," Dovin said. "I suspect he's a bantam. They're smaller and never get much bigger than that. They also rarely breathe fire."

"I wonder if I can get him used to Gregor."

"Just keep him fed and I'm sure you can."

"We don't have time for that right now," Mateo said. "We need to go back to the goblins."

"What?" Dovin asked. "I thought we talked about this."

"We can make a difference," Mateo said. "The king was listening to Odie, and I made them some cookies. They were all so impressed, I bet I could get them to do anything for more."

"Why did you leave?" Kaylee asked.

"We're trying to figure out a way to make us invisible," Odie said. "Then we could figure out what Garin is really up to. We went to the giant village to talk to the giant Mateo met. A fairy told us the giant was captured and Kaylee and Claret. We came back here to get Dovin."

"Hundo and Zute were both captured by the witch," Kaylee said. "The witch captured them because they helped us. She confuses me, though. She seemed to treat her captives well."

"That's because she was showing them off to her friends," Claret said.

"Yeah, it was like a zoo. Do you have zoos around here?"

"I don't believe so," Claret said.

"It's a place where people keep animals and you can go look at them."

"I've never seen one except on Earth," Dovin said.

"Well, we need to go back to the goblins," Mateo said. "If we don't, they'll get suspicious and never trust us again."

Dovin sighed. "Very well, but be careful. Avoid Garin."

"We will."

"What about us?" Claret asked. "What should we be doing?"

"I should teach Claret to teleport," Dovin said. "And Kaylee could use a sword lesson."

"I already took fencing when you told my mom I should."

"Yes, but that wasn't a real sword. You should be using the Blade of the Phoenix."

"But what if someone tries to steal it?"

"Don't let them."

15

—·—

CHAPTER 15

Odie stood in the goblin castle down below the throne. He'd asked his question and then stood there in silence while King Ummi tapped his finger against the armrests.

"You want me to tell you a secret that is only known to the goblins?" his father finally asked.

Odie tossed his feathered cape over his shoulder. "You always said I was a goblin deep down."

Kind Ummi twisted his black ring around his thumb while he studied Odie. "So you are. Still, only a few goblins know how to make a potion of invisibility. It is difficult and dangerous. If it wasn't, we would use it more."

"I'm better at making potions than any goblin."

Kind Ummi tilted his head.

"All right, so I have made a lot of messy mistakes along the way, but I get there eventually and I do it on my own. If I already have the instructions, it's a breeze. Besides, I could use it to our advantage. I can make sure Garin isn't plotting against us or doing things you don't know about.

The king rubbed his temples. "How do I know I can trust your friend?"

"He doesn't have to know the entire list of ingredients, and I trust him. If you don't tell me, I'm going to end up blowing things up until I figure it out."

King Ummi muttered something under his breath. "Fine. I will tell you, but you must promise to tell no one else. You must memorize it and never write it down. Do you understand?"

Odie nodded eagerly. He had been waiting for this for years. He hoped the list wasn't too long if he had to memorize it.

"Come near, Odious. No one can overhear what I am about to tell you."

Claret sank down on the dirt and wiped sweat from her brow. Her long maroon dress was going to get dirty, but she didn't care. "I can't do it."

Dovin paced back and forth under the shade of the trees and rubbed his chin. "This is so confusing. I've taught several people to teleport, and they never had trouble. Mateo was the first one to struggle past the initial lesson, and now you."

Claret felt the urge to cry, but she wouldn't. She couldn't seem to do anything these days, and her confidence was plummeting.

"Don't get upset," Dovin said. "I don't think it's your fault. I wonder if there's something different about teaching it down here."

"But you and Durdessa can still do it."

"Yes, but we were already doing it regularly for years. Mateo did learn, in a sense, it is just taking time."

Just as he said that, Mateo and Odie appeared by their side. They were still running, and they tripped over each other and fell in a heap.

Dovin shook his head as they untangled themselves and stood. "You see? That isn't ideal. I'll have to think about it. Perhaps a different approach would be better."

"Hey," Mateo said. "Where's Kaylee?"

Dovin gestured at the castle. "She's practicing swordplay with Durdessa."

Mateo grinned. "That I have to see." He turned and hurried away.

"Don't give up, Claret," Dovin said. "We will try again tomorrow. All right?"

Claret nodded, but she still wanted to melt down. Being the weak link among everyone she knew was frustrating.

"I'll see you back at the castle." He turned and followed Mateo.

Odie squatted down next to Claret and his eyes scanned her face. She pushed a stray blond hair from her face and tried not to think about how terrible she must look.

"Are you all right?" he asked.

She tried to smile. Why did people have to ask someone if they were all right when they looked like they weren't? Didn't they know that was just going to make the tears spill out? She bit her lip and tried to laugh, but it might have sounded like she was choking. "I'm fine. Why do you ask?"

"You just seem a little... I don't know. You aren't usually sitting in the dirt."

"Dovin was trying to teach me to teleport. It wasn't going well."

"It must be hard. Mateo isn't getting much better about it."

"At least he can do it."

Odie pointed to a large scratch on his arm. "Yes, but the landings aren't very good."

"I can't seem to do anything," Claret said.

Odie frowned. "That's not true."

"I can't teleport, I can't run a kingdom, and I'm never helpful." She shouldn't be pointing her faults out to Odie. A queen should pretend to be confident and never let others see her weakness. Another thing she was failing at. She especially didn't want Odie to see her as a failure.

Odie stood and grabbed her hands, then pulled her to her feet. "That is the stupidest thing I've ever heard. You're a great queen."

Claret's lip trembled, and she felt a tear escape. Not again! She spent years holding in her emotions and now she was crying in front of Odie for the second time. She wiped the tear with her hand and sniffed.

Odie's eyes widened, and he looked terrified for a moment. The look quickly changed to something Claret couldn't place. His eyes narrowed, and he put a hand on her shoulder. "You were young when you became queen.

You worked so hard to prove to the people that you could do what needed to be done. I'm sure you overworked yourself and now you are feeling the effects of it."

She shook her head as another tear threatened to fall.

He dropped his hand and hung his head. "I'm sure I'm to blame for a lot of it. If the goblins had left you alone, you wouldn't have gotten overwhelmed. I'm sorry."

She sniffled. "It's not your fault I'm weak."

He looked up. "You aren't weak. I used to be a little scared of you, in fact."

The corner of her mouth twitched up slightly. "You were not."

"I was. You have that perfect posture and a glare worthy of a queen."

She laughed softly. "I try."

One side of his mouth turned up. "You succeeded."

Her mouth turned down. "I've made terrible decisions lately. I followed the witch even though Kaylee thought it was a bad idea."

"Anyone can make a mistake."

She chewed her lip. It was sweet of Odie to try to make her feel better, but that didn't fix the way she must appear to everyone. If the people of Riviand began seeing her as a joke, she didn't know how she would continue to rule.

"You need more help," he said. "Riviand is a big place."

She nodded. "That's what Durdessa and Kaylee were saying. We don't have time to figure it out. I don't have time to be weak. I need to pull myself together and deal with the goblins and Isadora."

Odie put a finger under her chin and gently lifted her face so she was looking at him. "Everyone needs a moment of uncertainty. Even a moment of weakness. It's all right to cry and take time to get your emotions out. Everyone needs that."

Claret tried to smile. "Is that what you learned from the goblins?"

"No. I've never seen a goblin cry. It's what I learned from life."

Claret nodded and felt another tear run down her cheek. "Thanks, Odie. You're a good friend."

She stepped forward and wrapped her arms around his waist. He went stiff for a moment and then put his arms around her. She wasn't going to let herself fall completely to pieces like she had when she was in the goblins' dungeon. Her heart felt less heavy when Odie didn't push her away or release her.

Claret rested her head against his shoulder and sighed. She knew she should step away and go back to the castle, but hugs were not something she got a lot of, and she was beginning to think they were something she needed. Odie rubbed his hand over her back and she squeezed her eyes shut. It wouldn't be hard to fall for her ex-enemy if she wasn't careful, and nothing inside of her wanted to be careful.

Odie hadn't felt this terrified since the time the spiders had fallen all over Claret in the dungeon and she'd clung to him crying. Odie hadn't been hugged a lot in his life and he felt like something missing was being filled in his soul. He knew it was a dangerous thing to think about. Odie could fall in love with Claret in a minute if he let himself, and there was no way the queen of Riviand was going to fall for the prince of the goblins. She could have anyone she wanted, and he was sadly lacking.

Claret pulled back slightly, and her eyes intently studied his. He tried not to flinch. Her eyes were shiny and filled with something Odie wasn't sure of. She released her hold on him and he wanted to sigh with relief and disappointment. He didn't even know what he was feeling. His insides were such a mess of nerves.

He slowly released his hold on her, and just as he was about to step away, she put her hands on his shoulders and went up on her toes. His eyes widened as she softly pressed her lips to his. His hands went back around her as he returned the kiss. This couldn't be real. Her arms went around his neck and he knew he could die happy right at this moment. He knew she was upset and letting that guide her, but he would stew on that later.

Claret ended the kiss and hid her face against Odie's shoulder. He hoped he didn't smell. "I'm sorry," she said. "I don't know what I was thinking."

He tried to think over the loud pounding of his heart. "Don't worry about it." He wished he could see her face. "Just don't do it again." She stiffened in his arms. "Not unless you mean it."

Claret looked up at him. "I did mean it."

Odie arched his eyebrow.

"I like you, Odie. A lot."

If Odie thought his heart was beating loudly before, he'd been wrong. Now it was deafening. There was no way Queen Claret of Riviand was telling him that she liked him—but she was, and from the look in her eyes, he almost believed her.

Odie went against his insecurities and ran his hand over Claret's soft cheek. "I like you, too." Before he could change his mind, he leaned down and kissed her again.

"Ahem," said a high voice from behind. Odie released Claret and spun around to see Padmire. The bungle had his arms folded, and he was tapping his foot against the ground. "Don't look at me like that. I waited patiently for longer than I wanted to."

Heat crept up Odie's neck, but he tried to look indifferent. He didn't dare look at Claret.

"What do you need?" Claret asked.

He scratched his blue head. "It's time for supper. I don't know why I've become the messenger. I've had my fill of adolescents and their awkward moments. I don't know why I am privileged to witness them so often."

"We're coming," Claret said.

Padmire nodded and disappeared into the trees.

"I guess we should go," Odie said, following after him. He hoped everything wasn't going to be awkward from now on. He turned to see Claret a few paces behind watching him. She hurried to catch up and laced her fingers with his. She leaned her head against his shoulder and they walked to the castle in silence.

When they entered the castle, Durdessa came around the corner. Odie dropped Claret's hand but not soon enough. Durdessa crossed her arms and frowned.

"Hello, Auntie," Claret said, a little too high-pitched. "Are you going to supper?"

"Yes, I am," she said, her eyes shooting daggers at Odie.

"Let's go together, shall we?" Claret linked her arm with Durdessa and steered her toward the dining room. Odie smiled as he watched them go. Nothing good could come from forming too close of an attachment to Claret, but he would worry about that when the time came.

16

CHAPTER 16

Mateo hadn't been able to find Kaylee and Durdessa, so he started for the dining room. He was starving, and it had to be close to suppertime. He rounded a corner and almost stepped on Padmire. "Whoa, sorry, Padmire."

"Hrumph," Padmire said, jumping back a few steps. "I need to find something more useful to do so I'm not the one sent to collect everyone for supper. My legs are too short for this."

"Is that really the worst job you could have? Is Kaylee already there? I can't find her."

"Yes, she is," he said, giving Mateo a terrifying smile. "And how do you feel about your friend dallying with the goblin human?"

Mateo laughed. "What?"

"I had to collect your friends and I tell you, I am tired of adolescents and their awkward relationships. Kissing is such a strange thing. Whoever decided it was a good idea to press their mouth to another mouth? It's ridiculous if you ask me. I always thought she would fall for you and not that pretend goblin."

All the humor left Mateo's eyes. "Wait, she was kissing Odie?"

Padmire grinned with his sharp yellow teeth. "Yes."

"And she didn't slap him or anything?"

"No. In fact, I'm pretty sure she started it."

Mateo rubbed his lips together and tried to process what Padmire was saying. Kaylee had never shown any indication of liking Odie. How had he missed something this big? "Are you sure you saw it right?"

Padmire nodded. "I saw it twice. I have excellent eyesight."

Mateo narrowed his eyes. The bungle was enjoying his job as the messenger. He knew it would annoy him, and he'd been happy to relay it. Mateo turned and stomped toward the dining room. Punching Odie in the face would only make things worse, but he sure wanted to. If he did, Kaylee would never forgive him. He couldn't believe she'd kissed him first. Padmire probably made that part up.

When he got to the dining room, everyone was waiting for him. Dovin and Durdessa were talking quietly amongst themselves. Williams was half asleep in his chair, Kaylee and Claret were laughing about something, and Odie was sitting next to Claret, staring into space and smiling slightly. Mateo clenched his fists and forced himself to sit down. He left a space between him and Williams. He didn't feel social. Padmire climbed onto his stool and grinned as he looked from Mateo to Odie.

The fish and potatoes were served, and normally Mateo would dig right in. He took a small bite and watched

Kaylee. She could kiss anyone she wanted. He didn't have any right to get angry. Still, he thought Odie liked Claret.

He took another bite and cringed. Padmire said she kissed him. He didn't even have a reason to be mad at Odie. Mateo had hated Odie when they first met, but Odie was a good guy and it was too hard to keep disliking him. Now he wasn't sure. Odie knew he liked Kaylee.

"Does anyone know what a pryka plant is?" Odie asked. "I need one for something I'm working on, and my father said the only time he was able to get one was from the king, and that was years ago."

Dovin nodded. "In Basura, they are extinct."

Claret dabbed at her mouth with a napkin. "Prykas are almost extinct here. They are a type of cactus. My father kept one around for emergencies. We still care for it. They are really powerful but dangerous."

"Do you think I could have a piece?" he asked.

Claret turned to him and frowned. "I am not exaggerating when I say they are dangerous. One poke and a person could die."

"I'll be careful."

Claret twisted her napkin around her fingers. She stood and walked to a large window facing east. "Look over there," she said, pointing. Odie stood and joined her. "Do you see that glass building?"

Odie squinted. "Yes."

"That is where all the valuable plants are. They are guarded just as much as the Blade of the Phoenix is."

"Can I get a piece?"

Claret sighed and kept her gaze out the window. "I'm not sure. It is very poisonous."

Odie put his hand on Claret's back and leaned toward her. "I won't touch it. I can extract it without coming in contact."

Mateo jumped to his feet. Something in his brain told him to sit back down and mind his business, but he wasn't letting that thought through. He rushed across the room, grabbed Odie's arm, and pushed him away from Claret. "What do you think you're doing?" he asked. He heard Padmire snicker.

Odie's eyes narrowed. "What are you talking about?"

Mateo clenched his jaw. He told himself to count to three, but as soon as he got to two, his fist flew through the air, connecting with Odie's eye. Odie stumbled backward and fell to the floor.

"What are you doing?" Claret yelled as she dropped to Odie's side. Mateo could hear Dovin and Kaylee yelling something at him, but he was mad and he couldn't take time to listen.

Odie popped up and threw his own fist, connecting with Mateo's jaw. Mateo hadn't expected it, and he was thrown back a few steps.

He growled and took a step forward, but before he could attack, Williams had him by the arm. He dragged him across the room and pushed him into a chair. "Sit."

Mateo rubbed his jaw and glared at the coach. Mateo might think he was tough, but he knew Coach Williams could flatten him if he wanted to.

Mateo stared down everyone in the room. Odie was holding a hand to his eye and Claret was wringing her hands next to him. Kaylee was glaring and crossing her arms. He was sure to get a lecture from her about not solving problems with violence. Durdessa was shaking her head and Dovin was standing next to Williams, frowning down at Mateo. Padmire sat on his stool, smiling while he ate.

"What was that all about?" Dovin demanded.

Mateo crossed his arms and his eyes narrowed as he looked at Odie. "Why is everyone looking at me? You should all be glaring at Odie."

"I thought you two had resolved your differences," Dovin said.

"So did I," Odie muttered.

"That was before he went off kissing Kaylee and five minutes later cuddling up to Claret by the window." Six sets of eyes blinked at him in surprise. Padmire chuckled and kept eating. Everyone turned to stare at Odie, except Kaylee, who was looking at him with her forehead furrowed.

"I didn't kiss Kaylee," Odie finally said.

Kaylee rolled her eyes. "I would never kiss Odie. No offense, Odie."

Odie grinned slightly and shrugged.

Mateo frowned and looked at Padmire. "But Padmire said..." He closed his mouth. Padmire had said Odie kissed Mateo's friend. He never said Kaylee. Claret was standing tall, but her cheeks were a pretty shade of pink. Claret had kissed Odie, and Mateo was an idiot.

"Padmire said what?" Padmire asked with a sneer.

"You did this on purpose."

Padmire grinned. "I did nothing. That was all you. I told you your friend kissed Odie. I thought you were all friends. How was I to know you would jump to conclusions?"

Mateo glanced at Claret. The pink in her cheeks had changed to a fierce red.

Durdessa glanced at Claret. "You know better."

"I need to be excused," Claret squeaked. She turned and fled from the room.

Odie looked from the door to Durdessa. Durdessa's eyes were on fire and Odie looked terrified.

"I'll go with her," Kaylee said, getting up. "Don't be more of a dork than you already are," she said to Mateo as she left.

Now Mateo was alone with all the adults and Odie, and they were all staring at him. He wondered if he could sneak out as well.

"What did we talk about back on Earth?" Dovin asked. "We don't solve problems with our fists."

Mateo didn't know how to respond. This was all on him, and he couldn't pass the blame, except maybe to Padmire, who seemed to be enjoying the entire thing. He rubbed his eyes with his fist. "I'm sorry. I don't know what came over me."

Williams chuckled. "The same thing that came over you when you flattened Chad. You have Kaylee under your skin."

"Chad deserved it." At least Mateo could say that confidently.

"You aren't going to get Kaylee to like you by punching people," Dovin said.

Mateo grumbled under his breath. "Can I leave?"

Dovin shared looks with Durdessa and Williams. "I suppose, but I want you to apologize to Odie."

Mateo looked at Odie. "Sorry, man. I shouldn't have lost it."

Odie nodded. His eye was slightly swollen. "It's all right. I get it."

"And, Odie," Durdessa said, "You can't—"

Dovin put a hand on his wife's arm. "Durdessa…"

"No," she said. "I know you're going to tell me it's none of my business, but Claret has no one else to protect her. Odie, you cannot kiss Claret."

Padmire hadn't stopped grinning since he'd come into the dining room. "In all fairness, she did kiss him first."

Odie swallowed hard and looked like he wanted to be anywhere but here.

Durdessa sighed. "Claret hasn't known a lot of young men. It makes sense that she might gravitate to the first one she spends time with."

Odie looked like he'd been punched in the gut.

Mateo stood and walked toward Odie. "Me and Odie are going to leave. Anything else that is going to be said is only going to be more embarrassing than it already is. How about we all decide to never talk about this again? Come on, Odie." Mateo clapped him on the back and they exited while the adults stood watching. He heard someone mutter something about teenagers.

"Ignore Durdessa," Mateo said. "Claret chose you. I've been around plenty. She must really like you if she chose you over me."

Odie grinned and shook his head. "I'm going to have a black eye, you know."

"Probably. Sorry. You know you hit a lot harder than I expected," Mateo said, rubbing his jaw.

"I still can't believe you thought I kissed Kaylee."

"Padmire is definitely going down. He did this on purpose." Mateo grinned, ignoring the pain in his face. "So, you and Claret?"

Odie's smile fell. "I don't know. I think Durdessa might be right. Claret can have any man she wants. Why would she choose me?"

Mateo laughed. "Don't ask me. Maybe she likes guys who wear all black and talk to puffins."

"Who is Chad?"

Mateo sighed. "A guy back on Earth who kept bothering Kaylee. He made me look like an idiot, then he grabbed her arm and wouldn't let her go."

"So you punched him?"

"Yeah."

"You might want to think of other ways to solve your problems."

"Probably."

Kaylee followed the fleeing Claret to her bedroom. She caught the door before Claret could slam it. She entered and shut the door quietly behind herself.

Claret sat on her blue bedspread and covered her face with her hands. "That was the most embarrassing experience of my life."

Kaylee smiled and sat next to her. "I bet."

"I think I'm going to hide in here for the rest of my life."

"That seems reasonable," Kaylee teased. "I'm sure plenty of queens lock themselves in their rooms and never come out."

Claret peeked over her hands. "What do I do?"

Kaylee shrugged. "Nothing. Just pretend it didn't happen."

"Is that what you're going to do?"

Kaylee grinned. "For the most part. I might go slap some sense into Mateo, though."

Claret smiled weakly. "He must really like you."

Kaylee blew out a breath. "It seems that way."

"What are you going to do about it?"

"Nothing. I like Mateo but not the way he might want me to." Kaylee knew it wasn't one hundred percent true. She could fall for Mateo if she let herself, but she wouldn't. Mateo wanted to stay in this world, and Kaylee belonged on Earth.

"Durdessa still distrusts Odie."

"I understand why. He did a lot of low-down stuff for the goblins."

"Yes, but I understand why."

"And you kissed him," Kaylee said, smiling.

Claret closed her eyes and her cheeks turned pink again. "Yes, and I would do it again."

Kaylee giggled. It was funny to think about the proper queen falling for the boy who wears a puffin-feathered cape.

"I felt so useless and down today," Claret admitted. "Then Odie came and talked to me and everything seemed better. Then when we kissed—But then that blasted turtle had to come and ruin it."

Kaylee shook her head. "Padmire is a mystery. I wonder why he told Mateo. It's almost as if he wanted the boys to get into a fight. I'm a little shocked. When did you stop liking Mateo?"

Claret wrinkled her nose. "What are you talking about? I've never liked Mateo—at least not like Odie."

Kaylee put her hands on her hips. "But that time on the roof. You said he was handsome when we were looking down at him."

Claret shook her head. "Mateo is handsome, but I was talking about Odie."

Kaylee laughed and felt relieved. "I didn't think for a second that you were talking about Odie."

Claret smiled. "Because you were thinking that Mateo was handsome?"

Kaylee ignored her. "So now what?"

Claret sighed. "I need to take Odie to get the pryka. I'm going to feel weird around him now. He might think I'm forward or something. He did kiss me a second time, but I feel odd about the whole thing."

"Just act normal and see what he does."

Claret nodded.

"We could go get the pryka and give it to him," Kaylee suggested. Then you don't have to take him.

"It's a hard thing to work with," Claret said. "We could get it if we're careful."

"Then the boys would leave and we wouldn't have to deal with boy problems for a while."

"That sounds good," Claret agreed. "Should we go now?"

Kaylee thought for a minute. "Let's go tomorrow. I think I need to go talk to Mateo first."

"I don't know how you can do that so casually," Claret said. "Isn't it awkward since you know he likes you?"

Kaylee shrugged. "Not really. I'll be back soon, all right?"

Claret nodded.

Kaylee went out in search of Mateo. She passed Odie in the hall. "Do you know where Mateo is?"

"He went to his room."

"Thanks." Kaylee jogged down the hall and knocked on Mateo's door.

"Who is it?" he called.

She rolled her eyes. "Kaylee."

He opened the door and peeked out. "I'm a little busy."

She crossed her arms. "Busy hiding?"

He grinned. "Maybe."

"Well, let me in."

"Why? So you can tell me not to punch people?"

Kaylee let a small smile escape. "Something like that."

"No need. I'll just rethink the last time we had that conversation and save you some time."

Kaylee shook her head. They couldn't have unsaid things between them. Mateo sighed and opened the door wider. She went in and faced him.

"I shouldn't have punched Odie in the face. Blah, blah, blah, I'm sorry, okay?"

"That's not really what we need to talk about."

"Oh?"

"You punched him because you thought he kissed me. You didn't even wait to get the real story."

"I know."

"And even if he had kissed me, that's none of your business."

He clenched his jaw and looked up at the ceiling.

"Nothing is ever going to happen with me and you. We're friends. That's it."

Mateo nodded. "Fine. Are you done?"

Kaylee frowned. He was angry, which wasn't what she wanted, but she didn't know what else to say. She nodded, and he shut the door. Kaylee took a deep breath through her nose and let it out slowly.

17

CHAPTER 17

Claret walked through the glass greenhouse and breathed in the humid air. "I haven't been here in a long time." Three rows of plants stood before them. She'd forgotten how many beautiful colors there were in here.

"There are so many strange plants," Kaylee said. "I've never seen any of them before."

"Don't touch them. I don't know what all of them do." Claret used to come here with her father and he would teach her about some of them. Since he'd died, she lost interest. "Here is it," she said, pointing at a deep blue cactus. It was two feet high and had long needles.

Kaylee smiled. "Cool. I've never seen a blue cactus before."

"Did Odie need a spine or part of the actual plant?"

"I don't think he said. We can get both." Kaylee pulled on a pair of elbow-length gloves. They probably wouldn't protect against a poke, but if she brushed against it, they might be helpful.

Claret pulled on her own. She grabbed a pair of tongs from a brown bag. "I'm not sure we can get anything except a spine with the tongs."

"Well, I guess we can get that, and if it's wrong, come back with something else."

Claret hesitated.

"Do you want me to do it?" Kaylee asked.

Claret shook her head. "I've got it." She grabbed a spine with the tongs and wiggled it until it broke loose.

Kaylee held open the bag and Claret dropped it in. Kaylee swung the bag up on her shoulder and grinned. "That was easy. Let's go show the boys."

She nodded, but Claret wasn't excited to see them after the last encounter. She was the reason they had both punched each other in the face, even if she hadn't meant it to happen. It was hard to feel normal around people after that. She had purposely missed breakfast this morning and grabbed something from the kitchen.

They strolled casually back to the castle. When they got to the castle steps, the door opened, and Mateo and Odie came out.

"We've been looking all over for you," Mateo said. "Can we talk about the cactus thing now? We need to get back to the goblins soon before they think we're up to something."

Kaylee held up the bag. "We already got it."

"Did you need part of the plant or one of the needles?" Claret asked without making eye contact with either of them. "We only got a needle."

"I think we actually need part of the plant," Odie said.

"Great," Kaylee said, dropping the bag to her side. Her eyes widened. "Oh no."

"What is it?" Claret asked.

"It just poked my leg through the bag."

Claret dropped to her knees and pulled up Kaylee's pant leg. Kaylee sat down and pulled it higher. Under her knee, there was a small red spot.

Mateo frowned. "What do we do?"

Claret didn't want to cause a panic, but this wasn't good. "Mateo, go burn the needle so no one else touches it. Odie, go get Dovin and Adler."

"It doesn't hurt more than a bug bite," Kaylee insisted.

"And don't burn the needle," Odie said. "It could release toxins into the air. Bury it or something."

Mateo frowned. "I'm not leaving."

"What's going on out here?" Dovin asked.

Claret frowned. "The pryka poked Kaylee. We need to get her to the healer, now."

"I'll go find him," Odie said, running inside.

"Really, it's not bad," Kaylee said.

"Let's all get inside," Dovin said, motioning to the door. They all went in slowly, and Claret wanted to scream. No one was taking this as seriously as they should.

"Hurry. We need to get you to your room," she said.

Kaylee sighed. "I don't need to go to bed. I don't feel weird or anything."

"You will," Claret muttered.

Dovin linked his arm with Kaylee's and began guiding her toward her room. "If Claret thinks this is serious, then we are going to have this checked."

"Fine," Kaylee said. "But... Wait, what were we talking about?" Her eyes narrowed, and she fell to the floor.

Mateo dropped to his knees and touched Kaylee's arm. "Kaylee? Are you all right?" Her eyes were closed, and she wasn't moving.

"Can you get her to her room?" Dovin asked.

Mateo nodded and scooped her into his arms. Standing was a bit of a challenge, but once he was up, he rushed down the hallway. Claret ran ahead and opened the bedroom door. Odie and Adler, the healer, were almost to the door as well. Mateo hurried into the room and put Kaylee on top of the light blue quilt.

Adler was carrying a bag and frowning. "Where is the wound?"

"On her leg," Mateo said, pointing.

Adler rubbed a hand through his messy gray hair and sighed. He looked up at Dovin. "I've only seen two people who were ever poked by the pryka. Both suffered for a week before passing."

Mateo sucked in a breath. "There has to be something you can do."

"I can try, but I've never heard of it being healed."

Mateo glared at the older man. "Well, do something! We need to go find some more healers. If you can't do it, maybe someone else can."

"Adler is the best healer in Riviand," Claret said. "If he can't fix it, no one can."

Mateo clenched his fists and paced a few feet from the bed. "There has to be a way."

Claret bit her lip and hugged herself. Dovin was pacing on the other side of the room.

"I'll do my best, but I don't believe in giving false hope," Adler said, pulling something from his bag.

Dovin stopped and turned. "Odie? You must get your father to let you leave Riviand."

Odie frowned. "I don't think he will."

"It's Kaylee's only hope. You and Mateo need to get up there and you need to find Kaylee's cousin."

Mateo shook his head. "What good will that do?"

"Long ago, there were healers that used magic to help create medicine. Their magic with the medicine could help even people close to death. The magic was lost and there hadn't been a healer who could come close to what the healers of old time could do. When Graham came to our world, he had a talent, and when he went through Padmire's cave, he came out as one of the best healers in our day. He can heal people that no one else can. You need to find him and get him here."

Mateo's heart sped up. He would do anything to help Kaylee. "How will we find him?"

Dovin rubbed his chin. "Graham is in Akkron. Have you been there?"

Mateo nodded.

"You will need to teleport there as soon as you get out of Riviand. Graham has made a name for himself, so he shouldn't be hard to find."

"I've met him once," Mateo said. "So we find him and jump back into Mermaid's Demise?"

"I'm afraid so. We will keep someone watching for you."

Odie threw his hands in the air. "You are all assuming my father will tell us how to leave. I don't think he will. I didn't know anyone could leave Riviand until he sent me with the Blade of the Phoenix and he didn't let me know how I got there."

Mateo glanced at Kaylee. Her face was scrunched up in pain and her breathing was labored. "We have to convince him, and we don't have time to discuss."

Odie's brows came together, but he nodded.

"I'm going to take us right into the throne room of your father. Ready?"

Odie grabbed Mateo's cape. "Let's go."

They took three running steps and Mateo teleported them into King Ummi's throne room. They ran three more steps before stopping smoothly. He would normally take time to brag a little, but they didn't have time.

"What magic is this?" King Ummi said from his throne.

Mateo turned to him. "We don't have time to explain. You need to send us out of Riviand."

The king twisted a ring around his finger and glared at Odie. "That is impossible."

"No. It isn't. Please. Send us up. It's an emergency."

"I cannot let Odie leave."

Odie stepped forward. "We'll be back. Please, Father. I wouldn't ask if it wasn't really important."

The king sighed. "I cannot send you. Only my brother has that power."

"Vork?" Mateo asked.

"Yes. And you must promise never to tell anyone else how you did it."

"I promise," Odie said. Mateo didn't respond. He hoped Odie's promise was enough.

"You must go higher up the mountain. There is a cave there. Go inside the cave, clap three times, and stomp once. That will summon Vork. I cannot promise he will help."

"Is it the cave you always told me to stay away from?" Odie asked.

"Yes. I am trusting you, Odious. Do not betray that."

"I won't." He looked at Mateo. "Let's go."

They rushed out of the castle and past the guards. Mateo followed Odie as he began climbing up the black mountain.

"I can't believe he told us," Odie said. "I thought we were going to have to bribe him."

"He must trust you."

"I noticed you didn't promise not to tell anyone."

Mateo shook his head. "I couldn't. Someday, me and the others are going to need to go back home."

Odie nodded.

"How far up is this cave?"

"If we run, we can get there in fifteen minutes."

"Then let's run."

Odie and Mateo entered a narrow cave entrance. The ceiling was low, so they had to duck. Odie had always wanted to see inside the cave, but he'd obeyed when his father told him not to. Mateo held up his hand and a ball of light appeared, illuminating the small cavern. Odie was disappointed. The cave was only about twenty paces across. The black walls looked like the rest of the mountain. Odie had found limestone caves on this mountain that were much more impressive.

"I don't see any snakes," Mateo said, glancing around.

Odie smiled. Mateo was terrified of snakes. Odie remembered the time he'd hid one in Mateo's bed. Mateo had been mad, and Odie was scared enough from that confrontation to never try that again. He'd been relieved when Mateo let him off with a warning. Odie touched his black eye. There hadn't been a warning that time.

"So we clap three times," Mateo said, clapping, "and we stomp." He stomped his boot against the earth.

They waited a moment, and the ground rumbled. The air in front of them ripped open and Vork stepped out. Goblins from the upper continents dressed differently from the ones in Riviand. Vork had a cloth around his waist, and that was all. He folded his gray arms and glared at Odie with his large eyes.

"What are you doing here, and how did you know how to summon me?"

"We don't have time," Mateo said. "We need to get to Akkron. It's an emergency."

He raised his dark brows. "It always is, isn't it? Your problems are not mine. I don't see any money on you, so you cannot bribe me."

"Come on, Uncle Vork. Do it for family," Odie said, half worried that would anger him more.

"I have never seen you as family," Vork said.

Odie was getting a pain in his back from not being able to stand straight. "Please. We need to go up."

Vork drummed his fingers against his arms. "I don't care that you need to come up."

"We can come back with Dovin," Mateo said to Odie. When Mateo first met Vork, he was with Dovin and Vork didn't seem to care for Dovin. Not that he seemed to care for anyone.

"Dovin cannot know of this place," Vork said. "He already knows too much about everything. I will send you but don't bother me again."

"Can you send us straight to Akkron?" Mateo asked.

Vork rolled his eyes. He waved his hands and before Odie knew what happened, he was slamming into the ground. He sat up and groaned.

Mateo was rubbing his jaw. "Man, I landed on the spot you punched."

Odie grinned. He wasn't a violent person, but it was nice to know he'd gotten a good hit in. Mateo was the one people thought of as having the muscle, but Odie had stood his own. He wouldn't think about the fact that Mateo had knocked him to the ground, and he'd only made Mateo stumble back a few steps.

They stood, and Odie looked around. His eyes went wide. They were in a city, and it wasn't small. People rode past on unicorns and he could see people flying overhead on alicorns.

"There are a lot of unicorns," Mateo observed. "That's a good thing. Years ago, their numbers were dropping."

Odie had been to big cities, but nothing like this. There were buildings lining the entire street and there were so many people. He was surprised they hadn't landed on anyone or caused people to stare when Vork threw them here. He'd always wondered about the upper world.

"There are a lot of people, but it doesn't seem much different from Riviand," he said.

Mateo shook his head. "It's different. We don't have time now, but just wait until you see flushing toilets. It will change your life." He stepped in front of a tall man. "Excuse me. Do you know where I can find Graham? I think he's a healer."

The man pointed down the street. "I've never met him myself, but he has an office down that way. It's a small brick building with a sign that says Graham's Medicine."

"Thank you."

"Does everyone know him?" Odie asked as they began walking in the direction the man pointed.

"I'm sure everyone knows of him. He helped save the world. That catches people's attention."

18

——·——

CHAPTER 18

Claret paced across Kaylee's room. She felt helpless. Kaylee slept peacefully thanks to something Adler had given her, but she hadn't woken up, and the injury on her leg looked awful. In the beginning, it had been small enough to miss, but now it was white and infected, with strange blue lines crawling against her brown skin.

Adler was trying everything he could think of, but nothing seemed to make it look any better. Claret was tired, but she didn't want to leave her friend. She hoped Mateo and Odie had gotten out of Riviand to find help.

Durdessa peeked in the door. "Claret, you need to go to bed. Wearing yourself out won't fix anything."

"I know, but I don't want her to wake up alone."

Adler was sitting on a chair near Kaylee's bed. "She isn't alone, and she isn't going to wake up. Go sleep."

Claret nodded and made her way to her room. They should have been more careful. If they had found a better container, they wouldn't be in this mess. She latched her door behind her and fell into bed. She wanted to cry, but the tears didn't come. Kaylee might die, and she might never see Odie and Mateo again, and all she could do was stare at the wall.

"I want my mermaid back," a voice said from behind.

Claret rolled over and sat up. Isadora stood next to her bed, wearing a long, red dress. Her lips had been colored and there was something black smudged over her eyelids. Claret had heard of women painting their faces to look more appealing, but this was the first time she'd seen it.

"Get out," Claret commanded.

Isadora raised her brows and glared. "You stole from me. I can handle the loss of the others but not the mermaid. Where is she?"

Claret rubbed her lips together and tried to think of a way to get past the witch.

"I know she's somewhere in the castle. I will have her back and Durdessa as well."

Claret couldn't tell Isadora where Jayah was. Jayah was fully human again, but she was still weak and didn't want to see anyone. The only person she would let in her room was Durdessa.

"If you want your friends to be safe, you must return her. The other mermaids miss her."

"She was a prisoner."

"No. She belonged to me, but she was more free than she had ever been. I allow the mermaids to stay in the water, and that is what they want."

"She chose to leave."

"But I'm sure she regrets it."

"If she does, she can come to you."

The corner of Isadora's mouth turned up. "You know I am going to make your life miserable, do you not?"

Claret took a deep breath and stood.

Isadora smiled. "The queen sleeps in her dress?"

"Leave."

"You have the power of a kingdom behind you, but you are young and you are weak. Even your magic is pathetic. You cannot defeat me, and I will make you pay for Vigh."

"He tried to kill me."

"Yes, and he failed. So pathetic. He was always a disappointment, but still. He was my disappointment. I won't rest until I see you fall. I could just kill you now, but where is the fun in that? If you give me Jayah, I'll let you live. I will still have my revenge, but it won't be your death."

Claret grabbed the lantern on her bedside table and swung it at the woman's head. It went through her. Claret's eyes widened in horror and the witch laughed.

"I didn't know you had that in you," Isadora said. "Good for you. I have some things to attend to and no time to waste with you. Think of what I've said. Send me Jayah and you will live."

Claret's eyes popped open. She was lying on her bed. She breathed deeply, then turned to see her empty room. It had been a dream. A frown settled on her face. It hadn't been a normal dream. Isadora had been in her head. If she could be manipulated through dreams, Isadora was going to win.

Odie and Mateo stood in front of a red brick building and knocked. It was small but looked well built. The door opened and a tall black man in his early twenties opened the door.

"Hi," he said with a smile. "Can I help you?"

"Hey, Graham. You probably don't remember me," Mateo said.

Graham tilted his head and studied him. "Are you one of Sen's brothers?"

"Yes, I'm Mateo. This is Odie. We don't have time to explain. We need you to come with us and bring all your medicines. In a waterproof container, if possible."

Graham raised his eyebrow. "Come where?"

Mateo sighed. "To Riviand."

Graham laughed. "Oh, is that all?"

"Is that Sen?" a feminine voice said from inside the building.

"Come in," Graham said, opening the door wider. Odie and Mateo entered.

The room had shelves lined with vials. Odie's eyes widened. If they weren't in a hurry, he would love to know what was in each of them. There was a wooden desk with a chair behind it, and in one corner, a beautiful young woman sat on a large cushion. She held a book in her hands, and a small green dragon was curled up at her side.

She stood and pushed her long red hair over her shoulder and adjusted her green tunic. The dragon yawned, and she placed her book on the cushion. She pushed her feet into a pair of black boots and came over to them.

"This is Sen's brother, Mateo," Graham said. "And Odie, was it?"

Odie nodded.

"They want me to go to Riviand."

She smiled. "I'm Wren. What do you want Graham to do in Riviand?"

Mateo let out a long breath. "We don't have time to get into it. Have you heard of a pryka cactus?"

Graham thought for a moment. "Yes... I think they're extinct."

"Not in Riviand. Our friend was poked by it. She's going to die if someone doesn't help her," Odie said. "The doctors there can't help."

Graham's eyes narrowed. "And you are from Riviand?"

Odie nodded.

"I've never heard your accent before."

Mateo rolled his eyes. "We don't have time."

"And you were in Riviand?" Graham asked. Mateo nodded. "Hmm. Sen told me you like to joke. I thought your family went to Earth?"

"We aren't joking. You have to come or Kaylee is going to die."

Graham's head jerked up. "Kaylee?"

"Yes. Your cousin, Kaylee."

Graham glanced at Wren, and she shrugged. He crossed his arms. "And how did she end up in Riviand?"

"It's a long story. Dovin can tell you when we get there."

Wren put her hand on Graham's arm and looked up at him. "Dovin said your cousin would come here someday."

Graham put his hand over Wren's. "I have to go."

Wren nodded. "So I guess Riviand does exist."

Mateo smiled slightly. "You might want to keep it quiet. People will think you're crazy."

She grinned. "I'm used to people talking about me."

Graham grabbed a cloak and pulled it over his shoulders. "How are we going to get to Riviand?"

"We have to jump in Mermaid's Demise."

Graham paused. "And you've done this before?"

"Yep."

"All right." He grabbed a brown leather bag and began putting things from the shelves into it.

"We have to figure out a way to get there fast. The healer said that the two people he saw get poked by the pryka died in a week. It took us too long on the boat last time and I'm bad at teleporting."

"I can teleport, but I don't know where it is." He grabbed a vial and held it up to the light. He frowned and stuck it in the bag.

The dragon walked over to Odie and sniffed his boot.

"Can I touch him?" Odie asked.

Wren nodded. "He's friendly."

Odie ran his hand over the dragon's head. "I wish I had a dragon."

"They're wonderful pets," she said.

"And we need a big one," Graham said.

"I'll go get Tal," Wren said. "His dragon is fast." She waved her hands and a shimmering silver portal opened in front of her. Odie watched with his mouth hanging open. The goblins could make portals, but nothing like this. It was beautiful. Wren jumped through, and it closed behind her.

"Wow," Odie said.

Graham smiled. "I know."

"Don't portals make you lose time?" Mateo asked. "We need to hurry."

"Most portals do, but Wren's figured some things out, and it's as good as teleporting when she does it."

"So we're going to ride a dragon?" Mateo asked. He'd ridden Dovin's dragon once, and it had been fast.

"Yes, if Tal agrees. Dragons are the fastest way to get around if you don't count teleporting and portals."

The silver portal reappeared, and Wren jumped back into the room. "Tal said he'll meet you out front in five minutes."

"Great." Graham grabbed another bag once the first was full. "I can't believe Kaylee is down there. I should have..." He sighed and let the sentence die. He placed something in his bag. "I don't think it will be hard to make medicine from the original pryka plant. It's still around, right?"

"Yes," Odie said. "We haven't seen it, but it's kept safe." Odie had to be honest. He couldn't let someone get trapped in Riviand without knowing everything. "It's possible you won't be able to leave Riviand."

Graham looked up. "Oh?"

"We don't know how to get back up. A goblin had to help us."

Graham looked at Wren and frowned.

Wren went over to him and wrapped her arms around him. "If you don't come back, I'll jump into the whirlpool and find you."

Graham smiled and leaned down to kiss her. Odie felt his face turn red. He looked at Mateo and Mateo glanced up at the ceiling. Couldn't they step into the other room before they did that?

The floor shook slightly, and there was a loud noise outside. Odie opened the door to see a large orange dragon on the street. A young man with tasseled brown hair sat on top. He grinned and waved. The dragon had four things that looked like saddles, only flatter. Graham stepped out.

"Climb up," the man said. "I'm Tal. Make sure you hook your feet into the stirrups and hold on to the tether."

Odie climbed up, his heart pounding with excitement. He sat on the enormous dragon and stuck his feet into the stirrups. Graham climbed on behind him, then Mateo.

"Love you!" Wren said, waving.

"Love you too!" Tal called back.

"Don't make me come up there, Tal," Graham threatened.

Tal laughed. "So, Mermaid's Demise?"

"Yes," Mateo said.

"And once we get there? What then, little Sen?"

Mateo scowled. "My name is Mateo. We jump into the whirlpool."

Tal moved his head to look at Graham. "You know I'm coming. If Riviand exists, I'm gonna see it."

"What about Sheba?" Graham asked.

"She can find her way back. Hey, Wren? Ming Li is at the bakery. I was supposed to help her with something later today. Will you let her know what happened?"

Wren nodded. "Sure. Be careful."

Tal looked at all of them. "Hold on tight. Sheba is lightning fast, and you don't want to get thrown off."

Odie wrapped his hands around the leather cord separating the saddles.

"Here we go!" Tal said.

The dragon took a few steps forward and lunged into the air. Odie felt like his face was going to slide off. He had never imagined speed like this. He closed his eyes as they shot higher and higher and hoped he wouldn't get sick.

19

— · —

CHAPTER 19

"What are we going to do?" Claret asked at break-fast the next day. "If Isadora can get into my dreams, does that mean she can read my mind?"

Dovin tapped his spoon against the table. "I don't think so. I've never heard of anyone reading minds in the last thousand years."

"And it might have only been your dream," Williams said. "She might not have been there at all."

"I suppose," Claret said. "It felt real."

"There was a time when powerful witches and sorcerers could walk in people's dreams," Dovin said. "I've never heard of one in my time, but I haven't been in Riviand long, so I don't know the history here."

"I've heard stories," Claret said, "but none of them were recent."

The door opened, and Durdessa and Jayah entered. Jayah was wearing a long yellow dress that flowed down to her ankles. Her short black hair was pulled back in small clips and she walked confidently. She still appeared tired, but she looked better than the last time Claret had seen her. Her eyes fell on Williams and then jumped away.

Dovin stood and held out a chair to Jayah and then Durdessa. They both sat and began to eat.

"Isadora was in my dream last night," Claret said.

Jayah looked up from her plate. "I've worried she'll find mine."

"So she can enter people's dreams?"

"Yes. She can manipulate dreams. She can see people's fears and desires and use them against them."

"That's like reading minds," Claret said, looking at Dovin.

Dovin shrugged.

"She can't read minds. It's more like she sees flashes of things when she's in the dreams."

Claret's eyebrows came together. "I don't understand."

Jayah put her spoon down. "If a person is afraid of spiders, she might see a spider. It will be dark and hazy. That's how she knows the person fears it. If she sees something bright, it is something the person values."

Dovin rested his elbows on the table. "Fascinating. And she told you this?"

Jayah nodded. "Isadora is obsessed with mermaids. She wanted us to be her best friends. She told us many things. I pretended to like her so she wouldn't harm me. The others were all grateful for being captured by her. They never have to leave the water."

"But you wanted to?" Williams asked.

"Yes. The water calls to me like any other mermaid, but I resist it. I'm drawn to the water, and I fear it."

"Are you from the upper continent?" Dovin asked.

Jayah nodded. "All of us are. I fell in two years ago. Isadora found me. I was grateful to her at first, but then she wouldn't let me go."

"Isadora wants you back," Claret said. "I think you're in danger."

Durdessa took a sip of water. "We need to get you out of here. Isadora will assume you're here."

"We can't send her into hiding alone," Claret said. "She doesn't know Riviand. All the time she's spent here was at Isadora's."

"I can go with her," Williams said.

Jayah raised her brows.

Claret shook her head. "You don't know Riviand either."

"No, but I know how to survive."

Durdessa glanced over at Claret. "There's a cottage for sale on the east side of Tyran. We could give Williams the money for it and they could hide there in plain sight. No one would expect that."

"We would have to change our names," Williams said. "At least Jayah would."

"It probably doesn't matter. I'm not that memorable," Jayah said.

"That's ridiculous," Williams said. "Anyone who has ever seen you would remember."

Claret agreed. Jayah was striking with her high cheekbones and smooth brown skin.

Jayah leaned forward, her eyes locked on Williams. "I don't know if I believe you, Magni."

Williams' eyes went wide. "How do you know my name? I never tell that name to anyone."

"I'm not so memorable," she said. "You don't remember me, and neither does Professor Dovin."

Dovin's eyebrows rose and then his eyes narrowed as he studied Jayah. "I never forget a student... ah! Jayah, I do remember you. You sat in the back corner of my class with your hood up. You never spoke, but you did well on your assignments. I can't believe I didn't see it before."

Jayah nodded and looked over at Williams. "You always got to be a captain when we played Octaball. You never chose me."

Williams leaned forward. "I'm sorry. I don't know how I could forget someone who looks like you. Sorry, I realize that sounds shallow."

She sighed. "I kept to myself. Still, I remember you. Your family moved away."

"Yes, we went to... another place."

"I'm not sure I want to spend all my time with someone who ignored me all through school," Jayah said.

Williams ran a hand over his face. "Sorry, Jayah. I spent my school days trying to be the best I could at everything. I wanted people to notice me for what I was and not for what I couldn't do. In trying to prove myself, I might not have been as mindful of others as I should have been."

She glared at him. "There's something you can't do?"

"Magic."

Her eyes widened. "You can't do magic?"

"No."

She blinked twice. "I never realized."

"That was my goal."

Claret finished her breakfast. "I need to go sit with Kaylee. Give them whatever money they need. Don't come near the castle unless you absolutely must. We can't have Isadora finding you."

"What if we destroy the locket?" Dovin suggested. "Without it, you can't be a mermaid, then Isadora shouldn't want you."

Durdessa and Jayah both looked horrified.

"Or we could hide it," he said.

Claret stood. "Give them enough money to live on."

Durdessa nodded.

"Don't leave us behind if you ever leave Riviand," Williams said to Dovin. "It's not bad here, but I'd like to go home, eventually. I guess I won't be able to help with school. Not that we've had time anyway."

Tal circled his dragon over Mermaid's Demise. They had to be right over it because the roar was deafening.

"Should we drop?" Graham yelled.

"How high are we?" Mateo shouted.

"Pretty high! I'll go lower!" Tal called.

The dragon dropped, and so did Mateo's stomach.

"Now would be a good time!" Tal yelled.

Mateo remembered the last time he'd gone into the whirlpool only too well. He would do it again for Kaylee. He freed his feet and leaped from the dragon. The water hit him hard, and he immediately began going around with the whirlpool. He closed his eyes and felt like he was falling asleep. He didn't remember that from last time.

Mateo jerked up and looked around. He was in his room in the castle. He scratched his head in confusion. Had it all been a dream, or had he ended up in the lake under Mermaid's Demise? Last time, it had felt like he'd gone around in the whirlpool for a long time. This time was so short. Maybe he had fallen in closer to the center.

Jumping out of bed, he ran out of his room and down the hall. He slid to a stop when he got to Kaylee's room. He pushed open the door and went in. Dovin and Adler were standing over Kaylee. Her breathing still seemed too sharp.

"Is she all right?" Mateo asked.

"She isn't well," Adler said. "I don't know how much longer she has."

"Graham just woke up," Dovin said. "He hasn't been in yet. He's washing his hands and changing his clothes."

The door opened, and Graham and Tal came in.

Graham had a soggy bag in his hands and a mixing bowl. He looked at Kaylee and his mouth turned down. "Wow. I wouldn't have recognized her. She's grown." He shook his head and walked over to her.

He kneeled by her bed and placed his hand on her arm. Kaylee's body convulsed and then went still. Her breathing was less dramatic, and she looked more relaxed.

"How did you do that?" Adler asked.

Graham shrugged. "I don't know how to describe it. It just flows down my arms and into the other person. She's still in danger, but she should be more stable. I need a piece of the pryka. I think I can use it to make something that will help."

"I'll go," Dovin said. "We can't have any more accidents." He turned and left the room.

"Can we pull this table over?" Graham asked, pointing at a square table against the opposite wall. Mateo and Tal helped him move it over. He emptied his bag and put all the vials on the table. Odie came into the room. His eyes widened when he saw Graham's supplies.

Graham started mixing things into a bowl and muttering to himself.

"You seem young to be a healer," Adler said.

"I'm twenty-two. It kind of just—happened. I have a talent for it. It's a long story and involves a bungle."

"So long as it wasn't Padmire," Mateo joked. "I'm getting tired of that guy."

Graham smiled. "It was Padmire. He was the guardian of a cave that gave people special powers. I wanted to be a doctor on Earth. When I went into the cave, Padmire gave me the gift to heal people in ways no one else can."

"Wow. He was actually useful?" Mateo asked. "All I've gotten from him is this bruise," Mateo said, pointing at his jaw.

Graham frowned as he mixed something green in his bowl. "I've never known Padmire to be violent."

"Well, he didn't do it, but he was the cause."

Odie grinned slightly. "I thought I was the cause."

Graham pointed at Odie's eye. "Did you two get into a fistfight?"

Mateo shrugged. "It was a misunderstanding. Caused by Padmire. I think he's getting bored here and wanted entertainment."

Graham stirred faster. "Padmire is here? Why?"

"I don't know," Mateo said. "He followed us. How long is this going to take?"

"It's hard to tell. You all should probably leave. I can't imagine Kaylee wanting an audience when she wakes up."

"Can I stay to see what you're doing?" Odie asked. "I'd love to know what you are mixing in there."

"You want to be a healer?"

"I never thought about it. I love making things, though."

"I guess that would be all right."

"I'm not leaving," Mateo said. "Not until I make sure she's fine."

Tal gave him a crooked grin. "It's like that, is it?"

Mateo crossed his arms. "I don't know what you're talking about."

"If you ever need my help, I'm here for you," Tal said.

Mateo's eyes narrowed. "What are you talking about?"

"I'm great at matchmaking."

Graham dropped his spoon. "What? No, no, no. Don't start, Tal. Not with Kaylee. She isn't old enough."

"How old is she?"

"I don't know... Sixteen?"

Tal grinned. "So the same age you were when you met Wren?"

Graham picked up his spoon and waved it at Tal. "That's not the same."

"Let's not start speaking of relationships with this group," Padmire said, entering the room. "We don't want them to start throwing punches."

"Padmire!" Tal said. "It's been a while."

"You have to take me with you when you leave," the bungle said. "It's boring down here. I have to make my own fun."

Tal laughed. "More boring than staying in your cave?"

"At least in my cave I have magic."

"I don't think Kaylee will appreciate waking up with so many people in here," Graham said. "Most people don't want anyone staring at them when they're unconscious."

20

CHAPTER 20

Kaylee knew she was having a dream. She was walking through a field of wildflowers wearing a long, flowing pink dress. She would never go walking through a field in a dress. Her hair was hanging past her waist in tiny braids. She never dreamed about anything worthwhile. Sweat ran down her back. That was odd. She felt terrible, but she couldn't figure out why. She felt like sleeping, but she was already asleep.

She bent down to rub a sore spot on her leg, and she wondered if she was unconscious and not asleep. Was there a difference? Did she pass out? She had no idea. What if she died? Claret said prykas were really dangerous.

It felt like someone was rubbing something on her face. She batted at the invisible hands but didn't make contact with anything. Her heart started pounding. She could hear voices, but they were muffled. A disgusting liquid ran down her throat and she fell to the ground and tried to spit it out.

She yelled out and sat up. She blinked. Was she awake? She shivered and glanced around her room in the castle.

There were several sets of eyes on her. Some she knew, and some she didn't. Her eyes landed on the person at her side. She scrunched her eyes. "Graham?" He was older, but it was her cousin.

He smiled. "How do you feel?"

"Sweaty. How did you get here?"

"Mateo and Odie brought me."

Her gaze jumped to Mateo. "You got out of Riviand?"

He nodded and came over and kneeled next to her bed. She scooted farther away. She must smell terrible.

She looked back at Graham and frowned. "You never came back."

His smile fell. "I know. I'm sorry."

"I'm sorry I was such a bratty kid. It's my fault you didn't come back."

Graham frowned. "No. I didn't think you would want to see me after I left. I know Aunt Temperance didn't."

Kaylee wanted to tell him it wasn't true, but Kaylee's mom had never liked Graham. Kaylee couldn't understand it. Graham was great. The two of them had been really close until Kaylee started taking lessons from her mom and acted horribly.

"Well, I like to think I've matured," she said. "Can I have some water?"

"I'll get it," Odie said, leaving.

"Why are there so many people here?"

Graham shrugged. "I tried to make them leave."

"I needed to watch," Adler said, holding up a paper. "I think I'll be able to make the same medicine."

"I can teach you some things before I go," Graham said.

Kaylee thought it was odd Graham could teach Adler anything. The man looked about a hundred.

"Could everyone leave so I can change into something less... sweaty?"

"Sure," Graham said.

"Don't leave Riviand without telling me," she commanded him.

"I won't."

Mateo squeezed her hand. "I'm glad you're better."

She gave him a half smile. "Thanks. And thanks for getting Graham."

"Sure."

"Come on, little Sen," a guy Kaylee didn't know said.

Mateo stood and scowled. "I'm the same height as Sen, and I could probably take him in a fight."

Graham and the guy laughed.

"I would never fight Sen," Graham said. "He has skills."

Kaylee watched everyone file out of the room. She stood carefully and waited for the spots to stop swimming in front of her eyes.

"So, young Sen," Tal said. "Can I call you young Sen? You are younger than him."

"Just call me Mateo. How would you like to be called by your brother's name?"

Tal shrugged. "I've never had a brother."

Mateo was sitting at the kitchen table, eating a sandwich with Graham and Tal. Going down a whirlpool made a person hungry.

Tal grinned. "I can see you've got your eye on Kaylee. What are you going to do about it?"

"Knock it off, Tal," Graham said. "No one wants your matchmaking here."

Mateo nodded as he bit into his sandwich. "Kaylee's my friend. Same as Odie and Claret."

"Claret is the queen?" Tal asked. "We haven't met her yet."

"Yeah."

Graham took a sip of his water. "So what's the deal with your jaw and Odie's eye? Most people don't punch their friends. I could heal your face if you want. It would take less than a minute."

"It's fine. Odie and I just had a misunderstanding." Mateo knew that wasn't fair. He'd had a misunderstanding and Odie was only defending himself.

Tal grinned. "Over what? Girls?"

Mateo rolled his eyes.

"Does he like Kaylee as well?"

Graham kicked him under the table, but Tal just grinned.

"No, he likes Claret. And I told you. Kaylee and I are friends."

"Because that's what she wants, or that's what you want?"

Mateo glared at him, then sighed. "It's what she wants. I don't think she's into guys who punch people over misunderstandings."

Graham tilted his head and studied him. "That's smart of her."

Mateo fidgeted in his chair.

"Do you punch people often?" Tal asked.

"Not often. But occasionally." It sounded stupid even to him. "The second to last time, the guy actually deserved it."

Tal laughed.

"You can't tell me you've never been in a fight over a girl," Mateo said.

Tal and Graham shared a look, but neither one responded.

"Do you want some advice about girls?" Tal asked.

"Not really."

"All right, but you're missing out." Tal took a big bite of his sandwich.

"Do you even have a girlfriend?"

"Of course I do," he said.

"Hmm." Mateo wasn't sure what he thought about Tal. He had an easygoing vibe and he might be funny if he wasn't trying to talk about Mateo's life.

"How did you and Kaylee get to Riviand?" Graham asked. "And why does Kaylee speak the language?"

"My parents sent me to live with Dovin in Missouri. I met Kaylee at school. I couldn't speak to anyone because of the language barrier. One day, I got partnered up with Kaylee and we found a sword near the school. Some goblins chased us, and we found out we both spoke Akkronese while this was all happening."

Graham rubbed his chin. "Why does Kaylee speak it?"

"Dovin was tutoring her. We ended up running into Coach Williams and he recognized the Blade of the Phoenix."

Tal's eyes widened. "You had the Blade of the Phoenix? I thought that was only a myth."

"Nope. It's real. Kaylee still has it. I can't touch it because only non-magic people can hold it. I learned that the hard way. Anyway, Dovin knew the blade was supposed to be in Riviand. We came down and saved the continent. Without the Blade of the Phoenix, the continent was beginning to rise and everyone would have been killed."

"Wow," Graham said. "That's quite the story. Why are you still here?"

"We couldn't figure out how to get out until we got you. Well, we still don't know how, but now we know how to summon Vork and he can take us up. He didn't want to help us."

"Once Kaylee feels better, we should all go back."

Mateo shook his head. "We can't yet. The goblins are preparing to go to war against the rest of Riviand. We need to make sure that doesn't happen. There's also a witch who's causing some problems."

"Maybe we should stay and help," Tal said.

Mateo shook his head. "This isn't your fight. Your lives are up above."

"I don't feel comfortable leaving Kaylee down here with all these problems," Graham said.

"Kaylee's tough."

Graham raised his brow. "Oh?"

"She knows how to sword fight and defend herself. She escaped from the witch. Dovin taught her a lot of stuff. He tutored her for years."

"I guess she was ten the last time I saw her."

"She missed you."

He let out a long breath. "I should have visited."

"It's not too late."

"I would have if I thought she wanted me to. We had a weird relationship. My aunt raised me against her will. I thought it might be easier for everyone if I were to disappear."

"It wasn't," Kaylee said, entering the kitchen.

"Well, I'll visit from now on. Even if your mom doesn't like it."

"She might not notice. She's too busy traveling with her husband."

"She remarried?"

"Yep. She married a surgeon. She didn't even care when Dovin said he was taking me somewhere for a month to a year. I get it. She has her life. She was just happy she could go to the Bahamas without worrying about me."

Graham stood and wrapped Kaylee in a hug. She looked short next to him. "I'm sorry. I promise to visit from now on. When are you planning on going home?"

"I'm not sure. Once we help Riviand."

"Do you feel all right?" Mateo asked.

"Just hungry."

Kaylee grabbed a piece of bread from the table and took a bite. Mateo left to find Claret. She still didn't know Kaylee was awake. No one seemed to know where the queen was.

"So, Mateo is a nice boy," Graham's friend Tal said.

Kaylee narrowed her eyes, then laughed. "A nice boy? That seems like a funny description."

"Well, isn't he?"

"Most of the time."

"When he isn't punching his friend in the face?"

Kaylee nodded. "He has a bit of a temper when it comes to some things."

Graham shot Tal a look that Kaylee couldn't decipher.

"Mateo is a good friend. I'll miss him and Claret and Odie once this is all over."

"You don't think you might want to stay here?" Tal asked.

Graham glared at him. "Why would she stay here? This isn't her home."

"Akkron wasn't your home, but it is now."

"That's different. My family was in Akkron."

Kaylee leaned forward. "What do you mean?"

Graham wiped his mouth with a napkin. "My parents were from Akkron. It's a long story."

"Coach Williams said something about being your uncle."

"My dad is his cousin. So we're like second cousins or something like that."

"Can we go back to Mateo?" Tal asked.

"Tal..." Graham shook his head. "Stop playing match-maker."

Kaylee frowned. "You're trying to match me up with Mateo? Did he ask you to?"

"No," Graham said. "Tal just gets crazy ideas sometimes."

"I don't know," Tal said. "I feel like there might be something there."

Kaylee shook her head. "Mateo loves this world. Not necessarily Riviand, but the upper continents. He wants to stay there, and he hates it on Earth. I'm going back to Earth. Trying to make a relationship from that is silly. Besides, I'm only sixteen. I can't make life choices based on which boy catches my eye."

"Ah ha!" Tal said. "So he has caught your eye."

Kaylee just shook her head. She needed to change the subject. "So are you one of Graham's weird friends who came to my house six years ago? All I remember was thinking it was weird you were all wearing capes."

"Yep. You've changed a lot."

"I hope so."

Graham nodded. "And now you're wearing a cape. It's weird what six years can do."

Kaylee grinned. "It turned you into an old guy."

He laughed. "Twenty-two is hardly an old guy."

"Maybe not. I'm glad I got to see you again. I really missed you. Like a lot."

"I missed you too."

"How long are you staying?"

"We don't know how to get out of Riviand. It sounds like we're going to have to talk the goblins into letting us go up. I'm not too worried about it, but with goblins, who knows? We didn't bring anything to bribe them. I should have thought of that."

"If Vork is involved, we can blackmail him," Tal said, grinning. "We can threaten to tell all the other goblins about the time Austra beat him up."

"Who is Austra?"

"A beautiful, proper member of the governor's council. He isn't going to want that to get out. Or we could threaten to send her after him."

Graham smiled and shook his head.

"If you aren't taking off, I'm going to go help Mateo find Claret. She'll want to meet you."

"Sounds good," Graham said. "We have time."

Kaylee smiled and went looking for her friends. She ignored the feeling in her stomach when she thought about Graham leaving again. He had been everything to her when she was little and after spending years thinking he didn't care, she now knew he did. No one would risk getting stuck on an underground continent for someone they didn't care about.

21

CHAPTER 21

"You're all right!" Claret said, rushing down the castle hallway toward Kaylee. She wrapped her friend in a hug. "I knew your cousin had fallen in from Basura and I hoped he would be able to help. I was so stressed I had to go for a walk until it was over. Sorry I wasn't there when you woke up."

Kaylee laughed. "It's okay. I had enough people staring at me when I woke up."

"So you're all the way healed?"

"Yes, I feel great. And I got to see my cousin, so that's a bonus."

Claret nodded. She didn't know what it was like to have a cousin, but she could imagine. "I haven't met him yet. I was told there was another person with them."

"Yeah, Graham's friend came with him. I'll introduce you to them. Graham's friend is pretty cute." Kaylee grinned mischievously. "Not that you care."

Claret ignored the comment. Mateo was approaching them, and he was frowning.

Kaylee turned. "Hey, Mateo."

"Who is pretty cute?"

Claret held back a smile. "Graham's friend, apparently."

Mateo shook his head. "Sure, if you're into older guys. He has a girlfriend."

"I'm sure he does," Kaylee said. "So are you ready to meet them?"

"Are they leaving soon? I'd prefer to change my dress first."

"I think they'll be here for a while."

"So I can meet them at dinner?"

"Sure."

"Thanks. I'll see you all then." She rushed off to her room. Odie had helped Claret a little with her feelings of being worthless, but meeting Kaylee's cousin was a bit nerve-racking. He'd helped save the upper continents. His friend was probably another one who had. She didn't want to be the silly queen who couldn't do anything. If she could just teleport, that would give her one thing to brag about over Mateo. Of course Kaylee's cousin probably wouldn't ask her if she could teleport. That would be silly.

Claret looked down the long, empty hallway. She could try to teleport from here to the other end of the hallway. No one would see her if she couldn't do it, so she wouldn't have to worry about embarrassing herself. She'd felt like a failure every time she couldn't do it when Dovin was helping her. He was kind and encouraging, but she thought she might need to try with no eyes on her.

She could try running like Mateo, but that sounded dangerous. She took a deep breath and closed her eyes. It might be better to try it somewhere out in the middle of nowhere, but she didn't have time to find the ideal place. Claret focused on closing herself. She felt some pressure on her shoulder and something happened that hadn't before. She felt like she was floating weightlessly in space.

Dovin said once you felt that, you needed to open yourself up. Claret focused on light and opening herself. She opened her eyes—and she was in the middle of a desert, not at the end of the hall.

"What just happened?" Odie asked.

Claret spun around. "How did you get here?"

Odie's eyes were still scanning the endless orange sand. "I saw you standing with your eyes closed. I worried you were about to faint, so I put my hand on your shoulder and the next thing I knew, we were here."

"I was trying to teleport."

"It appears you succeeded."

Claret smiled. "I did!"

"Why did you come here?"

Her smile fell. "That was an accident. I meant to go to the other end of the hallway."

"Hmm. What were you thinking when you closed your eyes?"

"That it might be better if I tried in the middle of nowhere."

He grinned. "Well, I guess that's where you took us."

Claret lifted her boot out of the sand and took a step. "Do you know where we are? I've never seen anything like this before. The only desert is near Dragon's Cove, isn't it?"

Odie scratched his head. "That's the only one I know of. I've never been here."

"If I remember correctly, the desert surrounds Dragon's Cove and keeps the dragons in."

"I think dragons are all right with the heat. The way I heard it, the desert keeps the people away from the dragons."

"I've never seen sand like this. It's pretty."

Odie nodded. "How long are we going to stay? It's pretty hot."

"We can go back. I wonder how I brought us here. Dovin said you needed to know the place you're going."

"Yes, but Dovin can teleport to a place he sees on a map. It must be enough to know where the place is."

Claret held out her hand, and Odie took it. "I'll take us back to my room. I don't want to pop up and scare anyone." She closed her eyes and focused on closing herself. Nothing happened. She squeezed her eyes tighter and tried again. Nothing. Her heart began pounding as she focused on her room. This had to work. They couldn't be stuck in the desert. They weren't prepared.

"It's not working," she said, looking at Odie.

He gave her a half smile. "Take your time."

She closed her eyes again and took a deep breath through her nose. She tried to close herself and feel the weightlessness, but everything seemed too bright.

"Dovin said once you do it the first time, it's easy," she said.

Odie looked around. "I have no idea which direction is which. If we need to walk, we should start now."

Claret frowned. She hadn't been able to teleport in front of Dovin, and she couldn't in front of Odie. Was she really that self-conscious? She looked at Odie. He wasn't going to do well in the hot sun. He wore his feathered cape and black clothing. His sleeves were even long.

"It's too hot," she said. "We won't make it."

He rubbed his lips together. "Not if we don't get moving." He unhooked his cloak and dropped it to the ground.

"You're going to leave it?"

"I can't take it. It will only make things more difficult. Come on."

"Which way?"

"Since we don't know, I guess it doesn't matter."

Mateo dug into his mashed potatoes. They rarely ate until Claret was at the table, but no one could find her.

"Claret is usually easy to find," Durdessa said, toying with her knife. "I can't imagine where she could be."

"She told me she would meet Graham and Tal at dinner," Kaylee said.

"Perhaps you scared her when you told her Graham's friend was cute," Mateo said, trying not to look annoyed. "I think Claret secretly gets nervous about meeting new people."

Tal grinned, and he lightly punched Graham. "I guess I've still got it."

"Thanks a lot, Kaylee," Graham said. "Tal doesn't need anything else inflating his head."

211

Kaylee narrowed her eyes at Mateo, and he shrugged. He probably shouldn't have said anything, but he'd been in a bad mood ever since he'd overheard Kaylee.

"Odie isn't here yet either," Dovin said. "They might be together." Durdessa frowned.

"Well, if they are together, I'm not going to look for them," Padmire said from his stool. "I've seen enough adolescent romance to last me a lifetime." He looked over at Graham and shook his head. Graham just smiled and took a bite of green beans.

"Is there a story here?" Kaylee asked, grinning at Graham.

"Padmire is full of it," Tal said. "He enjoys it or he wouldn't always be stumbling in on it."

"Dovin, will you go find them?" Durdessa asked. "I don't want Claret spending time with him."

Dovin got to his feet. "Come, Padmire. Since it seems you can sniff out romance, you might be useful."

Padmire grumbled but followed him.

"Where's Coach Williams?" Graham asked. "I haven't seen him since we came."

Durdessa cut her meat. "He's helping us with something. He won't be around the castle anymore."

Mateo took another bite. He wished Padmire had reason to spy on him. What did Tal have that he didn't? Tal was attractive, he supposed, but he was at least six years older. Maybe girls liked older guys.

"Hey, Mateo?" Kaylee said.

He looked up and shook his head to clear his thoughts. "Yeah?"

"Can we talk for a minute?"

He shrugged. "Sure." He got up from the table and followed her into the hall. "What's up?"

She folded her arms. "You were looking at Tal like you might want to punch him. I'm starting to recognize the look."

"I'm not going to punch him."

She arched an eyebrow.

He let out a breath. "I don't know him enough to want to punch him."

"I told Claret he was cute. I was just trying to get a reaction from her. You don't need to freak."

"So you don't think he's cute?" Mateo asked hopefully.

She rolled her eyes. "Don't be a dork. He's totally cute."

He frowned.

"You can't get angry every time a cute guy comes around. He's cute, but I don't care. You don't need to be self-conscious. You're hot, and I'm still not interested."

Mateo wasn't sure what to do with that information. "So it's my personality?"

She sighed. "I'm not looking for a relationship right now, all right? You belong here and I belong on Earth. There's no reason to even think about anything happening between us." She opened the door and returned to the dining room.

Mateo stood staring at the door. It opened, and Graham and Tal came out.

"You look like you just got punched in the gut. Are you sick?" Graham asked.

"No."

"What did Kaylee say? She looked annoyed."

Mateo ran a hand through his hair. "It doesn't matter. Just out of curiosity. Would you rather be called cute or hot?"

Graham laughed. "I take either."

"That girl, Wren. She's your girlfriend?"

"Yep."

"Was it hard to get her to like you?"

"She liked me before I liked her."

"Dang. So you didn't even have to try?"

He shrugged. "That doesn't mean we didn't have our awkward moments. And I did have moments of uncertainty and so did she." Graham lightly kicked Tal in the leg.

"Hey," Tal said with a grin. "I thought we weren't talking about any of that stuff ever again."

"I want to hear the entire story," Mateo said.

Tal shoved Graham. "Maybe someday. I'll give you my version."

"Did you ever punch your friend in the face over a girl?" Mateo still felt like he owed Odie.

"No," Graham said.

"That must be a family thing," Tal said with a smile. "Your brother threatened to punch me once because of a girl."

Graham tilted his head. "You never told me that."

"Relationships are hard," Tal said. "They seem especially complicated when you're young. Don't let it stress you. You have your entire life to figure it out."

Mateo nodded. He didn't know why he was seeking advice from Sen's friends. He barely knew them. Still, they had saved Basura, and they had a lot of experience with life. He glanced back at the door. Kaylee had been more than clear. He was going to have to respect her feelings.

22

— · —

CHAPTER 22

Odie had never sweated like this in his life. He pushed his sleeves up and tried to ignore the blistering sun. Claret hadn't complained once. He glanced over at her. She was sunburned and her lips were chapped. He licked his own dry lips and cringed.

A hot wind was blowing into them and Claret's green dress was covered in the red sand. She was blaming herself. He was miserable but glad he had grabbed her when he did. He couldn't imagine how worried he would be if she'd disappeared alone.

"What's that up ahead?" she asked, pointing.

He could see different colors but couldn't make out what it was. "I know the desert can play tricks on your eyes. It might be nothing."

"Well, let's hurry, just to be sure."

They picked up their pace and whatever was in front of them was getting bigger.

"I think it might be Dragon's Cove," he said. "It looks green. Dragon's Cove is supposed to be a thriving area surrounded by desert." He moved faster. He hoped that was where they were headed. They might see dragons. People avoided the area because dragons were said to be dangerous, but if Dovin was right, that might be a misconception.

"Where it's green, there must be water," Claret said, moving forward.

The closer they got, the more sure Odie felt. It was a large area. So large, they couldn't see the desert on one side of it. There were large trees and even small hills. When they arrived, it was like stepping into a different world. There was a line that was desert, and then a line of grass and weeds.

It was still hot, but the breeze was cooler.

"I hear water," Odie said. They hurried through a clump of trees and saw a small waterfall running into a small lake. Odie smiled. "Do you think it's safe to drink?"

"I don't even care," Claret said, rushing to the water, and dropped to her knees. She cupped the water in her hand and drank it. Odie did the same. It felt scratchy going down at first, but it felt great when it hit his stomach. He splashed some on his face and arms. He should really reconsider his clothing choice. If he hadn't been wearing thick, dark clothing, he would probably feel better.

Water hit him in the face. Claret giggled.

He smiled back. "You don't want to start a water fight with me. You didn't grow up with siblings. Tipp has never beat me in a water fight."

She cupped her hand and splashed him again. "I don't see how that matters."

"Have you ever been in a water fight?"

She shook her head.

"Well, you're about to lose your first one."

"I'm getting nervous," Kaylee told Mateo. "Odie does his own thing, but Claret is always accounted for. What if Isadora caught them?"

Mateo stood at the kitchen counter, stirring cookie batter. "I wouldn't worry yet. It's only been a few hours. They probably just went for a walk or something."

"I went to the dungeon where they're keeping the dragon. I thought Odie might be there. The guard said no one has been down there."

"Why are they keeping him there? It doesn't seem fair."

"The dungeon is pretty nice. At least for a dungeon. I think they put him there so he doesn't catch anything on fire. Claret's going to have him moved once she figures out a safe place."

Mateo nodded and added more flour. "Dovin said bantam dragons don't breathe fire."

"I don't think the people here know a lot about dragons."

"I still don't think Claret would not appear for dinner. You saw how worried Durdessa was."

"People do weird things when they start dating. My mom said it made my brother Miguel completely irresponsible."

"Are Odie and Claret dating?" Kaylee asked. "I'm not sure they talked about it. Do they even call it dating here?"

Mateo grinned. "I think they say courting. I don't know if they are or not, but they're at least kissing. That should go with dating."

"I think we should all be looking for them. If Dovin and Padmire haven't found them, they must not be at the castle."

"I don't see a reason for Isadora to take Odie."

"But if they were together, she might have. Plus, how often do you see a guy running around in puffin feathers? She might want him for her zoo."

Mateo laughed. "I guess. I think you're worried for no reason. They're probably off cuddling and watching the sunset or something."

"I guess." Kaylee stuck her finger in the dough and then in her mouth.

"Gross," Mateo said. "Aren't you worried about salmonella?"

She smiled. "Nope."

"Odie and I need to get back to the goblins soon. The king knows we left Riviand, but he's going to be expecting us back. Now that Graham gave us some of the pryka, we might be able to make the invisibility potion."

"Do people go invisible in Basura?"

"No. There's a trick you can do to make non-magic people unable to see you, but if you move too much, it doesn't work well."

Kaylee grabbed a stool and sat down next to Mateo. "I guess we wasted time on the whole Kaylee's Snakes and Bakes idea. I doubt we'll ever have time to do it."

"We might."

"Well, I can't wait for a cookie. Odie told me the goblins were impressed by your baking."

"Of course they were." He smiled. "You will be too. Can I ask you a question?"

Kaylee's mouth turned down. "I guess."

"Why do you want to go back to Earth?"

Her eyes narrowed as she thought about his question. "Well, that's where my mom is and my friends. There's also school."

"But you have friends here, and from what you say, your mom isn't around a lot. And you can go to school here." He dropped a handful of his homemade chocolate chunks into the batter.

"There are things besides that. Toilets, fast food, microwaves, phones. I'm already going through phone withdrawal."

"There's indoor plumbing in Basura."

"But it's still not home."

"Graham lives in Akkron. You could live there."

Kaylee frowned and watched him mix in the chocolate. "And you could live on Earth."

He cringed. "The air is bad there, and people don't live as long."

"How long do people live here?"

"I don't know about here in Riviand, but up above, people live twice as long as they do on Earth. The water is better and the air. You know Dovin is an old dude, right? He has a daughter who's like forty or something."

"He only looks forty."

"Exactly."

Kaylee swung her legs under the stool. Living longer would be awesome. Being near Graham would be nice as well. He might even let her live with him. He had to be better company than her mom. She didn't dislike this world. It was interesting but not what she was used to. She couldn't see herself living like this forever. Even though things were crazy, she had been happier here than she had been in a while.

"Now that I can teleport, sort of, I could take you to Earth anytime you wanted."

Kaylee tapped her fingers on the counter. "Dovin said it's harder to go from one world to another than moving from different places in the same world."

"I'll figure it out."

She sighed. She could see herself being happy in a place full of magic. The animals here were really neat. It seemed like too big of a thing to decide without a lot of thought. She didn't know what the upper world was like. She might not like it at all.

Mateo scooped cookie dough into a pan and stuck it in the oven.

The door opened, and Graham entered. "I was going to say good night but not if there's going to be cookies."

"It will be about twelve minutes," Mateo said.

"Hey, Graham?" Kaylee asked. "When you're in Akkron, can you teleport to Earth easily?"

"Sure. It only takes a second."

"So if I wanted to come and visit, you could get me whenever I wanted?"

"Technically, but I wouldn't know when you wanted to come. We haven't figured out a way to communicate between worlds without actually going there."

"But I could tell you to come get me in a week or something and you could."

"Yes."

Mateo crossed his arms and leaned against the wall. "Or you could live in Akkron and visit Earth whenever you wanted to."

"Why would Kaylee live in Akkron?"

Mateo shrugged. "Because it's awesome."

"I'm just trying to figure out what's possible. I'm not planning on moving," Kaylee said.

Mateo looked thoughtful. "I bet my mom will let me stay now that I've been here. She didn't want me to come before because she said I was too young. She let Sen stay when he was my age."

"Where will you live?" Kaylee asked. "It's not like you have a job and money here."

"No, but my brother has loads of money. I could probably live with him, but I don't really want to live where he is. I grew up in a city called Boztoll, but I always wanted to live in Akkron. It's bigger."

Kaylee's mind went back to Claret. "When do I get to panic about Claret?"

Mateo shrugged. "In the morning?"

"If I disappear one day and you wait to look for me until morning, I'm going to change my mind about not punching people to solve problems."

Graham rubbed his chin. "I would volunteer to stay and help you search, but the longer I stay here, the more worried Wren will be. I don't want her to grab the rest of our friends and come down here. We might miss each other and I don't want her getting stuck."

"That's all right," Kaylee said. "I'm probably worried for no reason."

"What if they ran off together?" Mateo said. "Claret's been a little... unstable lately."

Kaylee shook her head. "She wouldn't do that. Claret wants what's best for Riviand. She wouldn't abandon it, no matter how she feels."

Dovin wandered in and took a long sniff. "Whatever is baking smells wonderful. I just talked to the maids and one of them saw Claret and Odie teleport. At least that is what I'm assuming. She said they were there and then they disappeared. She was a little nervous and didn't want to talk about it."

"At least we know they're together," Mateo said.

Dovin covered his mouth and yawned. "Yes, but Claret couldn't teleport when I tried to teach her. They could be anywhere. I suggest we all go to bed and hope they are back in the morning."

"What if they aren't?" Kaylee asked.

"Riviand is a vast place. I'm not sure looking for them would do any good."

"I still worry about Isadora. If she can get into Claret's dreams, she can find her."

"That's not how it works," Graham said. "I've studied dream jumping and the person can't enter another's dreams unless they know where that person is. If the queen teleported to a random place, no one will find her dreams."

Kaylee felt a little better.

Graham chewed the side of his cheek and looked deep in thought. "I'm not sure I want to leave you here. There are too many things that might go wrong. You should go back with me."

She tilted her head. "You know I can't."

"You really have changed, you know that?"

She smiled. "You mean I'm not a selfish little brat anymore?"

Mateo grinned. "Well, you aren't little anymore."

Kaylee playfully bumped him with her shoulder. "You didn't even know me back then. I was a terror. I probably would have gotten along perfectly with you."

23

CHAPTER 23

Claret rolled over and her eyes slowly opened. She was lying on the ground under a tree. She yawned and then smiled when her eyes landed on Odie. He was sleeping with his mouth hanging open, and there was a grasshopper on his head. She wondered if she should try to teleport them while Odie was sleeping. If he didn't know she was trying, she might be able to do it.

Her clothing had dried in the night. She shouldn't have started the water fight with Odie because they had gone to sleep soaking wet. What was more, Odie had completely won that fight. He had scooped water faster than she could think and had eventually picked her up and thrown her in the water. She smiled. It was fun. Claret had never done anything like it before. Most people wouldn't dare throw a queen in the lake.

A noise behind the trees made her freeze. She thought about her sword in Tyran and closed her eyes. Summoning took a clear mind. She blew into her hand and the sword appeared. She let out a sigh of relief and nudged Odie.

"Hmm?" he muttered.

"Odie," she whispered. "There's something in the trees."

He sat up and ran a hand through his hair. "What? Claret?" He looked confused for a moment. "Right. Dragon's Cove."

"There's something in the trees."

"A dragon, maybe?"

Claret got to her feet and looked around. They hadn't seen a dragon since they'd gotten here.

A creature jumped out and growled. Claret screamed. It had the head of a tiger, the body of a man, the legs of something with hooves, and wings. Odie was up and pushing Claret behind him. Claret slammed her sword into Odie's hand and she grabbed a fallen tree branch. After Vigh, she never wanted to use that sword again.

"It's a vorcraw!" Odie said as the creature watched them.

"Vorcraws aren't real!" Claret said, grasping the branch with two hands and holding it in a swinging position.

"He looks real to me," Odie said, holding the sword out.

Vorcraws were supposed to be mythical creatures that could be summoned by a person of great magical power. Once they were sent to deal with a person, they never stopped until they were successful. The vorcraw took a step forward, then two more burst from the trees. They wore tunics and tan pants, just like anyone in Riviand might.

"If they kill us, I'm so sorry," Claret said.

"They won't kill us," Odie said. "I wish Gregor were here." The first vorcraw charged forward. Claret held in a scream as Odie ran to meet him. The vorcraw pulled out his own sword and swung at Odie. Odie blocked with his sword. The other two vorcraws ran forward to help their friend.

"Crash, bam, whack!" Odie said as he attacked.

Claret rolled her eyes. Why was Odie making sword sounds? Shouldn't the clanging swords be enough?

Claret ran at the vorcraws and skidded, falling to the ground, but swiped with her branch. She hit one of the vorcraw's legs, causing him to fall. She jumped back to her feet and slammed her tree branch into the other one's shoulder. He turned and roared. She ran and hoped they would both chase her and leave only one with Odie. She could hear the swords clanging, but she didn't dare look over. Both vorcraws chased awkwardly behind her.

It was said that a vorcraw was stronger than a man but that they were so oddly shaped that it made them slightly clumsy. Claret hoped that was true. She ran around the pond and looked back every chance she had. She couldn't see Odie anymore. The vorcraws' hoofed feet should be fast, but with only two legs, they were falling behind.

A twenty-foot-high rock formation came into view. A waterfall spilled from the top of it. Claret threw her branch behind her and began climbing as fast as she could. The rocks had sharp pieces that cut into her hands, but she barely noticed. She could hear the vorcraws climbing behind her.

She regretted wearing a dress and wished for a pair of trousers like Kaylee usually wore. She threw one leg over the top of the rocks and then the other. This wasn't too bad. It was amazing what adrenaline could do. She rolled away from the edge and jumped to her feet, looking around. The top of the rock formation was about thirty paces across. She grabbed the biggest loose rock she could find and threw it down on the highest vorcraw. He hadn't expected it, and he lost his grip and knocked over his partner on his way down.

Claret began flinging rocks as hard as she could. The vorcraws growled and tried to cover their faces from her attack, but they started climbing again. She grabbed a larger rock and threw it with all her might. It hit one vorcraw in the face, but he managed to hold on.

The waterfall came out of an enormous hole in the rock. She thought about jumping. It wasn't high, but she might be at a disadvantage if she was in the water. She didn't know any stories about vorcraws and the water. There weren't any more rocks to throw, so she waited.

When the first vorcraw put his hand on the top of the rock, Claret stomped on it as hard as she could. He roared but didn't fall. He moved faster and Claret kicked him in the chest with her boot. She watched him fall over the side, but unfortunately, he didn't take his friend down this time. Her heart pounded loudly in her chest. She looked out over the lake and saw Odie, still sword-fighting with the first vorcraw. She hadn't realized how skilled he was.

The next vorcraw reached the top, and Claret tried the same strategy. She stomped on his hand and then screamed when his other hand came up and grabbed her ankle and pulled. She fell back and rolled. Before she could stand, he had reached the top. Claret looked for any possible weapon. The vorcraw pulled himself up.

Claret took a deep breath, ran five steps, and jumped off the waterfall. She plunged into the lake below and quickly surfaced. The two vorcraws stood above, looking down. She swam to the side and pulled herself onto the shore. She looked around to see where Odie was. Her wet dress clung to her legs and made walking difficult. She pushed her hair over her shoulder and looked back at the top of the rocks. The vorcraws were gone.

She heard something running toward her. It was Odie. She ran up and threw her arms around him, avoiding the sword. He put his free arm around her back. "Where are the other two?"

"I don't know. They were on top of the waterfall."

"Vorcraws die in the water. Perhaps we should go into the lake and stay there a while."

"We can't stay there forever and if I remember correctly, they don't need to eat or sleep."

Odie nodded. "True. But let's stay near the water."

"Where is the one you were fighting?" she asked, scanning everything.

"He's dead."

She shivered.

"You need a weapon," he said.

"I summoned the sword. The only other I know where it is would be the Blade of the Phoenix and it has protections on it. Not that I could hold it anyway."

A deep growl made Claret's stomach drop. "Run!" She grabbed Odie's hand, and they went in the opposite direction from the growl. A vorcraw jumped out in front of them and they skidded to a halt. Claret ran to the side and picked up a rock. Odie charged it with his sword. Claret waited, ready to throw the rock as soon as she had a clear shot. The other vorcraw ran past her, sword in the air. He was going to hit Odie.

Claret threw the rock and hit him in the back. He stopped and turned to look at her, then turned back to Odie. He couldn't take on two at the same time. Claret held up her sopping dress and ran with everything in her. Jumping into the air, she landed on the vorcraw's back and clung to his neck. She pulled at his fur and jerked sideways, causing him to fall into the lake with her.

When she sat up, she watched steam float up in the air above the water. The vorcraw was gone.

Odie stepped toward her, a dead vorcraw near his feet. It caught fire and quickly disappeared. He held out his hand and pulled her up.

"That was the most amazing thing I've ever seen," he said.

Claret blushed, then smiled. "I was pretty amazing." She stepped out of the water and tried to wring out her dress.

Odie grinned. "Let's not forget that I killed two of them."

Claret raised her brow. "But I didn't see it, so I'm not sure if it was amazing or not."

He laughed. "Just take my word for it."

"You lose style points when you make your own sword sounds."

Odie grinned sheepishly and rubbed the back of his neck. "Tipp and I are pretty pathetic when we practice with swords." His smile fell. "I hope there aren't any more."

"Who do you suppose sent them after us? Vorcraws only go after someone when someone sends them. My guess is Isadora."

"It's possible," Odie said. "I wish we knew who they came for. If they were after you, I would say it was Isadora. If they were after me, my guess is Garin. I don't think he likes me."

"I bet they were after me. Vorcraws are only supposed to pursue the person they are sent for. You engaged one with the sword and the other two chased me."

"That's true," Odie said with a frown. "We need to get back to the castle."

"I didn't know you could fight like that."

Odie smiled. "When you don't have magic, you have to do other things to stand out. My father paid a man to teach me and Tipp when we were younger. Tipp and I practiced a lot, but it's different fighting someone taller. Tipp was always catching me on the knees."

Claret tried to shake the water from her sleeves. "It seems odd that we've seen no dragons. I would expect Dragon's Cove to be covered in them."

"They could be hiding from the vorcraws. Or us. We don't know what they're like."

"I won't be able to sleep another night here knowing there might be more vorcraws. I guess they can find me anywhere."

"If they do, we will deal with them. I won't let them hurt you."

Claret smiled. Odie filled her heart with something she didn't understand, and it made her want to burst with happiness. She went on her toes and kissed his cheek. "Thank you. And I won't let them hurt you."

Odie wanted to kiss Claret, but there was always that little voice in the back of his mind that told him she couldn't really like him. She was the queen, after all, and she was kind and funny. Even dripping water all over, she was beautiful. She was still standing close, staring up at him. Did she want him to kiss her?

He took a deep breath and bent down slightly. She inched closer, and it was decided. He met her lips and wrapped his arms around her. He was going to be wet.

She pulled back slightly and looked into his eyes. "It wasn't long ago that you were the last person I wanted to see. Now you are the only one I want to see."

He ran his hand over her cheek. "I'm sorry for before. I wish I could erase the past."

"The past is an important part of who we are. Just be glad that you were able to rise above what you were. You've come far, Odie. You should be proud."

He leaned in and kissed her again. This could definitely become one of his favorite things to do. It boosted his confidence when she reacted so enthusiastically. A growl sounded behind them. Odie broke from Claret and scooped her up over his shoulder, then carried her into the lake. He looked around. There had to be a vorcraw out there.

"Odie, you can put me down. I can walk."

"Sorry," he said, placing her carefully into the water. "In reality, you should have picked me up. You're already wet."

Claret smiled but looked cautiously into the trees. A blue dragon stepped out and watched them. Odie was excited and scared at the same time. He stepped from the water and walked carefully up to him.

"Hello," Odie said softly.

The dragon tilted his head.

"Careful, Odie," Claret said.

"But if we get on, he might fly us somewhere. At least get us away from the desert."

The dragon lowered his head and Odie rubbed his hand over it.

"Would he?" Claret asked. "I think they stay at Dragon's Cove. That's why we don't see many flying around."

"It's worth trying."

"Unless we fall off and die."

Odie turned. "You're scared of dragons?"

Claret wadded out of the water. "I've never thought about it, but flying on an untrained dragon terrifies me."

Odie walked over to Claret and took her hand. "I don't want to do anything that scares you, but what is our alternative? We could brave the desert and hope we make it out alive, or we could stay here and hope someone finds us someday."

Claret peered over at the dragon. Odie squeezed her hand, and she sighed. "All right." They approached the dragon, and it bent down.

"It's like he knows," Odie said. He lifted Claret and helped her sit on his back. She wobbled and then stabilized herself. Odie climbed up behind her and she leaned against him. "Hold on tight," he said. "It's faster than anything I've ever—"

The dragon leaped into the air and Claret's scream pierced Odie's ears.

24

— · —

CHAPTER 24

The dining room felt empty at breakfast. It was only Kaylee, Mateo, and Gregor. Dovin had given Graham and Tal a map, and they had teleported to the cave in the goblin mountain. They hoped to talk Vork into sending them home. Padmire had decided to go back with them. Durdessa and Dovin were trying to figure out where Odie and Claret had gone.

Kaylee took a bite of eggs. She wanted to help look for Claret, but Dovin was right. Riviand was huge and finding them by chance was small. Dovin knew some tricks he thought might help, and all Kaylee could do was stay here or get in the way.

"I still can't believe Coach Williams' name is Magni," Mateo said. "Did you all laugh?"

Kaylee looked up from her plate. "No, we aren't rude."

"I would have laughed."

Kaylee smiled. "I know."

"It's no wonder he didn't want to tell us his name. And now he's in hiding with a mermaid. I bet his life is in a different place than he would have imagined a few months ago."

"He's not the only one."

"That's true."

Gregor flew up to the table and Kaylee shooed him off. "Who cleans up after Gregor? Birds are messy."

"Odie taught him to go to the bathroom outside," Mateo said.

Kaylee narrowed her eyes. "Is that even possible?"

"It must be. There are a few windows that are left open, and he knows where they are. Odie said he just has to show him the window once, and Greg knows what to do."

"That must have taken a lot of training."

"It's not foolproof. Birds poop a lot, so if he gets shut in a place, it's bad. I heard a maid complaining one day."

Graham appeared in front of them, holding a book.

Kaylee put a hand to her chest. "Dang it, Graham! You should warn people before you do that!"

He grinned. "Sorry. I have some great news, so I thought you would forgive me."

"Oh?"

"Tal and I had a long talk with Vork."

Mateo chuckled. "I don't imagine that being fun."

"Nope. Still, we've dealt with him before and we've learned some things. We convinced him to tell us the way out of Riviand. And by convinced, I mean bribed."

Kaylee's eyes widened. "Really?"

"It's the cave Mateo pointed us to. You can teleport from the cave to the upper continents and from there to the cave. It's the only way to get up."

"That's great!" Kaylee exclaimed. "It's been stressful wondering if we would get stuck."

"I popped back home and grabbed this book and then came back." He handed the blue book to Kaylee. "I wrote this. It's about all the things I've learned about medicine. Riviand isn't as advanced as Akkron. Will you give it to Adler?"

"Sure." Kaylee stood and gave him a hug. "Thank you."

Graham patted her on the back. "Come see me before you go back to Earth."

"I will. And come down here and check on me now and then, just to make sure we weren't captured by trolls or anything."

Graham laughed. "I will. Trolls aren't mean, though." He disappeared and Kaylee put the book on the table and sat back down.

"I need to get better at teleporting," Mateo said. "That cave is small, so I won't have a lot of room to run."

"Dovin can do it."

"That's true. What are we going to do while we're waiting for Odet to come back?"

Kaylee tilted her head. "Odet?"

He grinned. "Odie and Claret. Odet."

Kaylee rolled her eyes. "I don't know."

"We could work on *Kaylee's Snake and Bakes*."

Kaylee wrinkled her nose. "I don't think that's a good idea. It sounded fun when we first thought of it, but we don't have time to open a bakery or take care of animals. If we ever get time, we know how to go home now."

"So we give up? Even after making that awesome sign?"

"For now."

"But what are we going to do? No one is attacking us or anything, so all we have to do is wander around the castle, making people wonder what we are up to."

"We could study for school. We're going to be behind. Dovin and Williams taught us for one day and that's not enough to help keep up."

Mateo flicked a piece of egg across the table at Kaylee. "I can think of a hundred things that would be more fun than that."

Kaylee ignored the egg. "Such as?"

Mateo rubbed his chin. "Uhhh, we could go fishing."

"Really? Fishing?"

"We could go check the stables to see if Willow made her way back."

Kaylee stood. "Let's do that. I was going to yesterday, but things were distracting."

Mateo stuffed an entire biscuit in his mouth and got up. "Mrfurafle?"

"I'm not even going to try to translate that. Come on."

Mateo watched Kaylee run her hand over Willow's nose. The stable master said that Willow had wandered in yesterday with Claret's alicorn, and they were both healthy and well.

"I wonder if we could introduce alicorns to Earth," Kaylee said.

"Nah. That would be too messy. People aren't ready for mythical creatures to appear."

"You're probably right. Do you want to ride her?"

Mateo narrowed his eyes. "No. I bet she's tired from flying around so much this week."

"You're still scared of her?"

"I'm not scared," he said, leaning over and putting his hand on Willow's back. "Let's let her rest. At least today."

"All right." Kaylee gave her a final pat. They left the stables and something charged into Mateo, causing him to fly into the air and hit the ground. He sat up, holding his ribs. Kaylee ran toward him and a large... thing walked behind her. It was as tall as a man, with the head of a tiger.

Mateo didn't take time to observe it; he jumped to his feet. When Kaylee reached him, he started running with her. He had never seen or heard of anything with a tiger head. Mateo reached out and Kaylee grabbed his hand.

"Three steps! One, two, three!" He teleported them to Kaylee's room in the castle. They ran two more steps and fell onto her bed. He wouldn't complain. He'd had worse landings.

Kaylee popped up. "What was that?"

Mateo shook his head and stood. "I've never seen anything like that before." He rubbed his sore shoulder. He hadn't realized it hurt until now.

"We have to warn people. Where do you think Captain Nerman is?"

"He's usually out running drills near the barracks. I thought you might want to grab the Blade of the Phoenix."

"Right," Kaylee said, dropping to her knees. She pulled a long box out from under her bed and opened it.

"Really? That's where you keep it?"

She glared up at him. "No one is looking for it, so it should be safe." She pulled out the bright sword and held it up. "The twine we put on the hilt to disguise it makes it look almost boring."

"Let's go."

They ran through the castle and ignored all the curious glances from the staff. Once outside, they ran near the barracks. Mateo had been right. There were at least fifty soldiers practicing different things. The sound of swords clanging rang in his ears.

"Captain Nerman!" Mateo yelled. Several soldiers turned and frowned at him. He didn't care.

Captain Nerman approached them, his mouth turned down in a frown. "Is Durdessa going to let us look for the queen? Waiting like this is careless."

"No, I don't know where Durdessa is. We were just attacked outside the stables."

He placed a hand on the hilt of his sword. "By who?"

"It was some type of creature. It had the head of a tiger."

"And wings," Kaylee added. Mateo hadn't noticed the wings.

Captain Nerman's brow furrowed, and he rubbed his mustache. "It cannot be."

"What?" Mateo asked.

"There is a mythical creature that only exists in stories. They were said to have the head of a tiger and the legs of a gazelle. There might have been something about wings. I don't remember. They are called vorcraws."

"What do they do?" Kaylee asked. "It was strong."

"They only come when summoned by dark magic. Once they're after someone, they never stop until they succeed, or the person who summoned them dies."

"Well, that's lovely," Mateo muttered. "We don't have time for this."

"It has to be Isadora," Kaylee said. "Who else has that power?"

"Even with the legs of a gazelle, they aren't fast on land. Only having two legs supposedly makes them clumsy, and they can be killed. You two go inside and we'll handle this." Captain Nerman whistled and all the soldiers stopped their exercises and turned to him. "Go," he said to Kaylee and Mateo.

Kaylee opened her mouth and shut it. She looked at Mateo and he nodded. He knew they weren't ready to take on something like that. It had thrown him like it was nothing. Before they could leave, there was a deafening roar.

The soldiers all turned, and Mateo's mouth hung open. There were at least ten vorcraws walking toward them. Only one carried a sword, and they were all growling.

"Fight!" Captain Nerman yelled, raising his sword. The soldiers all pulled themselves together and ran toward the creatures. "Go!" he yelled at Kaylee and Mateo.

Kaylee looked at the Blade of the Phoenix and set her jaw. Mateo frowned. She wasn't going to leave, and he didn't have a weapon.

The lead vorcraw waved his sword, knocking down the first two soldiers who approached him. He flew over the remaining soldiers and landed in front of Mateo and Kaylee.

Kaylee's eyes narrowed, and she swung the sword forward, pointing it at him. A blast of orange light shot from the sword, throwing the vorcraw back. A soldier nearby plunged his sword into it, and it caught fire and disappeared.

The others all cheered in support and began stabbing the other vorcraws. Soon, all the vorcraws were gone and there were only small mounds of smoke to show they had been there.

"I told you two to go!" Captain Nerman said, wiping blood from his sword onto his cape. "Go to the castle and stay there! Those things were after you, and if there are more, they will find you. I'll have extra guards placed around the castle, and I don't care what Durdessa said. I'm sending men to find the queen."

Mateo looked at Kaylee. She was breathing hard and staring at the captain.

"Go!" he yelled. They turned and ran to the castle.

"That was crazy!" Mateo said when they were safely inside the kitchen. The cooks all shot them disapproving stares.

"No swords in the kitchen," Cook said, wagging her pointer finger at them. "You might not respect all the rules, but I'm firm on that one." She patted her curly white hair. "Violence doesn't belong in the kitchen."

Mateo didn't have time to argue with Cook. They ran forward, then turned around when the door to the outside flew off its hinges and clattered to the floor.

A vorcraw stood in the doorway and gazed into the kitchen. The cooks screamed, and they all ran for the opposite door.

Kaylee clutched her sword in her hands, but before she could do anything, Cook was slamming a frying pan into the vorcraw's face. It stumbled back a few steps and then lunged at her. For being a larger woman, Cook was fast. She jumped out of the way and smacked it on the elbow with the pan. The vorcraw roared in pain.

"Look out, Cook!" Kaylee called.

Cook jumped out of the way, and Kaylee pointed the blade at the vorcraw and blasted it back with the orange lightning. The vorcraw flew through the air and hit the wall, then slid down and landed in a heap. Kaylee ran forward and stuck her sword into the beast. He caught fire and it turned into smoke.

"You see the consequences of violence in the kitchen?" Cook asked. "Now I have to go round up all those scaredy little cooks, and they are going to be worthless all day." She pushed a short curl out of her eyes.

Mateo grinned. "I would hate to be on your bad side."

Cook smiled and held her frying pan in the air. "Then I suggest you remember this day."

25

— . —

CHAPTER 25

"No," Odie muttered, his arms still wrapped around Claret.

"What?" she asked. They had been flying for a while, and she had finally calmed down.

"We're going toward the goblin mountain." Odie tried to lean to one side and get the dragon to go with him. It ignored him and kept going. He pulled harder but to no avail. The black castle came into view and the dragon dipped down with breathtaking speed. Odie clenched his teeth together and Claret held her breath.

The dragon landed in front of the castle and squatted so they could slide off. Odie went first and helped Claret down. As soon as her feet touched the ground, the dragon was off and into the air again.

Claret shivered. "Why did he bring us here?"

"I don't know, but we need to leave before anyone sees you."

The doors opened and several goblin guards poured out and surrounded them.

King Ummi stood at the top of the stairs and smiled. "Good job, Odie. You've brought the queen back. Now all is forgiven."

Claret's eyes shot up at him, and he swallowed hard. He didn't want Claret to think he betrayed her, but if they were both locked up, no one would know to look for them.

"Put the queen back in her cell and lock it this time," the king said.

Two of the guards grabbed Claret's arms and began pulling on her.

"Wait," she said. "You can't do this."

"Can I not?" King Ummi said with a smile. He adjusted his tall crown. "You have no power here. Did Odie give you our conditions for not coming to war against Tyran?"

Claret looked at Odie and frowned. He wanted to tell her to ignore his father, but he needed to be free to rescue her later. She shook her head.

Garin came out behind the king. He stifled a yawn and fastened his cape around his neck. "Let's get her locked up before we go through that, shall we?"

The guards pulled on her arms again and she followed. The king and Garin disappeared inside and the guards led Claret after them. Odie hurried to keep up.

They led her down a long black hallway and to the dungeon door. A guard standing near the door holding a spear opened it, and the king and Garin started down. This wasn't good. Odie made sure Claret didn't leave his sight as they walked down the dark staircase. No one spoke as they walked past the empty cells until they got to the last one.

Claret's bed was still inside from the last time she'd been here. Some of Odie's things were littering the hallway in front of it from when he had been guarding her. The guards shoved her inside and slammed the door, locking it.

Claret gave Odie one last blank glance before turning her attention to the king. She stood straight and didn't look scared. "How do I save Tyran from war? You know it would be careless of you to come against us. It isn't only Tyran you would fight but all of Riviand."

Garin smiled. "We do not fear you or Riviand."

Odie didn't understand Garin. He either had some plan that Odie couldn't understand, or he was a fool. Riviand could wipe out the goblins and any army they might gather.

"We do not want war," Garin said, "but you have ruled too long. A child should not be on the throne. King Ummi is the better ruler."

"And what say you, King Ummi?" Claret demanded. "Do you really think you will rule Riviand? This man does not appear to be the type who settles for second best. If you were to win against Riviand, which is highly unlikely, he is not going to let you rule for long. He will take over and leave you dead or worse."

"Ridiculous," Garin said, his orange eyes flashing. "I have no desire to rule."

"Then what is your objective? You want a war just to take me off the throne?"

"You don't have to be taken off the throne," King Ummi said. "If you agree to our terms."

She raised her eyebrows and crossed her arms. Odie was proud of the way she conducted herself. He knew she must be terrified, but he couldn't see it.

"What are your terms?" she asked.

The king smiled. "You marry Odious."

Claret laughed. "Excuse me?"

"Marry Odious and make Garin your advisor. Garin will report to me. Odious will rule with you, and he will have as much say in what happens as you do."

Claret's fingers drummed against her folder arms. "Odie isn't any older than me. So you want to use me as a puppet. Is that it?"

Garin's lips turned up. "She's smart."

"I won't be your puppet."

Garin shrugged. "Then we will take Riviand and you will rot in this prison. You have one day to think about it." He strode away, his cape flapping behind him.

"He's using you as a puppet," Claret said to Kind Ummi.

He frowned. "No. He is my advisor, not the other way around."

She raised her brow. "We shall see."

"Come, Odious," he said. "We've got things to do."

"Shouldn't I stay down here?"

The king's brows came together. "That didn't go well last time. We don't have to worry about her escaping, either. We will keep the cell locked and not allow any other prisoners down here."

Odie shot a look at Claret that he hoped she interpreted correctly. Her expression remained unreadable. He followed his father. He couldn't think of anything else to do. Garin was so far ahead he was almost at the stop of the stairs.

"Did you get the ingredients you were looking for?" the king asked quietly.

"I did, but I don't have it. It's with Mateo."

"And where is he?"

Odie shrugged. He didn't want his father to know there was any connection between Mateo and Claret.

"The queen is right, I fear. Garin is trying to use me, and the sooner we are done with him, the better. Still, getting the queen to marry you will be beneficial."

Odie frowned. "I am only sixteen, you realize? Getting married now isn't in my plans."

"It is now."

Odie ground his teeth. If he had to get married, he would pick Claret in a heartbeat but not now. He wished he knew what she was thinking. Did she trust him or think he'd betrayed her?

Claret stared after Odie until he disappeared. She walked over to the bed and sank down. Her heart was on the verge of bursting, but she didn't feel like crying. Instead, she was empty and cold. She pulled the blanket over her shoulders and stared at the gray cell wall. She could feel the sunburn on her face and arms, but that was the least of her problems.

Had Odie really brought them here? What were the chances that a random dragon would bring them here?

She shook her head. Odie hadn't deceived her. She didn't know what was going on, but he would save her. He would let her know somehow.

"Cold?" Garin asked. Why had he returned?

Claret startled and turned to see the man leaning against the bars. She hadn't heard him come. She turned back to the wall and ignored him.

"I can get you out of here, and it won't require marrying that young idiot. You can marry me instead."

Claret's eyebrow rose. "So that is your game. I thought it might be something like that."

"Better than war, isn't it?"

"No. Having a tyrant rule isn't better for anyone."

He ran a hand through his messy blond hair. "Tyrant? That's a rather strong word."

"So I am too young to rule but not too young to marry?"

He smiled and Claret tried to ignore the way his orange eyes flashed. "We both know your age isn't the issue here. There's no reason to try to deceive you. I want Riviand, and I will have it. The only thing to discuss is how hard you want it to be."

"The goblins can prepare for years, and they will never take Riviand."

"Maybe in the past. But now they have me to guide them."

"And I stand by my statement. The goblins are too few, and Riviand is prepared."

"You have a lot to think about. War will come, and prepared or not, it will not be good for your people. Even if we lose, you will suffer."

Claret wished she weren't wrapped up like a little kid in her blanket, but she didn't feel the strength to stand. "Leave," she commanded.

"Very well, but think about it. War or marriage to the ridiculous Odie. Neither one sounds like a great solution. I have a commanding presence and I can help you revolutionize Riviand. I'm from the upper world. Did you know that? They have things up there that you can't imagine. I can bring those things to Riviand and make your life easier. Think about it." He walked away.

Garin was an idiot if he thought he could sway her. She was going to get out of here and stop a war, and Odie was going to help her.

"Come on, Tipp. Help me out," Odie begged his brother.

Tipp crossed his small goblin arms and frowned. "If I open a portal to Tyran without Father's permission, I'm going to get in trouble."

"I need to get the pryka for my experiment. I can be in and out in five minutes."

"I dunno. If they see me in Tyran, they'll throw me in prison."

"You don't have to come. I can get back."

"How?"

"I just can."

Tipp kicked at the floor. "All right, but if I get in trouble, I'm blaming it all on you."

"Fine."

Tipp pulled his hands apart and ripped open a portal. Odie jumped through and landed on the steps of the castle. The two men standing guard both jumped and drew their swords. When they recognized him, they lowered them.

"Be careful," one said. "There are dangerous creatures roaming about. We've already killed several. People are out looking for you and the queen. Where is she?"

"I don't have time," Odie said, running inside, straight to Mateo's room, and flung open the door. Mateo and Kaylee were sitting at a small table, playing a game.

"Odie!" Kaylee exclaimed, jumping to her feet. "You are super sunburned! Are you all right? Where's Claret?"

"She's in the goblin dungeon. It's a long story. I need the pryka and I need to go back."

"I have it," Mateo said, hurrying over to his wardrobe. He pulled out a container and handed it to him.

"Can you come with me?" Odie asked. "I can't get back without you and I can't leave Claret."

Mateo glanced at Kaylee and frowned. "I don't want to leave Kaylee alone. There are these weird creatures called vorcraws, and they keep coming."

Odie's mouth turned down. "Some came for Claret and me as well."

"Where were you?"

"Claret accidentally teleported us to the desert. We found Dragon's Cove. That's when the monsters came. We killed three and then found a dragon. He flew us out but took us to the goblins and they locked Claret in the dungeon. She probably thinks I betrayed her."

Kaylee grabbed the front of Odie's shirt and pulled him close to her. She glared into his face. "Did you?"

"No!"

She pushed him back. "Good. Mateo, go with him. I'll be fine. I have the Blade of the Phoenix and Dovin will be back anytime."

Mateo looked from Kaylee to Odie.

Kaylee rolled her eyes. "Seriously. Go with him."

"Why don't you come?"

Odie wasn't sure that was a good idea.

"No. If something goes wrong, I can't come save you all if I'm there as well. Don't worry about me."

Mateo nodded. "All right, but stay away from anything that might eat you."

She rolled her eyes again. "Okay. Now go."

Mateo grabbed his cape from his bed and fastened it. Odie grabbed ahold of it and they ran three steps and right into Odie's room.

"I'm getting better at that," he said.

Odie nodded. "So long as there aren't any trees. You know, for all of Kaylee's talk about not solving problems with violence, she sure scares me sometimes."

Mateo laughed. "I know what you mean. Now what do we do?"

Odie held up the pryka. "Now we figure out how to be invisible."

26

⸺ · ⸺

CHAPTER 26

Kaylee copied the notes Dovin was writing into her notebook and sighed. It had been three days since Odie had come and gotten Mateo, and Kaylee was quickly tiring of being the only teenager in the castle. She wanted to keep up with her schoolwork, but it was hard when she knew her friends might be in danger.

Captain Nerman was preparing to storm the goblin castle to rescue Claret even though Durdessa was forcing him to wait a few days. Since Claret wasn't in immediate danger, Durdessa and Dovin thought it might be good to give Odie and Mateo a few more days to try to figure it out.

There hadn't been any more vorcraws, so Dovin figured it was time to get back to chemistry. Kaylee was always ahead in most of her subjects, but chemistry and math gave her some problems.

"Are you with me, Kaylee?" Dovin asked.

"Sort of."

"I don't want to go over this again. Where's your mind?"

"It's hard to think about this stuff when I don't know what's going on with the others. I should have gone with them."

"How would they have explained your presence to the goblins? I think it's best you stayed."

"So the others are with the goblins?" Isadora asked.

Kaylee jumped from her seat and spun around to see the witch standing by the window. Her hair hung in long ringlets, and she wore a gold dress. She looked entirely different from the first time they had met.

"Get out of here," Kaylee said, stepping back.

"Out of where? Your head?"

Kaylee looked over at Dovin for help. He sat at a desk, reading a book.

Isadora grinned. "He's not here. He can't help you."

"I'm asleep?"

"Of course. And now you've told me where your friends are. But why? Are they spying on the goblins?"

"Claret is in the dungeon," Dovin said, without looking up.

Kaylee ground her teeth. Her dream was betraying people.

"I went through a lot of trouble, sending the vorcraws after you. You weren't very welcoming to them."

Kaylee narrowed her eyes.

"I have to say, I was disappointed when the vorcraws failed, but you've given me another idea. If the queen is in the goblins' dungeon and your other friends are there, then I think I need to pay a visit to the goblins."

"Leave them alone."

"The goblins?"

"My friends."

"Tell me where Jayah is and I might consider it."

"No."

Isadora turned to Dovin. "Where is the mermaid?"

Kaylee concentrated as hard as she could, and Dovin disappeared.

"Very well," Isadora said. "I suppose you have chosen." She snapped her fingers and disappeared.

"Wake up, wake up," Kaylee told herself. She tried shaking her head and pinching her arm, but nothing changed. After squeezing her eyes shut, she pried them open. She was lying in her bed, staring up at the ceiling.

She breathed hard, then jumped out of bed and ran to Dovin and Durdessa's room. The hallways were dim, so it must still be night. She pounded on the door and waited a minute.

Dovin opened the door a crack. His hair was messy, and he yawned. "What is it?"

"Isadora is going to go after the others."

He raised his eyebrows. "How do you know?"

"She was in my dream. What should we do?"

Dovin rubbed his chin. "I think we should wait."

"Wait? Why?"

"What if it was only a dream? It's possible you dreamed of her because she'd been on your mind. If we go charging the goblins, that will start something we aren't ready for."

"It felt real. She was there. We should send the army."

"Give it some time. We will talk more in the morning."

"Fine," Kaylee grumbled. She hurried to the library. The library had books from ceiling to floor on three walls, and the fourth wall had cubbies full of rolled up maps. Kaylee began pulling them out and studying them. It only took five before she found one that showed the goblin mountain.

"Got it!" she said, rolling up the map and running to her room. She grabbed a bag and stuffed the map and a change of clothes inside. She pulled on her scabbard and stuck the Blade of the Phoenix to her side. With luck, Willow would be up for the flight. Kylee stopped in the kitchen and grabbed some bread and cheese and put them in her bag. Within fifteen minutes of leaving Dovin, she was on Willow's back and in the air. She only hoped she was going in the right direction.

"Vivi, Vivi, Vivi," Mateo said, shaking his head. "You burned them again."

Vivi crossed her arms and kicked the oven. "What magic do you use that you aren't telling me about?"

Mateo sighed. "It's not magic. You put the cookies in, wait twelve minutes, and take them out."

"That's what I did, and they still burn."

"No, I left you here twenty minutes ago, and you just took them out when I came back. Twenty is more than twelve."

Vivi grumbled.

"Don't you usually time things when you cook?"

"No, and no one ever cared until you came along. After the goblins all tasted your creation, they want things to taste better. You've ruined my peace."

"Well, you could fix it by taking the food out on time," Mateo said. "Oh, and use clean dishes. No one wants their food cooked in a dirty pan. That's nasty, Vivi. You don't want to be nasty, do you?"

Vivi fixed him with a hard stare.

"Hey, do you think I like this? I have better things to do than sit in here teaching an ancient goblin to make cookies."

Vivi laughed. "You are a fool, Mateo, but you are growing on me."

Mateo smiled. "Let's clean off this pan and try again. All right?"

"Very well."

Tipp ran into the room. "You burned them again, Vivi? Oh, Mateo. You're back. Could you make sure the cookies are better next round? A burned cookie is only slightly better than no cookie." He picked up one of the burned discs and tossed it into his mouth.

"I'm sure Vivi will get it," he said.

Vivi nodded and took the pan to the sink.

Odie poked his head into the kitchen. "Hey, Mateo? Can you come here for a minute?"

Mateo followed him out of the kitchen and down the hallway. "What's up?"

"I think I've figured it out," he said in a low voice.

"The invisibility potion?"

"Yes. Come on."

They hurried to Odie's room, and Odie picked up a vial full of blue foamy liquid. "This is what it looked like when my father gave it to me when I stole the sword."

"So we need to dump it on us or something?"

"No, it has to be ingested."

Mateo wrinkled his nose. "That sounds awful."

"And we don't have a lot of pryka, so we need to save it for the right time. Someone needs to test it first, though. We don't want to discover it doesn't work when we need it."

Mateo looked into the vial. "One of us has to ingest something that almost killed Kaylee?"

"It's been boiled and changed. It should be harmless."

"Who tries?"

"I will. I just wanted you to be here, just in case something weird happens."

"And what do I do if something weird does happen?"

Odie shrugged. "I don't know."

"Couldn't we test it some other way?"

Odie shook his head. "It has to be one of us."

Mateo grinned. "We could try it on Garin."

"Do you really want Garin to be invisible?"

"Good point."

Odie popped open the top of the vial and took a sip. Mateo watched in awe as he slowly faded into nothing.

"Wow," he said. "You did it."

"Yeah, and it wasn't as hard as my father made me think. The only complicated thing was getting the pryka."

"So are we wasting the time you're invisible, or are you going to do something?"

"Blast," Odie said. "I should have thought it through better. Should I go see what Garin is up to?"

"Yes. And I'll go back and make sure Vivi hasn't burned the cookies."

Kaylee sat by a small stream and waited for Willow to stop drinking. The map in her pack had done her no good. She wasn't even sure she had flown in the right direction and it had been a day and a half since she left. If she couldn't find a landmark that was on the map, she wasn't going to find the goblins or her way back to Claret's castle.

Dark clouds circled overhead, and Kaylee feared lightning. Flying through the clouds during a thunderstorm wouldn't be ideal. She hadn't felt any rain, but she was sure it was coming.

Kaylee wished one of her friends were with her. Being lost with friends wasn't as bad as being lost alone. A low growl from behind made Kaylee freeze. Willow looked up from the water and cocked her head to one side. She'd heard it too. Kaylee stood and quietly walked to the alicorn and mounted. As soon as she was seated, Willow leaped into the air.

A roar below caused Kaylee to look down. A vorcraw stared up at her. The monster ran forward and flew in her direction. Kaylee focused her attention forward and rubbed Willow's head. "Go as fast as you can." She didn't know whether alicorns could understand people, but Willow picked up speed.

Touching the Blade of the Phoenix, she frowned. If she tried to pull it out, she wouldn't be able to hold on. She should have dealt with the creature when she was on land. She tried to keep Willow low and out of the clouds. Rain began falling onto her face and she heard the vorcraw shriek. She looked over her shoulder to see it falling. She turned Willow around and watched the vorcraw hit the ground and go up in smoke.

Kaylee wasn't sure why the vorcraw had fallen, and she wasn't going to stay around for any more to find her. Rain pelted her in the face and she flew to the ground. It would be safer down here. She urged Willow on, and they galloped across the countryside. The wet weeds and wildflowers flew by. Without any trees, she felt exposed. With luck, she would run into a village before too long. She needed to find her way, and she needed to do it quickly.

She tried not to think about Dovin. He was probably so angry and worried. It had seemed like a good idea when she left, but she regretted it completely now. Not only because she was lost but also because it had given her too much alone time to think. Mateo kept popping into her head and she didn't want to think about him the way she was beginning to think about him.

Kaylee had slept against a tree last night. It was the driest place she could find. When she was about to fall asleep, she'd had the thought that it would be nice if Mateo were there to put his arms around her and keep her warm. The thought had made her suddenly wide awake as she'd tried to erase it from her head. She blamed it on being a half-asleep dream, but she couldn't stop thinking about it.

If that wasn't bad enough, she'd dreamed about him the rest of the night. With nothing but trees flying by, it was hard not to let her mind wander back to the dreams and she had to concentrate hard to think of anything else. When she did that, she thought about the time she told him there would never be anything between them. For some reason, that memory bothered her almost as much as the rest. She sighed. Trying to control her thoughts was giving her a headache.

CHAPTER 27

The hallways in King Ummi's castle seemed unusually crowded today. Odie took off his boots and placed them against the wall so no one would trip on them. As soon as he let go of his boot, it became visible. He moved away quickly, his stockinged feet almost silent. Now, where to find Garin?

The throne room was as good a place to start as any. King Ummi was probably there, and Garin seemed to follow him. Odie slipped through a crack in the door and entered the room. He frowned when he saw Garin sitting on King Ummi's throne. A woman with long, curly brown hair and a flowing red dress stood before him.

"You want me to believe you accidentally wandered into the goblin castle?" Garin asked the woman.

"It's an honest mistake," she said.

"No. It isn't. Why are you here? Are you a spy?"

The woman crossed her arms. "I wish to speak to the king, not the jester."

Garin's orange eyes flashed, and he leaned forward. "You can speak to me or to no one."

She tilted her head. "Interesting. Who are you?"

"That is the question I should be asking you."

"My name is Isadora."

Odie sucked in a breath. The witch was here? This couldn't be good. Garin's expression didn't change. He didn't know who she was.

"I am Garin. I speak for the goblins."

Odie rolled his eyes. How had his father ever let this man weasel himself into power? They needed to get rid of him before it was too late.

"And what do you say for them?" she asked.

He narrowed his eyes. "Tell me why you are here."

"I believe you have a prisoner in your dungeon."

"Go on."

"A very... important prisoner."

"And what? You've come to free her?"

Isadora laughed. "Free is an interesting word. I wish to take her off your hands and imprison her myself."

Garin's face was blank. "Why?"

"This conversation is tiresome. I can take her or you can release her to me. I will forgive you for not recognizing my name but not for withholding the girl from me."

"Why should I know your name?"

"Because I am the most powerful person Riviand has seen in over a thousand years."

"A witch?"

She smiled. "Yes."

"Why do you want her?"

"She escaped from me a while back and stole something that was mine. I don't forgive easily. Now why do you need her?"

Garin grinned. "It's no secret. To help take over Riviand."

Isadora ran a finger over her lips. "How very interesting. I knew the goblins were stirring, but they're hard to read. And how do you plan on using her?"

"I have my ways."

"Marry her or cause a war?"

"I'm undecided."

She laughed, and Odie frowned. He wished he had the power to take them both down right now.

"Of course you must be manipulating King Ummi. He must think he will rule?"

Garin didn't say anything.

"I assume you will get rid of him and eventually the queen?"

Garin watched her. "There's no reason to get rid of the queen if she obeys me."

"So marriage? That would secure things for you nicely. You aren't from Riviand. You are from above."

"How do you know that?"

"It was only a guess."

Garin frowned. "I think you should leave."

She took a step toward him. "Do you? Because I think we should form an alliance."

"I'm listening."

"Who better to rule than the two most powerful people in Riviand?" Odie ran his hands through his hair. This was getting worse and worse. Odie would never believe Garin was one of the most powerful people in Riviand, but he believed it about Isadora.

"What makes you think I'm so powerful?" Garin asked. "You do not know me."

She smiled. "I can see it. In your eyes. I recognize what others don't."

Garin narrowed his eyes.

"Don't worry. I won't tell your secret," she said.

"And how will an alliance work?"

"You marry the girl and let her lead. Once the people trust you, we get rid of her and you marry me."

Odie shook his head. If Garin agreed, he was stupider than Odie would have thought. What was to stop Isadora from getting rid of him as soon as she got what she wanted?

"I have to think on it," Garin said. "It is more complicated than that. The king wants his son to marry the queen."

"That won't be a problem once we get rid of the king."

Garin smiled. "I like the way you think."

Isadora walked up the obsidian steps to the throne. "I'll be back in two weeks. I have some loose ends to deal with. When I get back, you can give me your answer." She leaned over and kissed Garin on the mouth.

Odie wrinkled his nose. They had known each other for what? Five minutes? He stepped quietly out of the room and made his way back to his bedroom. He paced back and forth across the room until there was a knock at the door.

"Odie? It's Mateo. Are you in there?"

Odie unlocked the door and Mateo slipped in.

"So I'm guessing you're still invisible," he said.

"Yeah. It takes a while to wear off."

"Did you find Garin?"

"Yes, and things are worse than I could have imagined."

"How so?"

"He was talking to the witch Isadora. They were forming an alliance."

"Man, that's not good."

"Not for Claret. Whatever they decide is going to leave her dead or married to Garin," Odie said.

"Are you sure they're working together?"

"No. Garin said he wanted time to think about it. I'm sure he'll join her, though. She's... not unattractive, and she kissed him."

Mateo frowned. "I wonder how long they've known each other."

"They just met."

"Gross. What do we do?"

Odie shook his head. "I'm not sure. We need to get Claret out of here, and I might have to marry her."

Mateo snorted. "Marry her?"

"Garin is going to try to get her to marry him. If she marries me, she can't marry him. It's more complicated now that she might hate me."

"Why would she hate you?"

"I haven't been able to talk to her since they locked her up. She might think I tricked her and brought her here on purpose."

"Hmm. We should have acted faster and taken out Garin. If he makes powerful allies, we could have a problem."

"I wonder if we could get Vivi to let you take Claret her dinner. If she sees you, she'll know she isn't abandoned. My father won't let me go down since I helped her escape last time."

"It's worth a shot. I think Vivi likes me."

"Vivi doesn't like anyone."

Mateo grinned. "I grow on people."

Odie wouldn't bet on it. He'd known Vivi his entire life, and she wasn't the type to be swayed by the likes of Mateo.

"Of course I'll let you go down to see the queen," Vivi told Mateo. "The king only lets me down there, but the guards won't question me if you carry something."

"Thanks, Vivi," Mateo said. "You're the best. I've always wanted to see a queen."

"She's a pretty one, too. At least for a human. Polite as well."

Vivi loaded a plate of food onto a platter and motioned for Mateo to take it. He lifted it and followed her from the kitchen down the hallway. When they got to the dungeon door, the guards opened it and Mateo followed Vivi through. He walked carefully, making sure he didn't spill as they walked down the endless stairs. When they got to the bottom, there was a long stone hallway. On each side of the hall, there were cells.

"They put her at the end," Vivi said. "I guess the king wants me to get my exercise, making me walk all the way five times a day."

"Five? There are only three meals a day."

Vivi stopped and glared at him. "Two snacks."

Mateo grinned. He couldn't believe the goblins who wanted to take over the world gave their prisoners snacks.

When they got to the end, it was to see Claret, sitting on a large bed behind the bars. She held a book on her lap. Her eyes widened when she saw Mateo. She looked at Vivi and didn't say anything.

"This is Mateo," Vivi told Claret. "He wanted to see you. He's never seen a queen before."

Vivi unlocked the cell, and Mateo went in and placed the tray on a small table by the bed.

"Thank you," Claret said.

Mateo winked at her, and she gave him a half smile. "You're welcome."

"Now come out," Vivi said. "Queen Claret, this boy can make a thing called a cookie that I can't even describe. I'll have him make you some and bring them down later."

"Thank you. I'm sure I'll be here."

Vivi locked the cell, and they went back down the long hall. Mateo was glad to see Claret was at least comfortable.

"So how long have you known her?" Vivi asked.

Mateo looked down. "What are you talking about?"

"I saw the looks. She knows you. I saw hope in her eyes."

"You're crazy, Vivi."

She barked out a laugh. "No one doubts that. Is she your sweetheart?"

"No."

"Pity. I hear they are going to have her marry Odie. Odie is a good boy. I've always been tough on him, but I like him more than I like any goblin I know. Most of the goblins don't tolerate his presence, but I always found him interesting."

"He thinks you don't like him."

She laughed again. "That's the way I like it. I always thought he might need help someday, and if I helped him, no one would suspect." They walked up the long hallway. "You are a friend of Odie. I suppose the two of you are going to save her?"

Mateo didn't say anything.

"If you need my help, I'm here. Don't worry, I won't tell anyone."

Vivi tapped on the door, and the guards pulled it open. He wondered what she wouldn't tell, since he hadn't said anything.

They walked in silence to the kitchen. When they went inside, Vivi began putting things away.

"You better make the queen some cookies," Vivi said. "We did promise, after all."

Mateo laughed. "Did we?"

"I'm pretty sure. No one wants to eat my cookies when they can eat yours."

Mateo began gathering ingredients. He was more sure than ever that the goblins weren't as bad as they might want to appear. If it wasn't for Garin, they probably wouldn't be a threat at all.

28

— · —

Chapter 28

Claret bit into Mateo's creation. It was good. Of course it would be better if she were enjoying it at home and not in the smelly dungeon. She was feeling renewed hope since Mateo had come down. Now she knew she wasn't alone, and she felt more sure Odie hadn't betrayed her.

Every time she asked, Vivi would bring her a new book with her meals. They were strange books and not anything that interested her, but they were better than sitting in here staring at the wall. Time had no meaning down here. She couldn't tell if it was day or night, except when meals came.

She couldn't help wonder why it was taking Odie and Mateo so long to get her out. She shivered when the thoughts entered her head about Odie's loyalties. What if he was tricking Mateo? That could be the reason she was still here. She wondered what the king would say if he knew Garin had offered to marry her. It didn't seem like the king and his advisor were on the same page.

Claret paced across her cell until her legs were tired. She tried to come up with a way to escape, but she couldn't find one. The cell was secure and there were no windows. If only she could talk to Odie. Odie, who was one hundred percent going to get her out of here.

She sighed and sat back on her bed. What if she was wrong? What if Odie had been planning this all along? He had helped her escape last time, but maybe that was to get her to trust him. If so, it had worked.

It couldn't be. She had watched Odie battle his emotions the last time she'd been down here. He was conflicted by his loyalty to his family and his conscience. His conscience had won, and he had saved her. It couldn't have been an act. She bit her lip. It would all work out. It had to.

Kaylee was hopelessly lost and hungry. Her bread and cheese had run out yesterday and her stomach rumbled. Willow was feasting on grass and didn't seem to have a care in the world. Finding food in Riviand wasn't too hard, but she was feeling sick from too many berries and nothing else.

"Is that smoke?" she asked, peering into a grove of trees. "What do you think, Willow? Should we go see if someone is in there?"

Willow ignored her and went on eating.

"Come on, girl." Kaylee walked toward the trees, and Willow came slowly behind. Anyone or anything could be over there. It could even be Isadora. She made her way quietly into the trees and followed the smell of something cooking. When she came around a tree, she could see the back of a troll. She recognized him as a troll because of his long quill hair. He sat at a fire, tending to a large pot.

"Hello?" Kaylee said,

Zute turned and smiled at her. "I wondered if I could draw you over."

"How did you know I was here?"

"I was looking for you. I wanted to thank you and the queen for saving me from the witch."

"Riviand is huge. How did you find me? I don't even know where I am."

"Trolls can sense people and where they are. Humans leave a bit of a trail that is easy for us to pick up. I've made you some stew. Sit."

Kaylee sat down. Willow was already eating more weeds.

"What are you doing out here?" Zute asked. "A person shouldn't travel alone. Especially one so young."

"I'm trying to find my friends. They're at the goblin mountain."

"You are nowhere near the goblin mountain."

Her shoulders slumped. "I'm not?"

"No."

"I have a map, but it confuses me. I've never had to follow a paper map before." Kaylee thought of how convenient it would be to have her phone and to be able to use the GPS.

Zute handed her a bowl of stew. She tried to eat slowly and not devour it.

"Thank you. It's good."

"I cannot take you to the goblin mountain, but I can point you to the correct path and give you this." He handed her something round and metal.

"Is it a compass?"

"Yes."

She moved it around and watched a small needle change direction. "It points north?"

"No. You see these markings?" He pointed at some strange symbols.

"Yes."

"Each symbol represents a different place. They represent the troll village, the goblin mountain, Tyran, and one that we don't understand. If you turn the arrow to the one you want, the spindle will take you to them."

"Have you tried to get to the one you don't understand?"

"Yes. All that is there is a hill. Nothing extraordinary."

Zute took the compass with his thick hands and held it up. "If you point it at this dark symbol, you will find the goblin mountains."

"Thanks."

"You are a mystery to me," Zute said, taking a bite of his stew. "You and your friends seem to look for trouble."

"I'm sure it looks that way."

"The goblins cannot be trusted. Be careful. I wish I could help you more than I have."

"You've helped a lot. Now I know where to go, and the stew has made me feel a lot better. I didn't prepare as well as I should have."

He handed her a bag. "This food should last you until you reach your destination."

Kaylee swallowed hard. "You didn't have to do this."

"I know, but now we are even. I don't like to feel indebted to others. Are you aware of the monsters that follow you?"

"The vorcraws? Are there more of them?"

"Yes."

"Do you know where they are?"

"They come from many directions. I cannot see them, but I feel them. None are too close at the moment."

"Do you know anything about them? Their weaknesses?"

Zute scratched his head. "They can be killed with water. They are slow and clumsy. That is a good thing as you have been moving quite fast."

"Killed with water? How are they still following me? It's rained a few times since I left."

"They can go underground."

Kaylee thought of the monster that had fallen from the sky. "How much water kills them?"

"Any amount, I believe."

"How many vorcraws exist?"

"There is not a certain amount. They can be summoned forever and they will keep coming."

Kaylee sighed. "That's not very assuring."

"Who would send them after you? It must be a very powerful person."

"It was Isadora. She isn't happy that we freed everyone."

"Ah, I see. Then my debt to you isn't paid until there are no longer any vorcraws following you. It could take time."

Kaylee shook her head. "You don't owe me. Isadora trapped you because you helped me. It was all my fault."

"Not your fault. Her fault. You did not make her choices."

"Do trolls have magic?"

"In a sense, but not the way humans do. We can read things in the sky, and as I said, sense where people are. We can do several things like that."

"What can you see from the sky?"

Zute looked up. "It's going to rain."

Kaylee laughed. "I think you're right." It didn't take a troll to see that. "I was upset about the rain, but I guess it's a good thing if it keeps the vorcraws away."

"It is a blessing indeed."

"How is the sleeping draught coming?" Garin asked Odie. Odie mixed some hods bark into his gooey green mixture. He didn't want Garin in his room, but he didn't know a polite way to tell him to get out.

"I'm sure it will be ready in a week or two."

Garin crossed his arms. "A week or two? If you've made this before, it should be easy."

"It's a complicated thing, and I didn't write it down. My father wasn't happy with it, so there wasn't really a good reason to keep making it."

"I hope you'll put your focus on it."

"Sure."

Garin turned to leave.

"Hey, Garin?" Odie said.

He turned his head. "Yes?"

"Do you know a lot about dragons?" Ever since the dragon had brought them to the goblin mountain, Odie had wondered if Garin was behind it. Odie found it hard to believe the dragon just happened to bring them here. The chances of that were one in thousands. Garin was from up above where people rode dragons. If Odie had to guess, he would say Garin was responsible.

Garin raised his brow. "I know a fair amount."

"Is it possible to control a dragon?"

He rubbed a hand over the stubble on his chin. "I suppose, to a certain extent. Dragons can be trained the same as an alicorn or unicorn."

"People here fear dragons. I'm starting to wonder if it's an irrational fear. People are scared of them because they don't understand them."

Garin smiled. "Dragons are like any other creature. Some can be trusted and some cannot. You don't want to run into the ones that can't be tamed."

"They're vicious?"

"They can be. The worst thing about them is they are highly intelligent. They can plot." He smiled and his eyes flashed with something Odie couldn't read. "You don't want to get in the way of a dragon with a plan."

Odie blinked. Even when people talked about dragons, no one ever acted like they were conniving. Dangerous, yes, but not that they planned ahead.

Odie watched Garin leave and then went back to his mixture. He could make his sleeping draught with his eyes closed, but he wasn't going to let it fall into Garin's hands. Nothing he made could go to that man.

They needed to act soon. If they didn't, Dovin was sure to send someone after them or come himself. That could cause problems they didn't need. Odie liked to believe that Dovin could defeat anyone, but Garin was powerful. Garin needed to be taken care of before anyone got hurt and before any more goblins started following him. If he teamed up with Isadora, he shuddered to think of what might happen.

Claret slammed her book shut. She was going crazy down here. If Odie and Mateo didn't get her out soon, she was going to have to try to get herself out, and she didn't see that going well. Even if she escaped the cell, she would have a hard time getting past the guards up above.

"It's not bad," a woman's voice said, startling her from her thoughts. She looked up to see Isadora. "It would be nice if they did something about the smell."

Claret sighed. She must have dozed off while she was reading. "Get out of my head," she demanded.

Isadora smiled. "I'm not in your head this time."

Claret frowned. "Then how did you get down here?"

"I can go anywhere I want. I'm not bound by any rules."

"Do the goblins know you're here?"

"No, and I think we should keep it that way, don't you agree?"

Claret was tired and not in the mood for Isadora's games. "What do you want?"

"I just thought you might need a visit. It can't be much fun down here. Are they treating you well? The cell looks nice. Not as nice as what I was planning to give you, but at least the bed looks cozy."

"Just leave. Please."

She smiled and took hold of the bars. "You know this wouldn't have happened if you had stayed with me."

Claret narrowed her eyes. "What makes you think I would be happier locked up in your dungeon?"

"At least you would have had company. Would you like to make a deal? I can help you."

"I doubt it."

She leaned into the bars. "Would you like to hear it at least?"

"I suppose." Claret didn't trust anything Isadora said, but she might as well know what the woman was trying to get her to do.

"I've met Garin. Delightful man."

Claret wrinkled her nose. "Even if I didn't know you, I would have lost all respect for you after that sentence."

"Garin has a plan, as I am sure you know. It involves you."

Claret shrugged. "I'm not surprised."

"It doesn't have to be that way. I know you are part of his plan for taking over Riviand, but the more I think about it, the more it all seems too complicated, with too many steps. We could eliminate most of the plan if you chose to step down as queen."

Claret laughed. "Why would I do that?"

"Because if you don't, you may very well end up dead. Step down and appoint Garin king."

"Never."

"He will get there, eventually. Why put yourself through all of that? You can run off and hide with all your little friends and make a new life for yourselves."

"Do you really expect me to agree to this? What would you gain by it?"

She smiled. "I would be queen, of course. Just imagine the things I would have access to."

"You want to marry Garin?"

"I think I do. He's attractive and ambitious. You have to agree to that."

Claret tilted her head and thought of Garin. She supposed some would call him handsome. It was hard to get past his personality to see it, though. That and his eyes...

"I will never give Riviand to the two of you. It deserves a leader who puts Riviand's needs ahead of their own. You and Garin want power, and I won't see my land corrupted by you or anyone else."

"That's quite the statement coming from someone down here. We will take Riviand. I was only trying to make it easier on you."

Claret's eyes opened, and she was lying on her bed, her book on her lap. It had been a dream. Isadora had lied. She needed to talk to someone. If she could tell King Ummi what Garin and Isadora were planning, he would have to take her side.

29

—·—

CHAPTER 29

Mateo sat on Odie's bed, eating a roll. "We need to do something. How long are we going to leave Claret down there?"

"I don't know," Odie admitted. "Garin is getting impatient about the sleeping draught. I just don't know what to do."

"We hit Garin with the sleeping draught and lock him in the dungeon." It didn't seem like it would be that difficult.

"My father fears him. It makes me wonder if he is immune to magic or something. Why doesn't my father do something? He has magic. He can do all sorts of things, but he doesn't."

"We could slip something into his food."

"I'm not sure capturing Garin will fix things. My father was stealing from Riviand long before Garin came, and I don't see that stopping. When he had me steal the Blade of the Phoenix, Garin wasn't around, at least as far as I know. The problem is bigger than Garin."

"But Garin is a big part of the problem."

"Yes."

"So if we got rid of him, we would only be dealing with the goblins."

Odie shook his head. "And the witch."

"I forgot about her. I feel like we need to do something, though. Claret is probably stressed out down there and we aren't doing much of anything."

"I know. I worry any day Captain Nerman is going to come marching over with an army."

"And he should. They have the queen. The entire continent should be coming. Where are they?" Mateo was ready to be done with this place. It had been interesting at first, but now he was stuck making cookies all the time. He couldn't believe how demanding goblins were when it came to cookies.

"I just worry about moving too fast."

"We know Garin's plan. If we stop him, that should stop the witch, right?"

"Stop that plan, but she could make another."

Mateo frowned. "What are you afraid of?"

Odie threw his arms into the air. "I don't know! I worry about making the wrong choice. What if Claret gets hurt?"

"She's more likely to get hurt here."

"Let's give it a few more days," Odie said. "Then we can go invisible and go get Claret."

"Then what? We have to stop Garin."

"We can use the sleeping potion on him and hand him over to my father."

Mateo cocked his head. "That sounds like a bad idea. What if he decided to let him free? No offense, but your father isn't exactly ethical. And don't you think the longer you leave Claret down there, the more time she's going to have to wonder about you? She's going to think you are working with the goblins. That you tricked her."

"But I can tell her the truth once we get her out."

"Yes, but if she's already turned you into a villain, it will be hard to change her mind."

"She already changed her mind about me once."

Mateo arched an eyebrow. "But will she do it again?"

"I don't know."

"The queen is pretty," Vivi said as Mateo carried a breakfast tray down the dungeon stairs. "I guess it doesn't hurt to let you see her again, although I still think you know her."

He laughed. "Why would someone like me know a queen?" If he had to make Vivi think he had a thing for Claret, then he would do it. Their steps echoed across the dungeon floor. When they got to Claret's cell, it was to find her pacing. Her sunburn looked a little better, and her nose was peeling. Her eyes lit up when she saw Mateo.

"Good morning," Vivi said as she unlocked the cell. "How did you sleep?"

Claret looked at Mateo and then at Vivi. "I had a bad dream last night," she said. "It felt so real. There was a witch, and she was going to team up with a man to take over Riviand and use the goblins in the process."

Mateo placed the tray on her table.

"Dreams are funny things," Vivi said. "I'm just going to check the other cells and make sure they don't need to be cleaned." She walked out of sight.

Mateo raised his brows. The castle had maids, but he wouldn't call any of it overly clean, and the dungeon wasn't anywhere near clean. She was giving him time. But for what? He wasn't going to waste time wondering. He hurried to Claret's side.

"The dream was real," she whispered. "We need to get out of here. Garin is using the goblins."

Mateo nodded. "I agree. Odie is dragging his feet for some reason. He thinks we need to wait and be careful. We already know Garin is teaming up with the witch. The faster we do something, the better."

"Is Kaylee here?"

"No, she stayed at your castle."

"What does Odie hope to accomplish?" she asked.

"I don't know. I think he might be conflicted. He still cares about his goblin family, and he knows Garin is using them. He's worried about leaving them to him."

"I understand that, but the longer we stay, and the more alliances Garin makes, the harder it will be to escape."

"I agree. I'll talk to him again. How are you holding up?"

Her lip trembled, but she smiled. "I'm fine."

He gave her a side hug. "Don't worry. We won't take more than another day or two."

"Well, it looks good down here," Vivi said. "Let's get back up there."

Mateo gave her another squeeze and left the cell. Vivi locked it, and he followed her up the stairs.

"It looks like the queen likes you."

He didn't respond. Let her think whatever she wanted.

Odie grabbed one of Vivi's mixing bowls and began tossing things in it. Vivi could be back at any moment, and she hated when he used her things. He'd had a slight explosion in his room and he needed to wait for the smoke to clear. If he could make a quick batch of sleeping draught, he would feel almost ready to save Claret.

Odie grabbed a vial from his bag and dumped it in the bowl. He mixed quickly and hoped going fast wouldn't ruin it. He liked to take his time, but he wasn't in the mood to deal with Vivi. Vivi had taken to Mateo, which was weird. It must be the cookies.

The door opened, and Vivi entered, carrying an empty tray. When she saw him, her brows furrowed. "What are you doing here?"

Odie flashed her a smile. "My room is a little... smokey."

She grumbled. "I'm sure it is."

"It will only take a minute."

She put her hands on her hips. "You are using my good mixing bowl."

"I'll clean it."

She snorted. "I suppose there is a first time for everything."

Odie mixed faster.

"I hope you don't allow your friend to do anything foolish," she said as she watched him.

"Foolish?"

"He seems to be quite taken with the queen. I hope he doesn't try to save her or anything that might get him sent to the dungeon himself. He's grown on me."

"I'm sure there's nothing to worry about," he said, grabbing another vial from his bag.

"I've seen humans do strange things in the name of love."

Odie chuckled. "Mateo isn't in love with the queen."

"I don't know. They seemed a little cozy when we took her breakfast just now."

Odie looked up. "Cozy?"

She grinned with her pointed teeth. "Very."

Odie bit the inside of his cheek and kept stirring. Mateo entered a moment later, whistling a tune Odie wasn't familiar with. He glared at his friend.

"What is it?" Mateo asked.

Odie glanced at Vivi, then back at the bowl. "Nothing."

"Why are you doing this in here? Vivi hates it when you do."

Vivi nodded. "That's true."

"I blew something up in my room."

"And I missed it?" Mateo asked with a grin. Odie just shook his head. "We can use my room."

Odie dumped the mixture into a clean container and sealed it. "No need. I'm finished."

"Can I expect you at lunch?" Vivi asked Mateo. "Do you want to take the queen her meal?"

"I don't think I'll be around at lunch," he said.

"Got enough cuddling in for the day?"

Odie clenched his fist, then released it and put his things back in his bag.

Mateo laughed. "I can't get anything past you, Vivi."

Odie's eyes narrowed. If he were Mateo, he would have punched someone right about now.

Vivi laughed. "I'm as sharp as they come. Nothing gets past me."

Odie stormed out of the kitchen and into his bedroom. He almost slammed the door, but Mateo slipped in. Most of the smoke had cleared out, so he shut the window. It looked like it was going to rain.

"Thanks for not punching me in the face," Mateo said, grinning. "I don't know how much more of that our friendship can take."

Odie slammed his bag onto his table. "I'm still thinking about it."

Mateo laughed. "Claret needs to get out of there. She's scared, I can tell. I gave her a hug, that's all."

Odie took a deep breath. He could believe that. "Fine. Now what?"

"I'm not sure. She had a dream. She said it was real. The witch was in her head. She's afraid and with reason. We need to break her out. Tomorrow."

Odie nodded. "All right."

"Then we need to leave this place and never come back. You know that, right?"

"I do. I mean, I might come back to spy, but I'll make sure I'm invisible."

"How do we get out?" Mateo asked.

Odie scratched his head. "You need to get Vivi to take you down to Claret again. I'll follow, but I'll be invisible. My father has made it clear to everyone that I am not to go down there. Once the cell is open, I hand Claret a vial and get her to drink it. Then we run before Vivi knows what happens. No one will expect it, so we should be able to get past the guards with no problem."

"And I take some potion too, right?"

Odie shrugged. "I guess."

Mateo rolled his eyes. "It was a friendly hug, Odie. Get over it."

"I'm over it."

"If we are going to be invisible, do we need the sleeping potion?"

"I want to be prepared. Once we're all invisible, we need to grab hands and then, when we are out of the dungeon, we need to teleport."

"Okay. We need to run as soon as we get out."

Odie frowned. "How will Claret know what to do?"

"If we grab hold of her hands, I'm sure she'll follow us. It will be a breeze."

30

CHAPTER 30

Kaylee sighed. Coming up the back side of the goblin mountain had been a stupid idea. She should have flown Willow right up to the castle, but she didn't want anyone to see her. She'd told Willow to fly back to Tyran, which she hoped she did. Tethering her to a tree could be dangerous, and she wasn't willing to risk the alicorn getting hurt.

Kaylee had only been on this mountain once, and she was completely lost. She didn't know where the castle was, so coming up from the back hadn't been a smart idea. Her legs ached from walking up and she was scraped up from falling a couple of times. She must have chosen the steepest place to climb.

"Do you give up?" Isadora asked.

Kaylee's head shot to the side. Isadora stood in front of her in a spotless blue dress. Her eyes danced as she watched Kaylee brush the dirt from her knees.

"This is an interesting way to approach the castle. I assume that is where you are headed." Isadora took a step toward her, and Kaylee stepped back.

"Leave me alone."

Isadora smiled. "I just finished sealing an alliance with Garin. I told him the only thing missing was you. Of course we will have to lock up your other friends as well. Starting a war is tiresome."

"How did you find me?"

Her smile widened. "Once I find someone's dreams, it isn't hard to track them if they don't move around by magic. Let's not waste time." She rushed at Kaylee and the next thing she knew, they were standing in a black room.

Kaylee put a hand to her heart. Had they teleported? She looked around the room. Everything in it was black. A throne sat on a platform, with five steps leading up to it. On top of it sat a goblin. He wore a dark blue robe and a tall crown. He had on so much jewelry, Kaylee wondered how he could move comfortably.

Standing to the side of the throne was a man in black. He had blond hair and the strangest eyes Kaylee had ever seen. He must be Garin. Next to him was another goblin, wearing armor and holding a small shield.

"This is Queen Claret's friend," Isadora said. "She was snooping around the mountain."

"Very good," the king said. "When Garin told me you would be a great ally, I had my doubts."

Isadora smiled. "I can be useful. You won't regret having my help."

The king looked at the other goblin. "Tipp, go find Odie."

The goblin nodded and left.

Kaylee relaxed slightly. If she could figure out what was happening from Odie, she would know what steps to take next."

"Trying to free your friend?" the king asked her.

Kaylee folded her arms and refused to look intimidated. "My business isn't yours."

Garin's eyes narrowed. "You are not from Riviand or Basura."

"Oh? And where do you suppose I'm from?"

Garin smiled, his eyes flashing unnaturally. "I don't know, but I am eager to find out."

"We haven't time for this, Garin," the king said. "She isn't enough of a threat to take up our time."

The door opened, and Odie and Tipp entered. Odie's face fell when he saw Kaylee.

"You needed me, Father?" he asked.

"This girl. She is a friend of the queen?"

Odie glanced at Kaylee, then back at the king. "I believe so."

The king tossed a key to Odie. "Go with Garin and take her to the dungeon. If she wishes to see the queen, we will allow them to share a cell."

Kaylee frowned. She wasn't going to get anywhere if she was locked up.

"Very well," Odie said, his expression going blank.

"I can't stay," she said. "But thanks for the offer."

Isadora and Garin laughed. The king only frowned.

Odie grabbed Kaylee's wrist. "You seem to think my father was giving you a choice. Come on, Garin."

Garin nodded. "I'll follow behind. We can't have her trying anything."

Kaylee tried to yank her arm from Odie, but he had a good grip. He pulled her toward the door and she gave up resisting. She wasn't going to escape with Garin and Isadora there. She wondered what Odie's game was.

They walked down a black hallway to a large door that two goblins guarded. They opened the door when they saw them approach. Odie pulled her through the door and onto a dim staircase.

"Why is everything black?" Kaylee asked as they descended.

"Most everything in the castle is made of obsidian," Odie said.

"It's a bit gloomy."

Garin laughed. "The color of the castle should be the least of your worries." They walked in silence the rest of the way. Kaylee's boots seemed overly loud when they reached a long pathway lined with cells. It was set up just like Isadora's cages, except it was dirty and dark and there was no one in these.

"Where are all the prisoners?" she asked.

"We only use these for people we are keeping an extra eye on," Odie said. "There's another prison, but it isn't in the castle."

At the end of the hallway, there was a bunch of stuff that had been pushed against the walls, next to a fireplace. There was even a bed.

Claret was in the last cell. Her face appeared sunburned, just like Odie's. She stood and frowned when she saw Kaylee. Odie released her arm and unlocked the cell. She thought about running, but Garin was watching her closely.

Odie pulled open the door and motioned with his head for Kaylee to enter.

"We shouldn't put them in the same cell," Garin said. Kaylee rushed inside, hoping they wouldn't separate them.

Odie shut the door and locked it. "My father said they could share. It's fine. What are they going to do?"

Garin looked like he wanted to argue but changed his mind. He turned and walked away, his footsteps echoing.

"Don't try to escape," Odie told them. "If you do, things will only go poorly." He followed Garin.

Kaylee turned to Claret. The queen was watching Odie with a small frown. Kaylee gave her a quick hug. "Don't worry. I'm sure Odie is only pretending." She rubbed her wrist. "Still. He could have been a little more gentle."

"I keep telling myself he's only doing this until he frees me, but I admit, I'm having my doubts."

"About Odie?"

Claret nodded. "I teleported us to a desert. We ended up at Dragon's Cove. I've never heard of anyone actually going there. There was a dragon. We rode it and it brought us here. Why would it do that? Odie says he's never flown a dragon, but what if he lied?"

"I don't think he would."

"But why would the dragon bring us here? No one knew where we were."

"You teleported the two of you to the desert, right?"

Claret nodded.

"Odie had nothing to do with that. He had no way of knowing you would end up with a dragon. How could he have planned it?" They should be figuring a way out of here, but Kaylee could see Claret needed some reassurance.

Claret's frown softened. "That's true. He couldn't have. Mateo has come down a few times with the cook. I feel like he is trying to reassure me without giving himself away."

"Right, and we know Mateo isn't loyal to the goblins. So what do we do? Try to escape or wait for the boys?"

"I don't know. I'm worried Garin is going to pair up with Isadora."

Kaylee nodded. "She has. She was the one who caught me. I didn't even try to fight. I was so surprised."

Claret rubbed her temples. "That's not good."

Kaylee walked around the cell, inspecting the walls. She ran her hands across the walls and looked up at the ceiling.

"The only way out is the door," Claret said. "Vivi is the cook. She comes down with whoever brings the food. It's been Mateo a couple of times. No one can use magic down here, and I'm unsure how strong goblins are. We could grab her and throw her in here and escape the cell, but we would still have to get past the guards. Vivi is nice, so I would feel bad about that."

"I wonder if Dovin will come. He's going to be mad when he realizes I left."

"Dovin got us out last time. Dovin and Odie."

Kaylee couldn't see a way out. "I think we should wait. If we make a plan and the boys make a plan, we could mess each other up."

"That's true," Claret said. "So we wait?"

"I think so."

—⬧✦⬥—

"You put Kaylee in the dungeon?" Mateo exclaimed. "What were you thinking?"

Odie sat on a chair at his table. "What do you think I should have done?"

Mateo threw his hands in the air. "I don't know, but something!"

Odie didn't know how to deal with Mateo when he got angry. He was doing the best he could when things he didn't expect happened. "If I tried to disobey, the only thing that would have changed is that I would be down there as well. I was in a room full of powerful magic and I don't know if you've forgotten, but I can't do magic."

Mateo paced back and forth next to Odie's bed. "I know, I know. Sorry. This is just getting too complicated. Why did she come here? Maybe she knows something and came to tell us."

"I don't think we can figure that out right now. Perhaps you can go down with Vivi today and ask?"

Mateo frowned. "What are the chances she's going to give me time to talk like she did last time? I think she only did last time because she thinks I have something for Claret, and Vivi likes me."

Odie rubbed a hand over his eyes. He had an idea, but he didn't like it. "Ask Vivi beforehand if she'll let you have a few minutes with Claret. She might let you. Just don't hug her or anything."

"If Vivi thinks I like Claret, she's going to expect me to hug her. Especially since I did last time."

Odie's mouth turned down. "Fine, but don't linger."

Mateo laughed. "Maybe you should ask Vivi if you can come with us."

"No. Everything we do is suspicious enough."

"Probably."

Mateo held a large tray with two plates and waited for Vivi to open the cell door. Mateo had asked Vivi if he could talk to Claret for a minute, and the cook had not agreed like he thought she would. She said he could talk to her, but she would watch so that the king wouldn't think she was being neglectful in her duties.

Mateo entered the cell, and Vivi jumped up on the table that was just outside. She sat cross-legged and watched. Claret and Kaylee were both sitting on chairs that were next to the small table. Someone must have brought in an extra chair. There was also another bed, making the cell crowded. He was still shocked the goblins gave their prisoners nice beds.

Dirt smeared Kaylee's cheek, and her clothing looked like she'd slid down the mountain wearing it. Claret and Kaylee both watched him. He placed the tray on the table, then dropped to his knees.

Mateo felt ridiculous, but he took Claret's hand in his, looked into her eyes, and spoke softly. "Vivi thinks I'm infatuated with you. Play along, Claret. Why are you here, Kaylee?”

He couldn’t look away from Claret to see Kaylee’s expression.

“She came to warn us about Isadora,” Claret whispered.

“Don’t try anything,” he said. “You won’t be able to get out. Odie and I have it under control. Odie made an invisibility serum. Next time I come in, we’ll pass two vials to you. Drink them and grab hands. I’ll drink it too. With luck, we will be able to run upstairs with Odie, who will already be invisible. I’ll grab him and teleport us out.”

“We’ll be ready,” Claret said.

Vivi hopped off the table and turned to face them. “Time is up. Give her a quick kiss if you want and let’s be on our way.”

Mateo grinned at the horrified expression on Claret’s face. It was hard not to look at Kaylee to see what she was thinking. “Not this time, Vivi. Not with you spying on me.”

Vivi laughed as Mateo left the cell. “I would have turned away for a minute.”

He winked at her. “Next time.” He followed her back to the kitchen.

“I’m not sure the queen feels the same way you do,” Vivi said. “That doesn’t mean it can’t happen, but I think you should prepare yourself for disappointment. She looked a bit disgusted.”

Mateo chuckled. “I’ll be fine.”

“I can tell the friend doesn’t approve of you.”

Mateo lifted his eyebrow. “Oh? What was she doing?”

"She was glaring at you like you were a piece of mud on her boot."

Mateo leaned against the wall and folded his arms. "Hmm. Was it a disgusted glare or a jealous glare?"

Vivi laughed. "You better be careful about that big head of yours. Isn't having the queen's attention enough? She didn't actually seem terribly happy with whatever you were saying, either."

"It's hard to be happy when you're locked up, I'm sure."

"I suppose."

"I need to go find Odie. I'll come check on your cookies later."

She tilted her head. "My cookies are going to be as good as yours soon."

Mateo grinned. "I'm sure they will."

He rushed to Odie's room and rapped on the door.

"Come in," Odie said.

Mateo opened the door and locked it behind him. "I talked to them. Sort of. I told them to be ready tomorrow."

Odie was sitting at the table, mixing something. Mixing weird things and getting his brother Tipp to come in and test them seemed to be what Odie lived for. He'd turned his brother's fingers yellow yesterday. He was surprised Tipp let Odie experiment on him.

Odie was wearing one of his feathered capes, and he was placing something inside the pockets.

"Good. I'm ready. Now that Garin and Isadora are both here, it makes me nervous, and I bet Gregor misses me. Did you hug her?"

"Kaylee?" Mateo teased.

He rolled his eyes. "Claret."

"No."

"Good."

Mateo grinned. "Vivi promised to look away next time, in case I want to kiss her."

Odie glared at him. "There won't be a next time."

31

CHAPTER 31

C laret rolled over on her bed and yawned.

"Is it morning?" Kaylee asked from her own bed. "I never know, but I can't sleep anymore."

"Do you think Mateo's plan will work?"

Claret sat up and rubbed her eyes. "I hope so. I'm nervous."

"I can't believe that goblin was buying whatever Mateo was trying to do yesterday. Mateo looked like a dork, and you looked like you wanted to run away."

Claret giggled. "I did. It felt ridiculous sitting there while he held my hand like that. I can't believe the goblins are allowing him to come down since they want me to marry Odie."

Kaylee rolled out of bed. "They do?"

"Yes."

"I guess that's one way to take over."

"Garin's plan is worse. He told me one version of it, but I can see through him. He wants me to marry him. I'm sure he would kill me soon after and marry Isadora. I'm not as daft as he thinks."

"Do all these things have to end in you marrying someone?" Kaylee asked.

"I'm not planning on marrying anyone, so this plan of Mateo's better work."

"I wonder when they'll come. I would get dressed and get ready, but I don't have anything to change into. My hair must be a mess." Kaylee ran her hand over her black curls and pulled them back into a ponytail with a band she had around her wrist.

Claret ran a hand through her own hair. Her fingers got stuck almost as soon as she tried. She sighed. She hadn't brushed her hair in days, and the tangles fell down to her waist. With no bath down here, she must smell horrid. She jumped when she heard the door to the dungeon slam.

"Do you think this is it?" Kaylee asked.

"Perhaps. Be ready, just in case."

The two of them stood, watching the hallway. Vivi appeared, and beside her was Mateo. He carried a large tray in his hands. Claret hoped Odie was somewhere behind them.

Vivi stuck the keys into the cell door and pulled it open. "Can the two of you step out for a moment?" she asked.

Claret and Kaylee gave each other puzzled glances, but they stepped out of the cell. Mateo placed the tray on the table and joined them in the hallway. Claret startled when a hand took hers. It must be Odie's. She gave it a slight squeeze.

Vivi stepped into the cell and closed the door. "Lock it," she commanded Mateo.

Mateo ran a hand through his hair. "Excuse me?"

Vivi smiled. "I'm not an idiot, boy. I'd rather you lock me up than try to knock me out or something. If you lock me up, the king won't have any reason to be angry with me."

Mateo turned the key in the lock and then threw it down the hallway.

"Good luck," Vivi said. "You too, Odie. I know you're here somewhere. You might want to work on breathing quieter."

"Thanks, Vivi," Odie's voice said next to Claret. She jumped slightly.

Mateo handed Kaylee and Claret vials. "Drink it."

Mateo drank his own, and Claret watched him disappear.

Claret did the same. It tasted horrid. She couldn't think of a time she'd put something so foul in her mouth. She watched as her hand disappeared.

Kaylee made a gagging sound. "That was gross, Odie."

He laughed softly. "Sorry. Now everyone grab hands. We can't have anyone getting lost. I already have Claret's."

"Where are you, Claret?" Kaylee asked.

"Over here." Kaylee bumped into her, then they grabbed each other's hand. "Ouch!"

"Sorry," Mateo said. "I didn't mean to step on your foot."

Vivi snorted. "I'll be shocked if you all make it up the stairs."

"Come on," Odie said, pulling them in a line.

They went up the stairs as quietly as they could. They didn't want the guards above to hear them.

Odie tapped on the door, and it opened. He led them all out. Claret tried to breathe normally as they hurried past the two goblins.

One goblin looked into the dark dungeon. "No one's there."

"Impossible," said the other. "I suppose it could have been the wind."

"From inside?"

The goblin shrugged. Any second, Mateo would run, and they needed to make sure they didn't lose their hold on each other. Claret's arm was yanked in one direction, and she stumbled, hitting Kaylee. She let go of Odie as she crashed down onto Kaylee. Odie fell onto her, and she had no idea what was happening with Mateo.

"What was that? Who's there?" one guard said, holding out a sword. Claret bit her lip and held still. Kaylee and Odie were still as well.

"Run!" Mateo said. Claret didn't wait to ask where or why. She jumped to her feet and ran in the direction of whoever's footsteps she could hear. She glanced back to see the guards behind them standing with their eyes wide. They were too terrified to move.

"Turn here!" Odie said. Claret took a left, and they ran to a large black door. It opened and Claret ran out into the open air. Not being able to see her body in any way was making her run clumsily, but she managed to stay on her feet. She flew down the stairs and hoped her friends were with her.

Once she reached the dirt path at the bottom of the stairs, she kept going.

"Where are you guys?" Kaylee called.

"Here!" Claret said, moving toward her voice. She put out her hand until she ran into Kaylee's shoulder.

"We need to grab hands again and run and teleport," Mateo said. Claret felt someone bump into her. She held out her hand and grabbed whoever's hand it was.

"Look up there!" Mateo said, at her side.

"Where?" Odie asked.

"On the castle."

Claret looked up. Garin was standing on the roof, look-ing down. It almost seemed like he was staring at them, but that was impossible.

"Is he... growing?" Kaylee asked.

Claret looked closer. "I think he is."

"It's too far to know for sure, but he looks like he's changing color," Mateo said. "Let's get out of here. Is everyone ready? Run forward three steps."

Claret pointed up at Garin, even though they couldn't see her. "I think he's changing into a dragon!" Blue wings were sprouting from his back.

"We can't hang around to find out. Run!" Claret ran three steps and then felt herself falling. When she sat up, she was in the hall of her castle.

Dovin paced back and forth in Claret's sitting room, while Kaylee, Mateo, Claret, and Odie sat squished together on the sofa. Kaylee could see a vein on the side of Dovin's forehead poking out. They had all been sitting here watching Dovin pace for the last five minutes.

Kaylee leaned against the comfortable purple velvet sofa and waited. She'd never been in this room before. It was small, with lavender curtains, and only held the sofa, a matching chair, and a small table. A large window looked out over the stables. Kaylee worried about making the tidy room dirty. They should have bathed and changed into clean clothing before getting their lecture.

"How could you all be so careless?" Mateo said, mimicking Dovin. "Why don't you start with that?"

Dovin fixed him with a glare. "It was careless. I don't need to tell you because you all know. There will be no more going to the goblin mountain. We have been looking all over for you, Kaylee. You shouldn't have gone off on your own."

She shrugged. "I thought it was important."

"Don't do it again."

Kaylee nodded. She wasn't planning on it anyway.

"What if you hadn't been able to get away?"

"We figured you would come eventually," Mateo said.

Dovin sighed. "You cannot count on me to save you. I would have come, yes, but who is to say I would be successful? I want you all to try harder to at least communicate before you run into danger."

"But if we tell you, you try to stop us," Kaylee said.

"Yes, and if you had listened, you could have saved your-self some time in the dungeon."

"But Claret was there. We still would have needed to save her."

"Shouldn't we be talking about the fact that Garin can turn himself into a dragon?" Mateo asked.

Dovin's eyes narrowed. "Are you sure?"

Claret nodded. "It looked that way."

He sank down into the chair across from them. "This isn't good."

Kaylee leaned forward. "Have you ever heard of anyone doing it before?"

Dovin nodded. "There are legends. I've never seen it myself. Long ago, it was said there were people who could change into dragons. It's not something that can be learned. It runs in families. It was said they could control other dragons."

"That's all we need," Odie said. "Garin controlling dragons."

"They can't control them completely, but they are in-fluential to them. A dragon still knows its mind, but they find the people who transform very persuasive."

Claret glanced sideways at Odie. "He was the one who took us to the mountain."

Odie nodded. "Probably. I still don't understand how he found us, though."

Dovin rubbed his chin. "Have you ever heard of dragon shifters in Riviand, Claret?"

"No, never."

"We know Garin is from the upper world," Dovin said. "I haven't studied shifters, so I lack a lot of knowledge. We may have to go above to learn anything about them."

Odie frowned and twisted the black ring on his pinky. "I don't know how many times we'll be able to get Vork to send people up."

"We don't have to," Kaylee said. "We found out we can teleport from inside Vork's cave. He doesn't even have to know we were there."

"That's convenient."

Dovin nodded. "Very. We can teleport to the cave, then from the cave to Akkron. Of course I can't teleport us. I've never seen the cave. That leaves Mateo."

"So we're going to go up there and research dragon shifters?" Kaylee asked.

Dovin nodded. "Unless you have some knowledge we don't know about, then yes. And we don't have to take everyone. It's probably best that Claret stays here to keep worry down in Tyran."

Claret nodded. "I don't know that I will ever be ready to go up above."

"If you go up, I'm coming," Durdessa said, entering the room.

Claret and Dovin frowned.

Durdessa walked behind the sofa and put a hand on Claret's shoulder. "I will come back, but there are things up there that I need to do."

Kaylee wondered if it had something to do with her daughter and brother.

"I can stay or go," Kaylee said. "I'm up for either. Especially if we don't have to jump into Mermaid's Demise to get back."

"Mateo still has to show me a toilet," Odie said. "He promised."

Kaylee smiled, and Mateo laughed.

Dovin nodded. "Very well. Mateo and Odie will accompany me and Durdessa. Claret and Kaylee will hold things down here and stay in the castle. If anything happens, send Captain Nerman for Williams. Do you understand?"

Kaylee and Claret nodded.

"Good. We shouldn't be gone long. If I can manage it, we will only be gone a day at most. We can bring back books and study them here if we need to."

"I think we should assign Claret and Kaylee a guard," Durdessa said. "Someone who stays with them the entire time we are gone."

"That isn't necessary," Claret said.

Kaylee wrinkled her nose. "Not at all."

Mateo tilted his head. "Not necessary? There could still be vorcraws after you, and Garin could appear at any moment. Keep a guard."

"Fine," Kaylee mumbled. "But hurry."

Dovin stood. "We will. I think we have run out of time. The sooner we deal with Garin, the better."

Kaylee went to her room, took a bath, and changed into clean clothes. She wondered if they would be able to defeat Garin. They had no idea what power he possessed. She leaned against her window and looked out over Tyran.

People were busy going about their lives, not realizing what might be out there.

Something was flying across the sky, but it was too far to make out what it was. It could be an alicorn or a Pegasus. It could also be a dragon. Possibly Garin. She took a resolved breath. It didn't matter what Garin could do. They would figure out a way to defeat him. Whatever magic he had, however powerful he was, they would win. She felt it deep down. They had to win.

— · —

ALSO BY KRISTY DIXON

Cozy Mystery
Murder With a Side of Bacon
Murder With a Hint of Cinnamon
Murder With a Fudge Brownie to Go

Young Adult
Akkron (The Silver Eclipse Book 1)
Boztoll (The Silver Eclipse Book 2)
The Other Continent (The Silver Eclipse Book 3)
The Amethyst Crown
More Than Once Upon a Time
Trapped In Once Upon a Timen
The Beginning of Once Upon a Time

Coming Soon!
Mermaid's Demise (Riviand Lost Book 2)
Dragon's Cove (Riviand Lost Book 3)
Murder With a Splash of Vanilla
Murder With a Drizzle of Syrup

— . —

ABOUT THE AUTHOR

Kristy Dixon received a degree in English from the University of Utah. She started writing stories when she was seven and never stopped. She enjoys writing fantasy books for middle grade and teens and cozy mysteries. At home, she spends her time playing board games with her husband and kids and writing. Occasionally she takes part in a Super Mario marathon. She has six chickens and a cat that help keep life amusing. If she isn't playing with her kids or writing, she is usually eating cookies, or wishing she was eating cookies.

www.ingramcontent.com/pod-product-compliance
Lightning Source LLC
Chambersburg PA
CBHW061339310726
48974CB00001B/117